IN THE

TIME

OF

FOXES

JO LENNAN

SCRIBNER

LONDON NEW YORK SYDNEY TORONTO NEW DELHI

First published in Australia by Scribner,
an imprint of Simon & Schuster Australia, 2020
First published in Great Britain by Scribner,
an imprint of Simon & Schuster UK Ltd, 2020
This paperback edition published by Scribner,
an imprint of Simon & Schuster UK Ltd, 2021

1 3 5 7 9 10 8 6 4 2

Simon & Schuster UK Ltd
1st Floor
222 Gray's Inn Road
London WC1X 8HB

www.simonandschuster.co.uk
www.simonandschuster.com.au
www.simonandschuster.co.in

Simon & Schuster Australia, Sydney
Simon & Schuster India, New Delhi

A CIP catalogue record for this book is available from the British Library

Paperback ISBN: 978-1-4711-9538-9
eBook ISBN: 978-1-4711-9537-2
Audio ISBN: 978-1-4711-9885-4

Printed in the UK by CPI Group (UK) Ltd, Croydon, CR0 4YY

Praise for *In the Time of Foxes*

'Brilliant. I was constantly astonished. Each story
takes us into a new world, yet the collection is bound
together by a belief in the power of adaptability'
Michael Billington

'Each of these stories is a whole new world of experience
and meaning, and to read them together is to fall
utterly under Lennan's spell as a master storyteller'
Ceridwen Dovey

'Spanning Sydney, Kyushu, Moscow and the European surf,
these are some of the best stories I've read this year – possibly
ever . . . These are world class stories, tales that feel so palpable,
true and lived, they almost feel like an act of possession'
Benjamin Law

'Lennan is a master at creating worlds: above all,
she is able to make the small details stick'
The Saturday Paper

'I'm absolutely blown away by the short story collection
In the Time of Foxes by Jo Lennan. I can't imagine
how one person has managed to live so many lives,
because I'm completely convinced by each tale'
Jenny Valentish

'A commanding debut. Lennan is a talented storyteller
with a new, authentic voice and *In the Time of Foxes*
is brimming with life. Each tale feels like a novel
in waiting and will leave you wanting more'
Sunda

'Lennan crafts each story as
Sydne

Contents

In the time of foxes

In London, where Nina lived, it was the time of foxes.

There had never been so many. It was said there were ten fox families per square mile. Their numbers thinned in the countryside as they migrated to the cities, a great animal migration to match the human one. They trotted into town along railway tracks, scavenged in bins, scouted territories, pissed and shat, snoozed on manhole covers, bit the heads off chickens, left corpses and intestines strewn about back courtyards, lucky-dipped for frogs, and generally sniffed about. They went from garden to garden, heeding neither man nor fence.

Hackney Council sent a leaflet. It came through the door one day.

The red fox is a wild member of the dog family.

The fox year – a month-by-month guide to fox activity and behaviour.

(There was a chart with descriptions and colour illustrations.)

Foxes are very adaptable and extremely well suited to urban environments. They have the largest natural distribution of any land mammal except humans.

1

'Sorry, you were saying . . .'

Nina had other things on her mind the day the leaflet came through the door. She stood in her kitchen, looking through the French doors to the garden. On the phone, her faraway brother was questioning whether their mother should stay in her own house. She was trying to persuade him that yes, of course she should.

'That's what's best for her. She knows where she is, she has all her things, it's home.'

Outside, the garden was overgrown, the grass luxuriantly green. Nina spoke with her head crooked at an angle, sandwiching the phone between her shoulder and ear so that her hands were free to clean the coffee machine casket. Ronnie was at her legs, saying, 'Mama, Mama,' and frisking her jeans-clad thighs.

'Wait a minute, darling, Mama's speaking to Uncle Jared.'

When she looked up again it was to see two young foxes in a sunbeam. They were bounding and tumbling. *Cavorting*, she thought.

'Foxes, Ronnie,' she said. 'Look. They're cubs, fox children.'

As soon as she said the words he detached himself from her legs and hurried to the doors with his funny waddling almost-run. He put his hands out, stroked the glass, and let out a breathy *Oh*.

'Works like a charm every time,' she told her brother. But she knew something must be done. Foxes were breeding in the garden. There was a nest – a den? – back there.

With Ronnie entertained, they returned to their conversation.

'We can make it work with her at home,' she went on. 'I'll manage the invoices, I'll help.'

She knew it was hard on Jared. There was only so much she could do over the phone and by email. He was the one in Sydney, living closest to their mother (although he wasn't close enough to make the visits easy). She could tell he was unconvinced but he gave her the dates of his holiday, and she agreed to stay with Helen in his absence.

'Got it,' she said. 'I'll look at flights.'

She called the real estate agent next. 'We have a Fox Situation,' she said, emphasising the words. The animals were getting to be a problem, what with the holes they dug everywhere. Her son could fall and hurt himself. Anybody could.

'It's also the poo,' she said. The Poo Situation. 'You have to play hopscotch to miss them.'

'The foxes?'

'No, the poos.'

'Ah, I see. Sounds like we'd better have a look.'

When she hung up, the cubs were still revelling in the sun, snapping at blades of grass. Ronnie watched in wonder, mesmerised, until she told him, 'Okay, mister, time for your play date at the park.'

As she packed his bag, Nina felt a little guilty. With her call to the agent, she had set things in motion – there would now be a process, perhaps involving the council and men wearing dungarees. Or so she thought until the agent called her back the next day. Apparently the landlady wanted to be humane. Had Nina tried securing the rubbish bin and not leaving food about?

Nina was curt in response. She insisted on action. Afterwards, she told her husband she was going to have to be the baddie, the one putting her foot down. 'I've had my share of appalling landlords but this woman takes the cake. We can't be expected to run a sanctuary in the garden.'

The thing with the foxes was one more thing to sort out before their trip. The other things included work things, Ronnie's childcare hiatus, and plans for how to get from the airport in Sydney to her mother's house two hours south. She crowd-sourced distractions for Ronnie for the plane, putting the call out in a Facebook post.

Other things, so many things. She received a recommendation for a grief counsellor and hoped to squeeze in a session. It had been six months since her father had died, but she'd barely had time to grieve. *Grieve*: put that on the to-do list with everything else!

Nina was never not in motion, never not hurrying somewhere. She tag-teamed with her husband Brent on dinner-and-bath routines. She read children's books to Ronnie; she never read adult books anymore (or just 'books', as she used to call them). At best she read articles on her phone, scrolling mindlessly in the dark after checking her messages. She took her son on the tube to the co-working creche, which had an adjoining office where she could do a few hours' work, always feeling there was never quite enough time to make a dent in her projects.

On the days Ronnie was in childcare she went to her agency in Shoreditch. They had rooms that she could use for editing and meetings. Most of her work was directing arty-looking TV commercials and documentary-style content. Lately she had worked as one of the directors on a TV series, a comedy about the trials of parenting. The show was irreverent and funny and a lot of people liked it. In the background, she was also labouring on a project of her own, a script for a feature film. This took untold hours of writing, with much plotting and re-plotting, and sometimes she had the feeling that it would never be finished.

In between meetings and the odd brief creative burst, Nina made calls about the Fox Situation. The landlady was being silly. Securing the bins – ugh. She tried that. It didn't work. Researching online, Nina found the details of a fox rescue group that ran a catch-and-release program, but she ruled this out, guessing the foxes would return. She had started to get some serious side-eye from her neighbours, who saw her garden as a hotbed of fox activity. Her neighbour at number 40, a man with a military bearing, accused her of feeding them. Not knowing his name, she mentally christened him Old Gammon. He told her to have the foxes shot.

'From those French doors of yours. There's a man you can call for that,' he said. 'Get the nasty little Charlies. Wait till you hear them screaming in the small hours of the morning, that's when they have intercourse,' he told her with distaste.

She didn't care about the neighbours' dirty looks. But the smells, the defecation, the missing shoe of Ronnie's that delayed a trip to the doctor – these were things she didn't need. The trip to the doctor was a checkup; they wanted to check his vital signs and say what percentile he was in for this or that, was he tall or short or fat for a two-and-a-half-year-old. She found the shoe later, masticated, slimy with saliva. She rinsed it with detergent, thinking that would have to do. Worst of all was the morning when, on leaving the house, she saw there had been a hit-and-run. The body was inert. It made a neat crescent shape on the road. It was one of the cubs; she knew it by its ears, the colouring on its paws. The runt of the litter. Ronnie gazed at it, dismayed.

'What happened, Mama?'

'A car. A car is what happened, sweetheart.'

She was about to call the council when out came Old Gammon from number 40. Putting on a pair of gardening gloves, he lifted the lifeless fox and slid it into a heavy-duty bin bag, then dumped it in his wheelie bin like any other bag of rubbish.

'Pickup day,' he said to her. 'They won't be long.' Then he muttered something about needing to scrub the bin out later.

His tone said, I told you so, this is what you get for feeding them.

With her hand forced, she spoke to the agent and threatened to call someone herself. 'Name's Bruce. He's very nice. He has a .22 Winchester, pops them off from the back window.' She had seen this on the internet. It was legal, apparently. She saw her husband's horrified look as he glanced over from the sofa. He was gentle by nature; he never so much as raised his voice. She flapped her hand at him: don't worry.

'How does that sound, alright? We can send you the invoice when he's done.'

Her bluff had the desired effect. A fox man arrived promptly. He wore dungarees, looked the part.

'My word, they've had a field day. You've got yourself a breeding earth. That big old tree stump in the ground, it's rotted out from the inside. That's what they've been burrowing to get to. A bit of shelter for them – very cosy, I imagine.'

A breeding earth. So that was what it was called.

'Don't worry,' he reassured her. 'We've strict instructions from the client to be humane and sympathetic.'

'Hmm,' said Nina. 'That's why I'm worried.'

She said it needed a proper job, he had to get rid of the breeding earth. She took no pleasure in saying so. She didn't want to be the baddie; she knew the eviction of the foxes would distress Ronnie. He saw them as his friends, furry counterparts of a sort. How was she going to tell him that their homes had been destroyed?

*

She arranged for the work to happen while they were away. Flying Heathrow to Sydney for the second time in six months made her feel pre-emptively exhausted. They flew as a trio at the beginning of December: Nina and Brent, both with their laptops for emails, and Ronnie with his own small backpack of toys.

Nina's brother met them at the airport and drove them to Wollongong, to save them renting a car. He made one stop, to show Nina the residential home in Sydney's southern suburbs.

'It's on our way,' he pointed out. 'It'll take us twenty minutes.'

She was jet-lagged and unimpressed, but she agreed. They toured the home. It was nine in the morning when they reached the complex, the sun was rudely bright and Ronnie's hat was buried somewhere in their luggage. This was nothing to him, of course. He had slept well on the second leg and now tottered happily behind, holding his dad's hand. The home was well laid out as a series of share houses for three or four residents. Each house was fitted with special lights and special doorknobs, a manager told them. The lights were ambient and soft, and the doorknob for every room felt different, features designed to reduce disorientation. Nina listened politely. She duly admired the fittings. She whispered to her brother so the manager wouldn't hear her, 'This is overkill, Jared. She doesn't need this stuff.'

He pretended not to hear her. 'It's not like other old people's homes,' he said. 'There are no stupid crafts, which is good if you're like Mum and you've never been into crafts.'

When they finally reached the real house, Nina's childhood home, her mother was inside waiting, still wearing her floral cotton nightie. Ronnie launched himself at his nanna. He rarely saw her in person, but they spoke every week on Skype.

'Aren't you big, Ronnie!' she said, cuddling him and making him beam. But as Nina moved about the kitchen, putting out a plate of biscuits and sitting at the Formica table, she saw how much her mother had aged in the last six months. She was greyer, more stooped and uncertain, more defeated. Her brother had warned her, it had all come on so quickly. She was only sixty-three. Sixty-three! Unable to let her hands lie still, she kept smoothing her hair, her thighs, or rubbing her forearms, up and down, an incessant habit. Sometimes, when she remembered or Jared handed it to her, she squeezed a raspberry-pink stress ball with a nubby surface.

This was what Nina's mother's Alzheimer's was like. It seemed less like an illness of forgetting than a bad case of anxiety. She had always been anxious, had always rubbed her forearms when she worried, but now it was as if the worrier was the only part of her left.

It had been three years since Helen was diagnosed with the disease. Until then, Nina knew almost nothing about Alzheimer's. Working as a director, she'd made mini-documentaries for charities, short films about misfortunes that happened to other people. Blindness, for instance. Or having your life saved by the London Air Ambulance. For the macular blindness one, she used blurry and shadowed footage to mimic the progression of the illness. First a shot in which a mother adjusts her son's school tie, then a later shot where she can't.

In the Air Ambulance one, she filmed a road accident survivor. She took him back to the intersection and had him tell the story: how he was hit by a car while riding his bike, how the car ran him over, crushing his pelvis. Going over the footage later, she cut the part where the man cried, deciding to show him almost-crying instead. You had to hold something back, give the viewer room to feel. Her style played well with the British. They were crazy for stoicism, someone keeping it together. When she played a cut of the film, the reps from the client started crying. They hugged her and said they could not have been happier.

But Alzheimer's had been a mystery. Slipping away from the gathering in the kitchen to look around the house, Nina saw evidence of her brother's efforts and felt the familiar guilt. Thanks to him, the bathroom sported a new set of safety handles – plasticky, beige and sturdy; not very attractive. On the fridge door she had noticed instructions for the carers, a laminated mini-essay with the heading 'A Typical Day'. *Helen has two crumpets with honey for breakfast. There are crumpet bags in the freezer. If the left side of the toaster sticks, give it a jiggle . . .*

The house was otherwise little changed. It was in a working-class neighbourhood, a place of straight, unshaded streets to fly along on a bike. It was still the house of Nina's childhood, a postwar brick box with an upstairs addition. Taking their bags upstairs, she found that her old room had been taken over by the young couple who lived in the house rent-free, an arrangement that ensured Helen was not alone at night. They had timed their own holiday to coincide with Nina's brother's, but the space was full to bursting with their big upholstered bed, matching bedside tables, and throw pillows embroidered with motivational sayings. She closed the door on the room, which was hers no longer. She dumped the bags in Jared's old room, unfolded the sofa bed in the upstairs sitting room for Ronnie, and located a box of her brother's old toys: Transformers, Lego, Duplo, a train set.

Before long, Jared left them, taking the train back to Sydney and leaving his Subaru for them to use. There was a booster seat in the back (borrowed from a cousin, as Jared did not have children). He was taking two weeks' leave from his busy job in TV production to go on holiday with his partner. They would decamp that night to Queensland, somewhere with snorkelling and rainforests.

Once her brother had left, Nina made crumpets, pushing them down in the ancient toaster. A typical day, she thought.

She spread honey and made more tea, let the mug cool for a good five minutes, put it on the table in front of her mother.

'Love a cup of tea,' said Helen.

'Nothing better,' Nina said, though she herself drank coffee.

That first day and night, Nina saw just how much vigilance was needed. Her mother was now unable to notice when she was too hot or too cold, so Nina had to keep watch for the signs, put her cardigan on or take it off. She couldn't shower by herself, but she didn't like Nina to help her do it either. She preferred to wait until mid-morning when the carer came, whoever it was that day according to the roster. The one thing she could do without help was clean her teeth, but then she would forget and worry that she hadn't done it.

'Ronnie, let's clean your teeth,' said Nina.

'Did I clean my teeth?' asked Helen.

'Yes, Mum. You did.'

'Oh good.' To mask her embarrassment, she turned the exchange into a lesson. 'Very important to clean your teeth, isn't it, Ronnie?'

Waking at odd hours during the night, a jet-lagged Nina read emails on her phone. Remembering the foxes in her garden, she summoned justifications for clearing them out. It wasn't as if they were endangered. They were colonisers, really. Furry little conquistadors, making themselves at home, profiting from easy pickings wherever humans built towns and cities.

In the mornings they woke to birds. The birds! The sound declared the day as belonging to a different country, even before you were fully awake, before your brain kicked into gear. There were the normal suburban birds, raucous and loud, and the smaller twittering birds that were drawn to the nearby lake. On the second morning of their stay, when Nina rose and went downstairs in the quiet house, she found a pair of her mother's underpants laid out, wet, on the kitchen table. It looked as if she had rinsed them in the sink. Finding her mother in her room, she asked what had happened, but her mother knew nothing about it. She just kept smoothing the nightie over her bottom and thighs as if she felt self-conscious with nothing underneath.

In the two weeks that followed, Brent came and went from the house, taking the train to work in his company's Sydney office. He was the finance guy in a team that consulted on the redevelopment of old industrial sites, turning them into mixed-use precincts and waterfront meadows and so on. Having used up all of his annual leave on their last trip, he was working remotely this time and had to keep up with his projects. In his absences, Nina was often alone with Ronnie and her mum. It was always a relief when the carer came at eleven o'clock each morning. With the help of some government support and a great deal of wrangling, Nina and Jared had organised the carer roster after their father's death.

The best of the carers was Cath, a large, indefatigable woman. She came with her bulk and her cheerfulness and helped out for several hours. She showered and dressed Helen. She helped her to go to the toilet, making male visitors stay clear of the hall to preserve Helen's dignity. Cath was very particular about toilet-related matters. She had worked for a woman in a wheelchair who, when Cath was in the toilet, parked herself outside and kept up the conversation.

'I quit that job, don't worry! Some things should be sacred.'

Back in London, the fox man emailed to update Nina on the breeding earth. He attached a photo of the garden looking like a demolition site, which made her glad that Ronnie was well out of the way. Those dark voids in the earth made her think of her mother's mind, its mysterious workings. Had parts of the brain got hollowed out, leaving cavities? Was that where her memory had gone? Or was it all still there, intact, but unreachable somehow?

*

It took an outing to a shopping centre that Friday for Nina to realise how bad things really were. All the noise and light were too much for Helen, who became increasingly agitated. Then a chatty shop assistant happened to mention Christmas and this started Helen worrying that she wasn't ready. She needed to get her hair done. She needed to buy presents, something to wear. And what would they do for Christmas lunch?

Christmas was two weeks off, but it might as well have been in half an hour, the way she spoke about it. She had no grip on time, it concertinaed in her mind like an accordion being played by a deranged musician. The baggy folds were brought together with an alarming wheeze, and *voilà*! Time was compressed. Helen went into a panic.

Ronnie stood below counter-height, looking from Nina to his nanna. Trying to read the situation, he looked baffled and concerned. He knew there was a problem but could not pick what it was. Clamouring for Nina's attention as she tried to calm her mother, he started tugging at her top. 'Mama, Mama,' he insisted, his voice taking on a sharp new edge.

'Stop that, Ronnie. Come on, Mum. Why don't we go home? Alright?'

Nina had always harboured a special hatred of shopping centres, but this was a nightmare of a different order. She shepherded her charges out of the shop and towards the exit, placating and steering Helen, and making sure Ronnie followed. They had to cross the car park, an acre of softening asphalt lined with glinting windscreens. She opened all four doors of the car to let out the hot air, then made Ronnie stand and wait while she helped her mother into her seat.

It was almost six pm. Brent had been at work in Sydney and Nina hoped he'd be back soon. The drive home from the shops did not take long. Nina talked brightly the whole way, keeping up a running commentary to help Helen orient herself. At the house, she enlisted Ronnie's help to get his nanna inside, which was as much a ploy to occupy him as anything else. Nina was banking on her mum's calming down once she was home. The small, dated kitchen should have been comforting, familiar, but Helen remained confused and distressed throughout dinner. When Nina was clearing up afterwards, Helen suddenly stared wildly at her and demanded, 'Nina? Are you Nina?'

'Yes, Mum. It's me, Nina.' Looking around, she realised that the single unshaded bulb – the only source of light – was behind her head, meaning that her mother could only see her silhouette. Nina circled the table, moving into a position where her face was in the light. 'See, Mum? It's me.' But she couldn't reassure Helen, who leapt out of her chair and veered between the benches, a trapped bird trying to flee. Unable to calm her, Nina tried to contain her.

Standing in the doorway watching, Ronnie started to cry, then stopped. He looked through his tears, aghast at his nanna's behaviour. Here she was, a full-sized adult needing care and attention! His nanna, a full-sized adult having a meltdown! He couldn't say, but must have felt, that he was being upstaged.

Nina made a snap decision. She couldn't manage them both, and she judged Ronnie to be the more capable. 'Go outside and play,' she told him, even though it was already dark. He looked at her, astonished, but did as he was told. He went outside with his frisbee (a lightweight, travel-friendly toy). Nina tried to calm her mother, but when the frisbee bounced off the neighbours' fence it set the dog barking, further agitating Helen.

'Where's Ronnie?' she asked. 'I can't find Ronnie. I don't know where – I've lost him.'

Ronnie was the one person she never failed to remember, thought Nina.

'He's outside playing, Mum. He's fine.' God, why was Brent so late?

Helen wouldn't be consoled, no matter what Nina said or did. She flailed, wheezed, cried, and started hyperventilating.

And then finally Brent was home, coming in through the back door. Standing framed in the doorway, with the weight of his laptop bag dragging at his shoulder, he looked handsome, even heroic, in a creased sort of way. He sized up the situation, saw the state Helen was in. 'Right, hospital,' he said. 'This can't be right. It can't be.'

They all went to the hospital together. To Ronnie, this part of the crisis was a big adventure. Off to Emergency, a waiting room with hard plastic seats, a triage nurse, quite stern, other children to inspect. Two nurses came out with a trolley, and with some cajoling and manhandling got Helen onto it. Then the doctor, a slim woman with a tic in one eye from fatigue, examined Helen carefully, looked over her file and prescribed antibiotics.

'UTI,' she said. 'Urinary tract infection. These infections make them crazy.' She grimaced before adding, 'With this kind of Alzheimer's, there's no gentle forgetting, is there?'

No, there was not, thought Nina.

The hospital released Helen that night, but the stress of the evening stayed with Nina. It was still with her the next day when she debriefed with Jared. Up until this point of her stay she had tried not to call him, sticking to messages when she had questions or updates. She had called him briefly on the way to the hospital, and then again to let him know when Helen was released. He rang her the following morning and they spoke for a long time. During the call, she suggested that they get a valuation for the house. It was something they'd talked about before, though only in general terms, agreeing they would need to get one down the track. Now she volunteered to get the real estate agents in.

'Let's see what they say,' she said. Jared didn't need persuading.

Early the next week, she arranged to show two real estate agents around the house. The agents were awful, both of them, perspiring with eagerness in their suits. Nina put her mother (nicely dressed) in the good sitting room downstairs, perched on the beige sofa that even after several decades was still as stiff and unyielding as hospital-grade plastic. She gave Ronnie her phone to let him FaceTime his dad. This kept him occupied while she spoke to the agents and wrote down numbers on a card, estimates of the house's value. Once the second one had left, she had to hunt for the phone to call her brother.

'Where is the phone, Ronnie?'

But he was making a game of rolling on the sofa, from one armrest to the other, squirming roughly past his nanna at the point where her bottom blocked his route. He squealed with delight as he tunnelled back and forth, while his nanna sat helpless.

'Stop that, Ronnie!' Nina told him on seeing the distress on her mother's face. 'Stop it and say sorry to Nanna.'

She could see he was struggling with the idea that his nanna was somehow vulnerable, defenceless. Actually, she couldn't blame him. She was struggling with this too. Nina thought of her mother as someone who was good with kids. Helen was – had been until recently – a capable primary school teacher, the one exercising patience in a room full of little horrors, giving out colouring-in tasks and reading picture books aloud. It was only four or five years ago that she retired from the job, saying she was making way for someone younger and quicker on their feet.

It was confronting, the change in Helen. Confronting for them all. Nina had kept up with her mother over Skype, but most of their calls were taken up with Ronnie-and-Nanna time, and her exchanges with her mother were brief and incidental. *And how are you getting on?* she'd ask, trying to gauge how Helen was. She regretted the talks they didn't have when it was still possible to have them.

In the end, she had to extract the apology from Ronnie. He finally mumbled a *sorry, Nanna*. Maybe she shouldn't have forced the issue. She'd read online that most children his age did not yet have the empathy that was needed for a real apology. Parenting articles blithely suggested alternatives, such as asking the toddler to offer help to the wounded party. One had described, as an example, a child at a playground being prompted to say to another child, 'Are you hurt? Can I get you a wet towel?' And Nina could not imagine a universe in which Ronnie would say that.

That evening, however, he did say something that surprised her. 'Mama, I want to go back to London.'

She looked down at his upturned face, briefly lost for words. She had always lazily assumed that her son would love Australia: the open space, the beaches, the outdoorsiness of it.

'Soon, Ronnie,' she said with a sinking heart. Then she took him upstairs and read him *The Wind in the Willows*.

There seemed to be no end to this wood, and no beginning, and no difference in it, and, worst of all, no way out.

Onion sauce! Onion sauce!

It shouldn't have been so surprising that he would want to go back to London. He had his routines there, his friends, the fox cubs in the garden. It was where they had their lives as a family. It was where Nina had her friends, her work. It had taken a while to establish herself there, but now that she had, doors were starting to open. People were taking notice, especially after her credit on the comedy series. None of this had come easily. It hadn't happened overnight. It was the result of a lot of hustling, countless coffees and mentorships, the usual long apprenticeship for overnight success.

The next morning, she opened an email from her agent in London. He was writing with big news: Nina had won a grant from the British Film Institute to develop her feature film. Nina blinked at the screen and read her agent's words again, not quite able to believe them. She had put in the application so long ago she had almost forgotten about it. The grants were tightly contested and it had seemed too much to hope that she might win. The film was a psychological thriller about a romantic getaway gone wrong. Now her agent was asking her to write a treatment of the film so he could send it to investors. Reading this, Nina paused, suddenly deterred. In normal circumstances, she would start work on the treatment straight away. Aim to make a good impression, show she was on the job.

But she couldn't do it now. Not this week; there wasn't time.

She would do it soon, she wrote back.

The agent would understand. Or not. Instead of worrying that she was not doing enough, she surprised herself by deciding it would happen when it happened.

The end of their stay was fast approaching. Brent stopped commuting and worked from home. On Friday afternoon, they made an excursion as a foursome, driving out to the cemetery where Nina's dad, Syd, was buried. Nina had noticed that Helen never spoke of him, but she had to know, at some level, that he had passed away. Otherwise she would surely ask them where he was.

They made the trip for Helen, wanting to help her to understand. Nina also wanted to see the grave for reasons of her own. She hadn't been to the cemetery since the day of the funeral. She wanted to have the feeling of visiting her dad, or at least of making time to pause and think about him. And she hoped that Ronnie would remember his grandad in some way.

Nina and Brent weren't sure how Helen would handle the grave visit. Maybe the grief counsellor would have had tips for this situation, Nina remarked with a wry smile. As it turned out, the visit itself was uneventful. Helen was unperturbed, Ronnie curious and watchful. They left flowers, stood about, and finally drove away. It was only on the way back that Helen came out with a question, piping up to ask, 'Has Syd gone to live somewhere else?'

As if her husband had moved out. As if, having reached the ripe old age of seventy-four, he had taken a flat somewhere or moved into a sharehouse with hipsters in Wollongong.

*

A world away in London, foxes carried out fox business. They stared with tawny eyes, trailed their tails behind them like rudders, came to grief in hit-and-runs, dying or limping on, went bald from mange and mites, picnicked in parks under the cover of darkness, traversed the top of garden walls, and were captured and released. They slunk under the cold gaze of CCTV cameras, startled commuters and carried on.

Fox news winged its way to Nina. The workmen had dug out the rotted tree trunk and roots, or as much of them as they could.

They doused the holes with repellent, gave it a few days and came back. They filled in the cavities with loose earth. Finally, to be certain, they paved a neat rectangle of ground over the top. While they were at it, they cut back the bushes at the rear, rebuilt the retaining wall and repaired the fence.

It was time to return. Over a weekend in mid-December, the trio flew back to London and reoccupied the flat. Having held it together for the trip, Nina came apart at home. Halfway through the unpacking, she slumped to the floor and cried. Brent made coffee, brought it to her, and took Ronnie out to play, bundling him into his coat and boots. 'You're not in Australia now, Toto,' he said. Remarkably, Ronnie had no jet lag. He launched back into his life like a happy duckling into water. He did not ask about the foxes, and Nina realised that this was the talent of small children: their love had the character of sunlight, falling on whatever or whoever was there with them. They gave no thought to what was missing. They mourned nothing and no one. The task of grieving fell to adults.

So it's down to me, she thought. She thought of the foxes. She was not immune to their charms. She had watched them playing in the garden and known them all by sight. She thought of the cub with the four black socks using its hind paw to scratch its ears. And of the cub with black-tipped ears and orange-white hind legs. She thought of the vixen, her tall ears drawn smartly back, in rude health with no trace of mange, a sleek white bib of fur lining her undercarriage.

They weren't her foxes but she loved them. She wasn't supposed to but she did. What was it about them? Their animal natures. Their ability to be themselves, which was its own sort of talent. The ease with which they moved, assuming that the world was theirs and everyone else just lived in it.

Now they were gone. She did not know where. As for the workmen, they'd left some gear rather carelessly at the back. A bag of cement, a few paving stones, a shovel. These items delighted Ronnie, who looked on them as toys. They were not at all suitable as toys but that did not stop him for a second. He thought it was Christmas – and in fact it almost was. Nina pulled herself together and they all went shopping for a tree. Choosing a furry pine that brought the smell of a forest into their home, they stood it in a pot next to the French doors.

Gazing past it to the garden, she saw no sign of the tree stump. She nodded when her husband said the new patio was nice – they could use it in the summer, eat there on warm days, and in general make more use of that part of the garden. Yes, she agreed, though summer seemed a long way off. She felt guilty about her mother, leaving her behind. She felt guilty about the foxes.

In the night she woke to a noise. She thought she'd heard a wail, a heart-rending, plaintive cry. Her husband slept on undisturbed while she lay awake thinking of the breeding earth. It was now obliterated; it was as if it had never been. In the small hours of the morning, she mourned the loss of her childhood home. Of her mother's memories, and of herself in those memories. She mourned the loss of her father, whom she'd barely had time to think of. He had been a popular man, her dad, a former steel worker. He had a big funeral, a big wake. Everyone was there, his workmates, his friends, the guys from the footy club. They had the wake in the backyard, a lot of food on trestle tables, everyone coming by to say how sorry they were.

In the morning, she called the workmen to pick up their tools and the cement. Then she called her brother. She told him, 'You were right.'

'I don't want to be right.'

'I know. But you are. I should have listened.'

They agreed to sell the house to pay for the residential home. They would put their mother on the waiting list to get in and hope the money lasted as long as she lived.

Nina rummaged to find the forms from their real estate agent of choice, the slightly less awful one. Looking up from the paperwork, she was startled to see a fox. They were still in the neighbourhood, people said.

Now one was in her garden again. The sight of the cub through the glass doors stopped her in her tracks. It was the one with the black-tipped ears, but bigger now, long-legged. He looked dirty, feral, wild and take-your-breath-away beautiful. If he was here, she thought, the others could be too. They could be out there, not far off, flitting through alleyways and gardens.

'You little beauty,' she said, standing still as she watched him go.

The invitation

Of the two of them, it was Nikolai who impressed Paul most at first.

Nikolai Kalinin, fortyish and greying, with his urbane good manners and habitual frown of concentration. Darya, at a decade younger, was not in the mould of a glamorous second wife. She dressed neatly but plainly and did not go in for makeup. Her lank fawn-coloured hair was pulled back in a practical bun, and her jutting lower jaw gave her a look of determination. When Paul got to know her, he thought her beautiful, but she was not the sort of woman he noticed on the metro, not among the striking faces he saw in the carriages, the faces of people from across the old republics who came to Moscow to try their luck.

He had come to Russia for his own mundane reasons. After working a year at a scruffy school in Luton, he'd been told that his next contract would not start until autumn. He was known for being fair, even-tempered, unflappable. Mild-mannered Mr Cullen. A geography teacher three years out, he knew how to settle a class, although one or two boys thought they could tell him to fuck off, *sir*, and the girls could switch quickly from flirtation to insolence. The idea of going to work in Moscow came from his college friend Julius. He was working there as a private tutor, making the faintly obscene amount of forty pounds an hour. He said he'd send Paul's CV to the agency he used. 'Come for the summer,' he said. 'This place is literally insane.'

Russia appealed as something bold, a wide impressive country. Paul imagined Moscow to be a place of machinations and intrigue, of old state power giving way to new liberties and glitz. Even though it was May, he pictured a snowdome city of images from the news: Red Square, St Basil's confectionary colours, the bridge over the Moskva River, flag-waving protesters in Bolotnaya Square.

Initially the reality was something of a let-down. His first job, through the long and cloyingly humid summer, saw him living in an outlying gated community, working for a family who had made it big in fertiliser. He was tasked with tutoring their twins, an identically sullen pair of boys. He was supposed to be grooming them for an English boarding school – the prospectus had been sent for and was shown to him when it came – but he couldn't have cared less about polish and etiquette. Julius had decamped, which was a Julius thing to do; he had followed his girlfriend to live in St Petersburg.

In August, Paul received an email from Luton. There would be no new contract, he learned, the numbers had shifted; very sorry, but there we are. This was when Nikolai stepped into the breach. He had asked the agency for a native English speaker, Oxbridge preferably, available at short notice. In an informal interview he spoke to Paul as an equal. Engaging him in conversation on EU monetary policy, which was in the news with the debt crisis, he sounded more like a technocrat than an oil executive. He touched briefly on his work as an 'operations guy', saying, 'People

don't know how much care and expertise goes into oil production. I work on brownfields, mature fields. To maintain output
is complex, delicate. It's jeweller's work, as we say in Russian.'
He spoke frankly about his family situation: his estranged wife
had been diagnosed with lupus, an illness that left her constantly
tired. Nikolai had recently brought their son, four-year-old
Anton, to live with him and his girlfriend. He led the shy boy
into the room, prompting a 'Hello, Mr Cullen.' When Nikolai
checked his watch, Paul was encouraged to see that it was not a
flashy statement brand, just an ordinary plastic Casio.

He started work soon afterwards. His new employers, thank
Christ, were nothing like his last. Instead of sequestering themselves in an outer suburb, they lived in Yakimanka, in the centre
of Moscow. The Kalinin flat was large, solidly comfortable, and
showed no sign of having been updated since it was built in the
fifties. Nikolai had a love of animals, and the entrance hall was
hung with framed photos of his horses, as well as several shots of
red foxes in the snow, with their whiskers and black-tipped ears
shown in sharp detail. He had taken the wildlife images while
out hiking in his younger days, before work took over.

'Foxes are misunderstood by humans,' he told Paul when he
saw him pausing in front of the prints. 'They're not deceitful in
the least. Just marvellous survivors, the way they live and thrive
in the most extreme conditions.'

Paul's job came with a modest flat several floors below the
Kalinins'. Here he was to tutor Anton every morning, Monday
to Friday. When it was time for Anton's lesson, it was usually
Darya who brought him down in the lift, before she went out to
run errands, or, as the weather cooled, before she went nowhere
at all, staying home to binge-watch *Breaking Bad*. He learned
that she used to work selling TV advertising but had given up the

job because she was away too often with Nikolai, accompanying him to the dacha near Tula (this was where he kept and rode his beloved horses) or on work trips further afield. 'At least I have this one,' she said brightly, tousling Anton's hair. Belting her coat securely, she would run out to buy cigarettes, only ever paying cash so Nikolai wouldn't know.

Paul did not meet Anton's mother, but she was present by her absence. Her disease was almost lunar, the way it waxed and waned. It confounded her doctors and by extension Nikolai, who had a rationalist's faith in medical science. Mrs Kalinin's condition was frequently discussed, and there were times when it looked like she might take Anton back. Paul had to wonder what Darya made of this. She had an ex-husband too, but he was practically never mentioned. Paul knew only that he had fought in Chechnya; Darya would later say, in a comment he found shocking, that it would have been better if he had died there.

Paul's focus was Anton; he tried to bring him out of his shell. His young student was placid. Not fast to learn, but willing. He liked the flash cards Paul used, he counted in English, and he grew better at stringing sentences together. Paul was surprised to find that he enjoyed the work. Not that anyone kept tabs on what he did. Paul saw less and less of Nikolai as the autumn went on, and whenever he did put his head through the door of the flat he had an embattled look. His divorce from Anton's mother had gone halfway then stalled. Perhaps it was the lupus; perhaps he was under fire at work.

The cold was deepening, but Paul was getting to know the city. Flush with his earnings, he booked a walking tour. He selected a guide named Angelica from the Real Guides of Russia website. Her page had great reviews, so he put aside the fact that her photo was slightly corny, showing her sniffing a daffodil. But she turned out to be a woeful guide: she drifted rather than led, took him to a closed cathedral, and muddled up the tickets for the Kremlin. He had hoped to be dazzled by tales of Napoleonic battles but she knew as much history as an indifferent high-school student. Still, he didn't mind too much; he enjoyed her company. Over a drink, she helped him to say her name correctly, with the softer Russian *zh*: 'Zh for *zhuk*, butterfly.' When he helped her into her champagne-coloured puffer coat, they agreed to meet again.

But it was Darya, not Angelica, who seized his attention, by initiating a brief affair. It took place over four nights in mid-December. For Paul, the whole thing was unexpected, even miraculous. Anton was at his mother's and Nikolai was away on back-to-back trips (first a work excursion to one of the oil company towns that dotted the tundra of the subarctic north, and then a few days' skiing with his brother in the Khibiny Mountains).

This was how it happened. Darya, feeling reckless or lonely or both, came to Paul's door wearing a wrap and towelling slippers. Walking in when he opened, she took his hand and put it on her breast under the wrap. Her hair was damp from the shower but she hadn't shaved her legs, and in what followed her stubble grazed lightly on his shins. His main contribution to the unfolding of things was to offer her vodka (her reply: 'I can't stand vodka') and to find a condom in the bedside drawer.

That was the first night. He didn't have time to feel guilty. It just happened and then she left; there was the muffled clunk of the door behind her. But then he wondered how to account for it. Had he unwittingly invited her approach, given her signals? It was true that he'd begun to feel drawn to her, but he thought he'd been careful not to show it. Perhaps he had given away more than he knew with all that effortful not-looking, his studious attempts at professional disinterest?

When she returned the following night, he didn't feel bad about that either. This time she had shaved her legs in an act of premeditation. Tracing his abdomen, she asked, 'Why do you look like this?' He thought it a strange question and laughed, saying, 'Rowing, I suppose.' Their conversation was light and inconsequential. She spoke about herself without revealing much, supplying cameo-like glimpses of a Russian childhood. She had grown up in St Petersburg and spoke fondly of the boulevards and canals, the wide Neva River, the walk to Vasilyevsky Island and her father's office in a building made of granite. He would have liked to reciprocate with stories of his own, but he thought his childhood dull, too boringly suburban to be of any interest.

The third night, she showed up with a bottle of chablis. 'What are you doing here, Paul?' she asked in a wondering tone, the same tone she'd used when asking about his physique.

'What are *you* doing here?' he said.

'You mean here, in this room?'

'I mean with Nikolai.'

'Let's not talk about Koly.' She pronounced her pet name for him like the first half of 'cauliflower'. But after they had sex she spoke of him anyway, venting her frustration. He wouldn't talk about his divorce, she complained; he said he had other things on his mind. But that hadn't stopped him from going skiing. *'Skiing!'* she repeated.

The worst part, she said, was that he wasn't even close to his brother. The guy was boorish, disrespectful. He had made money, it was true, although it was unclear how. 'Where does his money come from?' she asked Paul, as if he would know. In the past, Nikolai had ignored his brother's invitations to go hunting on the Kola Peninsula, saying he had no wish to kill animals for sport or to sit around with his brother's cronies, drinking and singing. Darya couldn't understand why he was spending time with him now. Nikolai was making his own way in the world, rising on his merits. 'He doesn't need anything from his brother,' she declared, annoyed. 'But enough of that,' she said, lighting a cigarette. 'Let's talk about you.'

Paul obliged with a change of topic. He wanted to travel to see Russia's far-flung reaches. He was thinking of those vast, snow-covered landscapes in Nikolai's photographs, extraordinary swathes of white touched only by fox paws. He recalled in minute detail a Werner Herzog film, *Happy People*, depicting the people who still lived in the wilderness, solitary hunters who spent whole winters in the forests. Darya listened impatiently, then cut him off with a lecture on what she called 'the reality picture': Russia's regions were depressed, there weren't enough jobs, petty crime was rife and heroin cheap. She swigged her wine but was not drunk; there was something controlled in her. Before long she made her exit, ending the evening on a low.

He thought he'd blown it. He really did. On the fourth night, he waited. When he finally went to bed he lay awake thinking about the danger in what he was doing, the risk of Nikolai discovering what he'd done. Paul tried to guess how he'd react. Would he confront him, irate? Throw him out on the street without a job? And then there was the question of what he would do to Darya.

It was after two when he heard Darya knock. Having relented after all, she had come down wearing a tracksuit. Paul forgot his fears as soon as he let her in. This time they had sex with more urgency than before. Then she fell asleep with her arm across his chest, so that he lay awake not daring to move, despite a tingling sensation and then a spreading ache. When he woke shortly before dawn she had already left.

Nikolai returned, and Paul worried about how their first meeting would go, but as things worked out he didn't see him. Several days passed in which he didn't even see Darya, and then he flew back to England to spend Christmas with his family.

'How are the Reds?' Nan asked, a gleam in her eye. She had been removed from her aged-care home and brought to his mother's place in Ashford, where she sat at the table's head like a wizened sexless queen. She gave Paul, her favourite, most of her turkey slices. The dining room felt cramped, with the five of them squeezed in among the knick-knacks and clutter. Paul's brother Richard had brought his girlfriend Elle, and they sat across the table discussing bathroom tiles for their flat in Dartford. On Paul's other side, his mother asked how his job was going. With her constitutional horror of inequality, she suspected he was working as a kind of servant. When she said the word 'tutoring', her voice betrayed her doubt; it was as if she were stepping on a pane of glass.

There was no way to reassure her, and he found her questions grating. As soon as he could he removed himself from the house. He spent an enjoyable New Year with Julius and his girlfriend Susan. They holed up in a cottage in the Welsh countryside that belonged to Julius's parents. Paul was fond of the place, as it was where he and Julius had crammed for their finals in their last year at Cambridge. Susan regaled them with stories of working for Russia Today, the state-owned English TV station. 'We cover anything to do with dead Romanovs, basically. There are always calls to dig them up to test some theory or other.' They played Monopoly and Susan was gleeful when she won, grinding on Julius while singing, 'I'm rich, I'm rich, I'm rich!'

Another night, they played cards, and Julius told them a Russian joke. 'A bear, a wolf and a vixen are playing cards.

The wolf is shuffling and he warns, "No cheating! If anyone is cheating, her smug red furry face is going to hurt."' He looked pointedly at Susan.

Susan laughed and protested, 'I insist you take that back. I've never cheated in my life!'

'Spoken like a woman.'

Paul felt his own face burning, but neither of them noticed and the moment passed.

*

He returned to the deep cold of Moscow. He expected to find tension. What if Nikolai had found out? Or what if he looked at him and *knew*? Instead, he got back to find his employers were still away. He occupied himself by going to the gym, cooking, watching TV. In the third week of January, he caught one of Susan's segments on Russia Today. She was covering the custom of Epiphany ice-swimming, in which the faithful dunked themselves in a hole in a frozen lake. Susan took part herself, in a black Speedo swimsuit (modestly cut, but still showing a lot of side-boob). In a later shot, wearing a polar fleece, she said, 'That's certainly one way to ring in the New Year.' And Paul, suddenly lonely, retrieved Angelica's number, Angelica with a *zh*. He sent her a message, and another when she replied, and after that he started seeing her often.

Early February brought his employers back to the city. He found Darya carefully neutral, Nikolai oblivious. Yet something had changed. In a reversal of roles, it was Nikolai who now brought Anton down each morning. Darya mostly stayed in bed, probably watching a new series. Taking the boy back upstairs after his lesson, Paul might hear a toilet flush, or some other muffled sound indicating Darya's presence, but she did not come out to greet him. Nikolai said she had the flu, and maybe she did. When she did at last appear she looked off-colour. Where once she had smelt of cigarettes, she now smelt faintly sour. She had given up smoking just as she had given up Paul, and these days when she went out it was to buy crisps and orange juice.

One day, bringing Anton into the kitchen at the flat, he glimpsed Nikolai's supposedly boorish brother. A man – he looked quite normal – came to the door, then disappeared into a room to talk business with Nikolai. Paul shot Darya a glance. 'They look thick as thieves,' he observed.

She pursed her lips. 'Brothers should stick together,' she said. Then she softened slightly. 'Before, I didn't know this, but Nikolai has been having problems.' She set out pastries on a plate and shook her head. 'You know, six years ago, when we had the oil crash, his fields kept the company afloat! And now that they're looking at doing some big deal, they're trying to force him out, trying to get what's his.' Apparently Nikolai held his shares on the strength of a handshake deal with the chief of the company, an old school friend, someone he had trusted. 'Poor Koly!' she said without irony.

Going by her newfound loyalty, he guessed the divorce was back in motion. Well, good for her, he thought. He was determined not to mind. He was dating Angelica, and while their relationship was strangely distant, even a little formal, he enjoyed its element of mystery. She didn't add him on Facebook, for example, even though he knew she used it. He didn't press her about it because he remembered Millie Beecham, whom he'd dated at Cambridge, telling him he could be – her word – *intense*. 'You just push a bit too hard,' she'd said in an irritated tone.

Still, there were nights when he wondered if Darya might knock on his door again. The less attention she paid him, the more he wondered how she felt. By day, he had things to do. Anton's English was improving. Paul was reading him his old favourite, *The Cat in the Hat*. 'It is fun to have fun. But you have to know how.' The boy's mother was unwell, then rallying, then unwell. Yet in March, when the bad news came, it was not Mrs Kalinin, but Paul's nan back in Kent. She had broken a hip, gone to hospital and died. He was shocked by the news; no one had told him about her fall.

'Why didn't you let me know?' he asked his mother when he flew home.

She met him at Ashford Station, looking puffy yet drawn. 'I had strict instructions not to,' she told him in the drizzly car park. 'Paul will be having the time of his life, she said.'

Nan had left him her house. It was in Littlestone-on-Sea, a short walk to the beach past the caravan park. It offended his mother that the house went to him alone with no share for his brother. But his grandmother's will was clear. She also left a note, folding it into the coffee tin: 'You're a good boy, Paul. Sorry about the mess. Love, Nan.' He would find this months later, after he came back to the house – this and the wardrobe full of empty Gordon's bottles, the hidden evidence of years of dedicated drinking.

The week of the funeral, he had only just enough time to see about the roof, which had started to leak while Nan was in the home. For the time being, he asked a roofer to do a patch-up job.

'No guarantees,' he was told with heavy disapproval. He told the man he would have the money for a new roof by winter. He would have to hang onto his job. Keep his nose clean, Nan would say.

Nan – what would she make of the way he'd been carrying on?

He flew back on a red-eye flight, landing on a Sunday morning. While he had been away, Russia had annexed Crimea, seizing the peninsula like a chess piece on a board. He wondered what people in Moscow made of the whole thing. As far as he could tell, it was business as usual. Outside the airport doors, men hunched and smoked in their leather jackets. He took the Aeroexpress to the city, and sat staring at the ads for Citibank: from each one the model smiled as if possessed by a secret thrill to see him, extending her hand to shake.

The family was back from Tula, where Nikolai had been riding. Going up to their flat, Paul had the impression of having interrupted a private moment. They had just entered the flat, leaving the door open. They looked at him as if remembering he existed.

'Paul!' Anton cried.

Darya said, 'You're back.'

Nikolai said, 'Ah, good.' He had a slightly hunted look but offered his condolences. 'Coffee?' he suggested, pushing his hair back with a hand, and gestured to the sofa.

Unexpectedly, he issued an invitation. 'Why don't you come with us to St Petersburg at Easter? You ought to see the city.'

Paul felt a curious mix of relief and caution; it felt as much like an instruction as an invitation.

Nikolai added, 'And your friend is there, isn't he?'

How did he know that? Then Paul remembered that Julius had been his referee for the job. It was like Nikolai to recall a detail like that, a person's address on a CV.

Darya returned with a bottle of Evian and Nikolai said, 'I asked Paul if he'd like to come with us to Peter.'

'Oh? You should come.' Her voice held no enthusiasm but even so a surge went through him.

'What takes you to St Petersburg?' he asked, feeling cheerful.

'Family,' she said, just as Nikolai said, 'Business.'

34

Paul went on to give a polite refusal. The offer was very kind, he said, but he already had plans.

Nikolai, clearly expecting a yes, was nonplussed. All the same, that afternoon he offered Paul a ride; it happened they were both going out at the same time. The BMW slid up, shining in the bright spring day. Paul got in the back, plunging into the leather seat.

'Anywhere near Arbat Street,' he said.

Nikolai was listening with a frown to Echo of Moscow, a liberal station, and an interview in English with someone from an environmental group. The activist claimed that an oil pipeline had ruptured in pristine forest. 'It happens all the time,' he said. 'These pipes are old and rusty, Soviet era.'

Nikolai made a *tsk-tsk* sound to show his disapproval. This was not the jeweller's work he had once described to Paul.

The rest of the program continued in Russian and Paul got out of the car. In the cafe he forgot about his employer, and soon Angelica came in from the stinging air. This afternoon she looked troubled and said she had something to tell him. He felt immediately concerned, and drawn to her at the same time: her expression was fittingly angelic, appealing to him the way angels in paintings appealed to the heavens.

'My name isn't Angelica,' she announced. 'It's Maria.'

'Oh, I see.' He didn't see, but thought it could be a Russian nickname thing.

'There is an Angelica,' she went on cautiously, and told him about the real Angelica, a woman who had set herself up successfully as a guide. As more bookings came in, she had recruited other women with good English and dark hair. She still took all the bookings but, after skimming off a profit, divvied them up between her protégées.

'You're kidding,' Paul said, amazed. And yet things suddenly made sense. The daffodils to obscure the woman's face in the Real Guides photo. The way Angelica didn't always turn immediately when he called her name. The fact that she kept him at arm's length.

'I should have told you before,' she said, 'but I didn't know how.'

'It doesn't matter. Why should it?' Though he did feel slightly cheated – all that stuff about *zh* for *zhuk*! He saw her more clearly now, as if knowing her real name swept away any mystique. He noticed the smudges of foundation that didn't quite match her cheeks, and the bulbousness of her nose, pink after her walk.

She put her hands on his. 'I'm sorry.'

He didn't pull away, not wanting to be rude. Instead he waited for their drinks and then picked up his coffee, saying, 'Really, I understand. Don't even think about it.'

*

The train was bolting north, past birch forests and wooden dachas. Darya looked out at the scenery, sighed, and left the carriage without speaking, leaving Paul to rub his forehead. She hadn't wanted him to come, but here he was anyway, imposing.

It was the Wednesday before Easter and they were taking the fast train. Just the two of them, as fate had it. Nikolai had been delayed; he would follow with Anton later. This might have been a good thing but in fact Darya had hardly spoken, staring at her iPad to avoid his eyes. When she left the carriage, he spiralled into doubt and self-recrimination. It was impossible, he knew, for them to pick up where they'd left off, but he found himself unable to stop wanting to. Nor was he making things easy for Darya. He didn't want to be like this, didn't want to be this person, but he couldn't bear the thought of returning to a neutral, respectful distance.

He saw the blue dot of an email from Julius containing an itinerary he had written for Paul's visit. Before Paul could read it properly, Darya returned. Holding two Chupa Chups from the dining car, she offered him one with a proposition: 'From now on, let's be friends, let's be as innocent as children.'

He stared at her, then agreed. 'Alright,' he said.

She took her seat, looking relieved, and they unwrapped their lollipops. (Paul's was caramel, hers was a strawberry swirl.) The deal was all it took for the tension to fall away. Darya's smile made her look brighter than she had in weeks.

On easy terms again, they relaxed into the journey. He took out the English-language *Moscow Times*. The headline 'Ukraine launches military operations' topped a photo of troops holding firearms in a field. Ukrainian forces had retaken an airfield from pro-Russian militants. He asked Darya what she made of the crisis.

'Oh, I don't understand it,' she said with disarming frankness. 'You know, Russians, Ukrainians – we're all the same people.'

The train stopped at a town with a timber yard, continued on. Darya's iPad screen showed a page with information about Miami, Florida. It looked like a tourist website: palm trees, beaches, pink stucco facades, a windswept blonde with a baby in her arms.

'You want to go to Miami?' he asked.

'Oh, I don't know. Perhaps.'

'If it's beaches you're after, you really can't go past England,' he joked.

This made her smile. 'Oh can't I?'

He told her about Nan's house, which was bizarrely his house now, with the shore a stroll away. Pitting it against those white Miami beaches.

'Is it a sandy beach?' she asked, playing along.

'Shingle.'

'Shingle?'

'You know, pebbles and shells.'

'Ah.'

'You'd like it to be sandy.'

'If that could be arranged.'

It was his turn to smile. He was enjoying the game, which was a way of pretending that things could be different, that a person – that Darya – might pick Kent over Miami, shingle over sand, him over Nikolai. As they went on, the journey grew more picturesque – a shallow lake, nicer dachas, slanting light on Darya's cheek – and he felt the unmixed pleasure of anticipation.

The next day, a Thursday, he met his friends. He wasn't staying with them, having accepted Nikolai's offer of a hotel room.

'What's the hotel like?' Julius asked.

'I shouldn't snipe.'

'Go on.'

'Purple chandeliers in the lobby.'

'Amazing,' said Susan, who was in excellent spirits.

Together, she and Julius were adversarial and joyous. They asked after Angelica, smiling winkingly. Paul said she was well, which was probably true. Wasn't the real Angelica raking it in, profiting off the labour of her lookalike guides? He didn't say things were tapering off with Angelica/Maria, that he hadn't responded to her latest text.

Keeping to the itinerary, they went to the Dostoevsky Museum. There were letters home from the writer's travels in Europe, full of a disgruntled traveller's complaints. As they wandered around, Julius and Susan spoke of using their savings to buy 'a little house in Bulgaria' where they would grow their own tomatoes and write a television screenplay. 'Everyone's doing it,' Julius said. He planned to write a thinly veiled drama ripping off his experiences working for Russia's rich. '*The Nanny Diaries* but for Russia.' He was collecting little details for authenticity, and he tried to pump Paul for gossip about Nikolai and his family.

'You can't use people like that,' Paul said, stiffening.

'Why not? They're using you.'

'No, they're employing me.' The Kalinins, he explained, were not the badly behaved rich. 'He's actually very intelligent. So is she.'

'That's the thing about Russia. Even the ones with boob jobs have a view on Pushkin.'

'She doesn't have a boob job.'

'Ah! So you've been looking. Paul Cutter's back in business.'

Paul shook his head, annoyed. He had never liked the nickname.

Susan, who had been listening, asked, 'Why are you calling him Paul Cutter?' Turning to Paul, she said, 'I thought your surname was Cullen.'

'We call him Paul Cutter because he likes to cut other guys' lunches.'

'What do you mean?'

'Julius —'

'He hits on people's girlfriends.'

'God, I'd best look out.' Susan pinched Paul's bum.

That night, the three of them ate at a Ukrainian restaurant, where there was no indication of the brewing hostilities and beribboned women sang folk songs to the diners. Through one number, Julius translated, deadpan: '"I will put a spell on you, you will not meet another woman, you will be with me, you will have to be with me."' As they were waiting for their meals, he

39

turned to Susan and proclaimed, 'Ducky, I feel so guilty. Here you are, a high-flying broadcast journalist, and how am I helping you? Dostoyevsky had Anya to take care of everything. I'm going to be a better boyfriend-slash-secretary-slash-drudge.' Taking her phone, he started sorting her apps into labelled folders, while Susan said, 'You're so sweet. Isn't he sweet, Paul?' But Paul was sick of their cutesiness.

The next day, he ditched the itinerary, going off-piste to see a ballet with Darya at the Mariinsky Theatre. It was her idea; Paul was not a ballet fan. Nikolai was to join them but he expected to come late. Things were coming to a head at his company, Zolotneft. Darya had left him talking things over with her father, who, as a state geologist turned senior bureaucrat, had experience in the sector. It was quite a coincidence, Paul mused, that Darya's dad was so well placed to be useful to Nikolai. But he couldn't pretend to be sorry to have Darya to himself, and he shot a text to Julius to make his excuses.

He and Darya caught a bus from Nevsky Prospekt, and he felt childishly happy to be in her company. Arriving early, they strolled to the English Embankment, and as they walked along the Neva River he began to feel a strange sense of insurrection. He had always been a person of moderate wants, yet as they walked to the river (keeping a safe distance from each other), he was aware of wanting Darya more than ever, beyond reason. He didn't want to stick to the deal they'd struck, didn't want to be her friend.

Preparing to say as much, he glanced at the darkening river and remembered something he'd read about it – that although it looked like it flowed east, this was just an illusion, a trick of the wind, and in fact the current ran very strongly west, towards the Gulf of Finland and the Baltic Sea. He was like this river, he thought, with an unseen current: he had never really been all that moderate, not as even-tempered as others thought. He could want things as badly as any person on earth.

But they had wandered too far, forgetting the time. Now they had to power-walk back to take their seats in the theatre. Onstage Giselle flounced and leapt, an improbably doll-like athlete. A slender-thighed Albrecht was stronger than he looked, eliciting flurries of applause. Paul joined in the clapping, impatient for the intermission, but when it finally came so did Nikolai. He met them in the foyer, with his furrowed brow, his own over-riding atmosphere of drama, and after greeting Paul he hurried Darya outside to talk to her privately. Through the glass, Paul saw him thrusting papers at her. He watched with dread as he saw Darya turn pale. He wondered if it was something to do with Nikolai's work, though he'd never had a sense of her being involved with that.

Then Nikolai looked chastened and swung his coat around her shoulders. Ushering her back in, he declared, 'We need champagne!' Weaving his way to the bar, he returned with two flutes, passing one to Paul and raising the other. Noticing Paul's surprise that Darya was left out, he grinned and said, 'But that's why we're drinking – to the baby!'

The baby? Paul reeled. He looked at Darya, who was now flushed.

'I'm pregnant,' she said.

Pregnant – but since when? He did some arithmetic. She wasn't yet showing, and they hadn't been together since December. It must have been Nikolai, a conception in January or February, perhaps. Feeling unreasonably betrayed, he wished he could speak to her. At that moment the bell rang and he had to traipse back in. He should have been (according to the itinerary in his phone) eating dumplings with his friends at an Uzbek restaurant. Instead he had to sit through the whole of the second act, trapped in his seat in the bel étage. He was acutely aware of Nikolai putting an arm around his girlfriend, only removing it to clap and call, 'Bravo, bravo!'

*

Darya's father was an affable, donnish type. In a button-down shirt and cardigan at lunch the next day, he held forth on the oil industry in Russia. With a degree from the city's Mining Institute, he oversaw natural resources in the Northwestern Federal District. He lectured Nikolai on the perils of offshore drilling, which he called 'a cat in a bag'. For Paul's benefit, he explained, 'You never know what you are going to get.'

No kidding, Paul thought darkly. They were at Darya's parents' flat for an informal celebration. He took a slug of vodka. Darya was eating determinedly and refusing to meet his gaze. Her mother, in Art Nouveau pinks and greens, had gone into the kitchen where she was making a curd cake.

Talk to me, he wished to say, but Darya wouldn't meet his eyes. She stared at the TV with its low-volume news of skirmishes in Ukraine. Since he couldn't break through to her, he drank to pass the time. Before lunch, there had been a lot of tedious baby talk, and a discussion about Miami, which was where Darya wanted to have the baby. Nikolai agreed: American hospitals were superior, no question about it. She was dealing with an agency that could organise it all; it was their mailout that Nikolai had discovered. There was further discussion about Anton, who at some point would be sent to stay with his grandparents, and it jolted Paul to realise that he wouldn't be needed for much longer.

Later, escaping, he slept awhile in his hotel room. He woke

feeling groggy. After splashing his face with water, he went down to the lobby and sat in a tall-backed chair, tipping his head forward and fiddling with his phone. He waited until he saw Nikolai go out, then took the lift for the new wing and his employers' suite. When Darya opened the door, she told him to leave.

'I have to talk to you.'

'Shhh.' She tilted her head at the doors behind her, closed on the alcove where Anton was sleeping. She reluctantly let him in, asking, 'What is it?'

Speaking in a low urgent tone, he tried to tell her what he'd realised the day before at the river, about the strength of the current and his own powerful feelings. Yet instead of listening, really listening, she moved to the window and looked down at the river. Outside, the sky had turned a deep Byzantine purple. On the street below, people were gathering by a church, waiting for the priest to come out and speak.

It was true, Darya said slowly – and here he knew she had missed the point – the river flowed strongly out towards the gulf. 'You know, one night last year a man drove off the bridge when it was raised. His car washed so far down that it was days before the divers found it on the bottom.'

Why was she telling him this? He went to her and tried to put his arms around her but she said, 'Go. I need you to go.'

He did as she said, going out to the corridor and around a corner, where he stood for a moment with his back against the wall. Then he heard her ask, 'Are you there?' Her voice was quiet, lonely – the loneliest words he had ever heard, coming though they did from someone who had no reason to be lonely, who was going to be a mother. 'Are you there?' she asked again, more insistently this time. Paul straightened and went back, full of an unreasoning hope.

43

They made love quietly so as not to wake Anton. This was the end of things, he knew, but everything felt heightened. Whatever his previous doubts about her feelings, he did not have them in her presence. Here, in the hotel room, he believed that she loved him, even though later it would seem impossible again and he would start to believe she'd never felt anything for him.

Afterwards, he looked at her body before she could disguise it, glimpsing before she turned away the curve of her belly, the noticeable tilt above the pubic patch.

'You can't be here,' she said.

He left a second time. In his room he took out his phone and googled 'sex with pregnant woman harm to unborn baby?' Then he scrolled through the results, sagging with relief.

*

His job did not end straight away. He worked for the family until June. His departure, when it came, was unceremonious. Only little Anton was visibly affected, holding tightly to Paul's leg and refusing to say goodbye.

There were no other positions available, he learned at the agency. The recruiter, a polished woman, apologised and shook his hand, making the resin bangles clack loudly on her arm. It was the uncertainty in the air; everyone in Moscow was watching and waiting, business was on hold. No one was hiring. From what Paul could gather, the main activity was that of wealthy Russians shifting their money out of the country as the rouble slipped.

Flying back to England felt strangely like defeat. Paul moved into the house in Kent. He put buckets under the new leaks, lining them with towels to silence the drips. By mid-autumn he had a job. The school was posh, the kind of place that would once have made him feel like a sell-out. He had always told himself he would work in rougher comprehensives. But he liked the boys in his classes, their deferential manners. 'Tell us about Russia, sir,' they would say to put off a lesson.

Not long after he started, a reporter on the *Financial Times* called him. Owen Dorsey had got his number from Julius. Julius was still in Russia but was thinking of leaving too – not for the house in Bulgaria, which was no longer mentioned, but to work for his father's investment firm.

Paul knew Owen but only vaguely. Owen said he was working on a profile. 'Nikolai Kalinin, one of our lesser-known oligarchs.'

Paul, on his way home from work, pulled over to talk. Other cars were whooshing by, headlights flaring across the marsh. He frowned into the phone at Owen's use of the word 'oligarch'. 'That's a bit strong,' he said. 'I don't know if I'd call him that.' He knew bits and pieces from reports he'd found online; he knew Nikolai had done well. There was something oddly hurried about his exit from Moscow; it made Paul think there was a reason why he'd cut and run. Cannily selling his interests before the oil price slid too far, he had bought an estate in Scotland, stables included.

'Oh, come off it, Cullen. There's no need to be bashful.'

'Who else have you spoken to?'

'Everyone's keeping shtum.'

'What about his wife?'

'Which one?'

The question threw him for an instant. Then he understood. Of course, Darya had become the new Mrs Kalinin. Of course they were married, that was how things happened. Even so, he was caught off guard. The thought dogged him for days, recurring at odd hours in the night or during class.

Two weeks later, the newspaper ran the story. Paul read it on the pebbly beach. Sure enough, there was the stuff about Nikolai getting out handsomely, the Scottish estate and stables. There was talk of him buying a racehorse from the Queen. As for Zolotneft, the report gave details of a deal with a foreign outfit. Having won the licence for a bluefield site offshore, they had launched a joint venture to go into the Arctic proper. This must be the deal that Darya had mentioned; the only mystery was how Nikolai came out of things so well. The paper said the deal had nearly foundered over concerns about Zolotneft's environmental record, after the authorities gave notice of breaches in the Northwestern Federal District, but Nikolai had managed to broker a settlement.

It was cold on the shore and the breeze rattled the pages. The shingles were hard to sit on, and clung to his trousers when he stood up. Brushing himself off, he thought of how foolish he'd been, asking Darya to come here. She would have had a September baby, he thought, counting the months. She'd now be leaving Miami, if she hadn't already. Strange to think of her in London, passing through on her way to Scotland, but then her London was not his London. They were completely different cities.

How had Nikolai turned the tables? he wondered, walking back. How had he scuppered the attempt to do him out of his shares, getting one up on whoever had tried to cheat him? He recalled his comment about foxes, that first day at the flat. His admiration for them as survivors, living and thriving in the most extreme conditions. That applied equally to Nikolai.

Up on the street Paul saw that his neighbours' recycling bins were out. He remembered something more about that lunch in St Petersburg, with Darya's parents. After they had eaten, in that slow dragging hour, Nikolai had cut into the older man's speechifying and murmured something about going after the chief of his company. Paul understood the reply: 'You don't know what you're asking. You don't know where this will end.'

This didn't stop Nikolai, who pressed some papers at his host. 'What's this?'

'I want you to use it.'

A manila file fell open and photographs slid out, and Paul saw the images before Nikolai scooped them up. Shots of blackish oil clogging swampland and creeks. A report of some kind too, with the word 'Nenets' in the title, referring to the northern region where Zolotneft had operations. The older man looked appalled, sighed heavily and sat back so that his cardigan fell open at both sides of his belly.

That wasn't all Paul had forgotten about the lunch; reaching the bungalow, he remembered the conversation they had gone on to have next. With Darya glued to the television news, he had made a point of offering Nikolai the use of the house in Little-stone. It was, as he knew, a ridiculous offer. It would never be accepted, which was why he could make the gesture in an airy, offhand way. No one had to know that it wasn't a large house, wasn't the kind of place where people came down for a weekend. He described the beach, the canals – 'like St Petersburg's!' He was aware of Darya, who sat stiffly, listening. He meant for her to hear. He wanted to punish her, and so he took the game they had played together on the train, took what had been private and made it a general thing, open to all and therefore valueless. 'Any of you,' he said blandly to the room. 'You'd be very welcome.'

Darya had glanced at him before looking away. It was as if he had torn the house down before her eyes. And that was the moment he felt bad. More than bad, he felt ashamed. Even so, he did not stop talking, he couldn't stop talking. By then he had drunk a lot, as had the other men, but it was he who had got drunk. It was he who, on offering Nikolai a top-up, accidentally called him Koly, Darya's intimate name for him. His boss let out a harsh laugh and they stared at each other before Paul laughed too.

On the path outside Nan's house, he scrunched up the newspaper. The recycling bin was full, which meant he had to use some force to wedge the paper down the side, shifting the glass bottles so that they chinked in a cosy way. That morning, running out of coffee grounds, he had gone searching for the tin of instant. He had finally found it, plus Nan's note. *You're a good boy, Paul.*

The words had comforted him then, but tonight he wondered if there wasn't a hint of complicity in her words, something cynical and knowing. He was uneasy as he flipped the lid on the plastic bin, covering his work of the night before. That was when, labouring in darkness so the neighbours wouldn't see, he had tipped in bottle after bottle from the supply in the back room. Now he had only to grip the handle and manoeuvre the bin towards the street. Feeling sorry for himself, he shoved it in disgust. Before he could help it the bin toppled forward, and the glass came pouring out in an almost elegant cascade. Everything was breaking, and he felt he was breaking too.

'Damn!' he cried. Too late. He knew he had pushed too hard, and now he was terrified to think of the damage he had done.

Joyride

My boss at the cafe often flirted with men. She was petite, in her mid-sixties, and had the face of a woodland creature – small, inquisitive, bright-eyed, with blinking dark lashes. Years of wearing heavy earrings had dragged on her earlobes, making two vertical slits of the piercing holes, but this did not stop her wearing a pair of large gold hoops.

Sylvie was single and unencumbered and she liked to enjoy herself. If she forgot somebody's name, she breezily told them, 'Good to see you.' If she wanted to compliment someone, she told them they looked great. She disliked creepy men, shrinks and feminists, but she wasn't dogmatic. She made exceptions. Once, she told me she had seen Germaine Greer on TV. 'The interviewer said that her marriage had failed. "No," she said. "It was just short." I thought, good on her. She looked great.'

Sylvie had been married once herself, to a man who lived in France. Their union, too, was brief. It left no bitter feelings.

She had not dated for some time when I met her, but she hadn't gone off men, and flirting brightened her regimented life.

There was nothing austere in her habit of wearing black; she cut the front out of her tops to show her tanned décolletage. She owned the lease on the cafe and worked there six days a week. Each year she took a two-week break and holidayed somewhere warm; otherwise she worked nonstop, insisting, 'I feel great.'

The cafe was her dominion. It sat on a hill overlooking Sydney Harbour. Cut off from the city by a loop of expressway, it was almost, but not quite, stranded, kept apart from the skyscrapers. Inside, the sun streamed in through the old sash windows, striking the gleaming floors and jars of preserved lemons. Having been in business a long time, Sylvie got by on her wits, making use of her charm and cunning as much as her culinary skills. Forever afraid of losing her lease, she was shameless in courting the owner of the building, plying the old man with free lunches and wedges of chocolate torte. She hoped he wouldn't realise that he was footing her power bills, a detail that had slipped his notice for years.

She was a terrible flirt with the electrician too, sending him coquettish texts when the oven gave her trouble. When we teased her about it she pretended to be shocked. 'Don't be revolting, Rowan, I shudder to think,' she said, tapping out a message full of exclamation marks. Other times she would come clean. 'I know, I'm vile. I'm a dirty creature.'

There was also her boyfriend, as we called him. He was a former prime minister, one of the Labor greats. He would come in for lunch, taking a table near the counter with his back to the room. She had never voted for him but always greeted him with, 'Darling, *great* to see you.' She would sit down with him unasked, saying, 'The girls will bring you bread.' He was a willing participant, addressing her as 'doll', and they chatted together in low tones like long-time confidants. He liked to know how business was, and always complimented her cooking. 'You could call that a terrine,' he said of her veal loaf.

Sylvie had known a lot of famous people and was never overawed. She had once served Pompidou himself, she liked to say, selling him a newspaper in the ski town of Auron. The president of France did not expect to have to pay, but she asked him for the money regardless.

Her flirtations were harmless, confined to the cafe. But then she got a serious crush, one that went beyond the cafe walls, unfolding in the dizzying expansiveness of cyberspace, in a flurry of emails and texts. At first she tried to hide what she was doing, but it turned out that she was back in touch with her husband, Charles Bernard, from whom she had been estranged for more than three decades.

'And why not, I'd like to know? Why shouldn't I write to him?' she asked.

Sylvie loved email; she loved the thrill of a back-and-forth, the idea of conversations beaming across space. Her emails were like her texts: quick-fire compositions, never more than a few lines, with 'you' rendered as 'u' and wrapped up with strings of 'xxx'. She tapped these missives out in the glow of the bright screen, despatching each with an expression of unmitigated glee.

I glimpsed a photo of Charles's on her laptop one day, as I was walking past with some dirty dishes. A flash of red, a green background that might have been grass or trees, and sunlight glancing off a crop of silver hair. With the other waitress, Elise, I teased Sylvie about this long-lost husband of hers. We called him the Silver Fox. Until now, she hadn't mentioned him much. Her marriage hadn't been her longest relationship: in the seventies and eighties, she had spent sixteen years with a ceramicist named Erik. He had made the original brown-glazed cups and saucers for the cafe, most of which had since been lost through gradual attrition.

After some pressing, she showed us the photo. Charles, now retired, was wearing a flying suit and standing in a field with a helmet under one arm. He was smiling broadly and screwing up his eyes in the sunlight. Beside him was an aircraft that looked too flimsy to be real. The plane – was it actually a plane? – resembled a red toy. It was a microlight, Sylvie told us. Charles had taken up flying as a hobby. A grand passion, he called it. He was working towards getting his passenger licence. Below the photo he had written *Any interest?* and added a winky face. There was a link to a website with the banner *Microlighting is freedom!*

Like ur onesie, she fired back as we watched. *Not sure abt the jet.*

There was a whoosh as she hit send, the sound of her message taking flight. It went winging across the oceans. The years fell away. Distance was nothing and she was having a great time, enjoying the renewal of the old romance.

*

I worked for Sylvie for several years, while at law school in Sydney. Elise, a high school friend, had got me the job. The interview went for two minutes before Sylvie said, 'Can you come Sunday? Eleven sharp.'

She was a generous employer. She paid double the hourly rate of my last waitressing job. On quiet days, she sent me home on full pay to study. On busy days, when we did well, she slipped me extra money, tucking banknotes into my clothes as if I was a stripper. She smuggled bread and avocados into my bag, and the pages of my books suffered more than one green smear before I learned to do a search at the end of each shift.

Sylvie despaired for Elise, an art school graduate with masses of curly hair and big, startled-looking eyes. She sold as much as she could paint, but Sylvie thought she was squandering her talent, partying too much and making bad choices in men. 'You've got to be serious,' Sylvie told her. 'You can't sleep with just anyone.'

'Didn't you?' Elise asked.

'Darling, I won't deny it. But that was in the sixties. It isn't the sixties now. Do as I say, not as I do.'

For me, the job meant the ease of money, or more of it. Earning more meant I could buy the shoes I needed and the books I didn't. But it wasn't just the money that made life better and less constrained – Sylvie had a talent for living well, a knack for doing things in a certain style and enjoying herself, and in working for her some of that ethos rubbed off on me.

As well as the avocados, the job also brought a largesse of baked goods – baguettes, friands and other cakes. My boyfriend at the time liked the cakes especially; he ate them as he studied, dropping crumbs between the pages. As the sugar hit his bloodstream, he became more animated, looking up to read some passage out loud. David was a philosophy student, quite intense, with a widow's peak. Elise called him Dave, having picked that he would hate it. She claimed the guys I liked were interchangeable. I said the same about her. She always went for artists who gave off a woodsman vibe, wearing old boots and flannel shirts to show their earthiness.

At the cafe, we would eat lunch in the mid-afternoon, after the crowd had thinned and before the afternoon teas and coffees. We heaped salad leaves in bowls (serving put us off rich food) and Sylvie poured herself a tumbler of red wine with water, a way of drinking she had picked up when living in Nice. Now and again she spoke about her life – anecdotal revelations, always adding up to something less than a full account. She often deployed her stories to illustrate a moral. There was the summer she spent eating frozen grapes by the pool. 'I blew up like a balloon, you don't need that much fruit.' Or she would talk about the dishonest types she'd met over the years, wanting us to know we could never be too careful. Yet on the rare occasions she spoke of her erstwhile husband, it was always with an undimmed fondness. They had lived as flower children in keeping with the age. After meeting him in Sydney, she followed him back to Nice, to an apartment on the Boulevard Gambetta. 'The outside looked quite shit,' she said, 'but we had an entire floor.'

His family ran businesses in Auron, the Alpes-Maritimes ski town where she had her brush with Pompidou. They had a house in Vence, near the famous Saint-Martin hotel. You could lie by the pool, Sylvie told us, and watch the sheiks come in by helicopter. These were her everywhere years. 'We just floated,' she said. Going out to California, they stayed in San Francisco's Haight-Ashbury district. 'We went for the drugs, darling. We were very much into mescaline.'

Thinking of Joan Didion, I asked her what she wore. 'Oh, very little, very little. Swathes of ferns in the hair. Leaves.'

She described how they went to Mexico City for the '68 Olympics. The next year, back in San Francisco, they watched the moon landing in a hotel room, then had to leave the US when it was discovered they were working illegally. Back in Sydney for a time, they decided to get married. The ceremony was small. Sylvie wore a fluffy dress she had bought the day before and Charles put a daisy through his lapel. Back in Nice, they were plagued by a cocktail of destructive forces, all the usual things that went wrong for flower children. Charles had his problems and the drug use didn't help. Sylvie did not blame him.

She blamed the cold weather that winter. She hated Auron, she said. She hated it so much she used to go back to Nice on the bus alone. When a telegram came to say her father had passed away, she flew back to Sydney for the funeral, and that was it for things with Charles.

Speaking of that time, she didn't bring up her pregnancy at first. She told me about it eventually, in a later lunchtime conversation. The baby had lived to term but it didn't come out well. Something had gone wrong, though no one could say what. It could happen, she knew that now. It was one of those things, she said. At least she had seen her son briefly: a silent waxy creature, not pink like he should have been. She had given birth to him in Nice, in a ward under a picture of Jesus on the cross, a scarecrow of a man. When a nurse asked if they wished to speak to a nun, Charles scowled and said no – according to the Church, their baby would be going to Limbo.

Sylvie told me this story when speaking not of Charles, but of her mother, a woman she described as 'sharp as paint': severe and unforgiving. She didn't mean to be that way, Sylvie thought, she couldn't help being stiff; she was just not an expressive person. When Sylvie came back from France, they met at a restaurant, neutral ground. Her mother, immaculately groomed even in the depths of mourning, looked her daughter over and said, 'I have to say, you look good.' Caught off guard by the compliment, Sylvie said in a rush, 'Mother, I lost my baby.' Then she cried a little as her mother looked on, pained, and after a time they asked for the bill.

*

The rekindled romance continued all that year. The emails and texts were short but dense with information. Each was gaining a sense of how the other lived. Sylvie learned that Charles still had the old apartment on the Boulevard Gambetta. His father had died the year before, and the winding up of his estate allowed Charles to quit his job at Aeros Bassiel, where he had worked for some years as a glorified English teacher.

'He used to have to teach them space talk in English,' she told us. 'He taught the French and then the Russians and then the Chinese.' Now a man of leisure, he wore polarised aviators, colourful rubber Crocs, and drill shorts that exposed his still-muscular calves. He had his lustrous silver hair cut each month, trimmed close at the back and sides. A good move, in her view. It saved him from looking like her idea of a paedophile.

In an email to him, she described her normal day. She rose at five, drank her first coffee as she watched the American news, and then dressed and did her face. She shopped at the markets and did her prep at the cafe. When Elise and I arrived she had one of us make her second or third coffee. At five pm, after packing up, she put on driving gloves to go home. Refusing dinner invitations, she stayed in – these days, she needed to recharge – and usually watched a nature documentary. She especially liked shows about baby animals – an orphaned monkey in a zoo, a lion cub suckling from a pig. On Mondays, her day off, she refused to go anywhere. If the weather was warm, she lay 'like a lizard' by the pool at her building.

'I bet he wants a photo,' Elise said knowingly one day.

'I'm not sexting him, you creep.'

'I didn't mean that. I meant a normal photo.'

But Sylvie resisted. She didn't like to be in any photos, even with her clothes on. Charles, it seemed, was too much the gentleman to ask for a picture, although he sent lots of himself. There were shots of his aircraft too, with its tricycle-style wheels, and the wings angling upwards from the frame in a shallow V. Like a glider, it was controlled by a lateral bar, he wrote. It was powered from the rear by a sizeable propeller.

I tried to take Sylvie's photo when I dropped in to see her one day in April. I had started part-time at a big commercial law firm, which meant fewer waitressing shifts. Working in a skyscraper with blinding harbour views, I wasn't far from the cafe as the crow flew, but to get there was a roundabout expedition, up a steep hill and through a concrete subway that sheltered a camp of homeless people.

As near as it was, the firm was a different world. Rivers of money ran. There was a private-equity boom, which meant buyouts and spinoffs. In the mergers and acquisitions group, people high-fived when deals were struck. Firms competed with each other for the best graduates, courting them with lunches and cocktail parties. I heard a law student at one function admire a female partner's shoes. 'Let's swap,' the woman told her, not missing a beat. 'You look like a six, six and a half?' And she swapped her expensive heels for the student's much cheaper ones.

Elise was now painting more but still working at the cafe; she needed a steady wage. Seeing me losing the argument about taking Sylvie's photo, she said, 'She won't even let me paint her portrait for my show.'

'I will!' said Sylvie. 'I said I would. Get my diary. Choose a date.' But there was no budging on the photo for Charles. 'Don't make me wild,' she said. There was an edge in her voice, and if I hadn't given up I believe she might have hit me.

Photo or not, the Silver Fox showed no signs of cooling. He had a lot of time on his hands, his girlfriend having left him a year ago, moving to Lyon to be near her two sons. He was getting his miles up in the microlight. When he had his full licence, he hinted again, he could fly with a passenger.

I could see she was drawn, and now I discovered that this wasn't the first time he'd made overtures. Sylvie, forever cagey, had made it sound like they had been completely estranged for the past three decades, but he had invited her to visit in the early nineties. And she had gone. Single again – things had finished with Erik – she made the trip in the European summer. The story had a madcap flavour. On a long stopover in Rome to visit friends, she narrowly escaped a car bomb on a street out front a church, one of several bombings in the wake of new anti-Mafia laws. The blasts meant extra security at the airport and thus delays, and she passed the time shopping and drinking at the bar. Finally making it to Nice, she got off the plane drunk, shopping bags up her arms. She had told Charles not to come to meet her but when she passed through the doors there he was, standing on the tiles, dressed for the occasion in a suit and a Hawaiian shirt. On seeing each other they both started to laugh, and they kept laughing until tears streamed from their eyes.

But the wheels soon fell off. Charles had a girlfriend, about whom he had kept quiet. (To be fair, he had never lied; Sylvie had not asked him outright.) When the girlfriend showed up, a pretty but fading blonde, she looked dusty and displeased, having walked from the bus stop in impractically strappy sandals. She found them at the car, about to go for a drive. When she demanded an explanation, Charles rounded on her in anger.

'Get in the car,' he snapped. 'I'm taking you home.' She did as she was told and opened the front passenger door. 'No,' he said. 'In the back. Sylvie is my *wife*.'

Still, Sylvie did not regret the trip. In her mind the story stood for the comedy of life, for that moment of amusement when she and Charles had locked eyes and laughed at each other's middle-aged selves.

*

Sylvie was not my family. I had a family already. I saw my parents when their travels brought them near or through Sydney. My father had a sailboat, a 21-footer that he towed on a trailer to sail in different places. People think of sailing as the purview of the rich, but Dad went sailing like other people go camping, taking his food in an Esky full of melting ice and tooling around for days or weeks on some lake or stretch of coast. No marinas, no moorings, no popped collars in sight.

That April, when my parents were sailing on Lake Macquarie, I headed up to see them, taking public transport and finding them at a jetty. Having come in from the wilds, they had pulled up at the village of Wangi Wangi, right below the neon lights of the RSL club. They used the bathrooms to wash and drank wine as the sun set, my dad looking forward to dinner at the Chinese restaurant. They were enjoying themselves, but I found myself impatient before we had even started sailing. I had spent a lot of time on boats, long holidays adrift with no way to escape, reading on deck until I got sunstroke. This time I had brought Tolstoy, *Anna Karenina*. I was amused by the part where Levin deals with the auditors; it could have been lifted straight from the Enron scandal. I tore through the book. Tolstoy was a genius. Who knew?

We spent the next day sailing, tacking back and forth in a north-easterly wind. After that, I was glad to get my train back to Sydney. I was always relieved to get back to the city, as relieved as my parents were to get out of it. They were more and more averse to dealing with the traffic, and if they had to drive through it Dad planned his route on fold-out maps, preparing as if for a polar expedition.

Since starting at university, I had lived in a series of share-houses in the inner west, under the flight path. Stanmore, Leichhardt, and Marrickville, where Sylvie had once lived. I was in the area that used to be called the warren, because some settler landowner had brought rabbits out from England thinking they would make a good food source for the poor. When I lived there, Marrickville had excellent food; it was a predominantly Greek and Vietnamese suburb. Old Greek men and women felt free to berate me on the bus, reproaching me for the faults of young people in general. Once, when I bought a bunch of long plum branches in blossom, I wondered aloud how I would carry them home.

'Where's your husband?' the grocer asked.

'I don't have one,' I said.

'Get one,' he shot back.

'What, today? This afternoon?'

When I told this story over lunch with my family, Dad asked what the grocer's background was. 'You don't know with these people, men in his position.'

'What do you mean? In what position?'

'Men in positions of flower,' my sister quipped.

For a short time I dated a guy who lived a few streets away. He was a part-time model and a DJ, and a hair stylist as well, although he preferred to say he was a 'hair-doing guy'. He was so committed to his look that when an iced-tea company asked him to shave off his beard to play a monk in a commercial, he said no. He had very smooth skin and smelt of tobacco. Not a sad, stale cigarette smell, but the much nicer smell of actual tobacco leaves. We didn't have much in common, but sometimes he came around after playing a set somewhere, and it was convenient for us both because he lived so close. Once, I saw a photo of his previous girlfriend on a beach and he became self-conscious. 'I gave her that haircut,' he said. 'It made her look like a troll.' She did look a little bit like a troll – it was a layered, spiky haircut, very eighties rocker – but something in his voice told me he still loved her, and later I heard they were back together.

At the firm where I worked, I wasn't drawn to the other clerks. They had new suits, shiny hair and the glow of shared good fortune. They quizzed each other to find out who they knew in common, exclaiming, 'It's such a small world!' As for the lawyers, the best of them were joyless, too tired and overworked to show much interest or spark. I shared this opinion with another clerk on my floor, before adding offhandedly, 'I guess if I had to be stuck in an elevator with any of them, it would be Chris from Insolvency.' I was mildly embarrassed when she started seeing Chris; two years later, when they got married, they sent me an invite.

I started seeing another David, David the Second. He wasn't uptight like the first; he was happy to go by Dave. Insisted on it, in fact. We met at a party where everyone adored him. He was a few years older than me and drinking peaty scotch whisky. He was smart and funny and raffish-looking, and I had been waiting for someone who was smart and funny and raffish-looking. He loved that I had read the books he liked, especially Norman Mailer, because it gave him an opening to talk about war novels and boxing. There was an incongruity to his attraction to boxing; he couldn't have looked less like a boxer if he'd tried. He was tall and bow-legged with unkempt hair, and when he sprawled on a bed or swam in the ocean or a pool his limbs splayed akimbo like those of a frog. He had a natural enthusiasm; he liked an escapade. One night, we climbed over the high fence into the Botanic Gardens, whispering and laughing, and fooled around on the grass until we gave up because of the bugs.

Dave worked as a speechwriter for the state premier, and he made it sound like he was writing Lincolnesque speeches rather than editing remarks about a train station expansion. He meant to be a writer, and he lived much as I did, with a mattress and a desk surrounded by piles of books, although he also had a nicer room in his parents' house over the bridge. He was less inclined to schlepp out to the inner west, so I was always going from place to place with my stuff stashed in a bag. He came to the cafe, though. He met Sylvie. He *loved* Sylvie. She's brilliant, he said.

She took to him as well, but she didn't know about his drinking, which was partly what gave him that glittering quality he had. I couldn't keep up with him. I tried for a time, but at some point I had figured out that marks actually mattered. Not just for getting jobs but for scholarships overseas, and one of my lecturers told me I should be thinking about these things. So I knuckled down. I studied. My essays bristled with footnotes. At the firm, I racked up billable hours and trawled through rooms full of binders. I wrote pro bono briefs. I was mentored by a senior lawyer over shots of wheatgrass juice.

I was serious at work. One day, another clerk tried to high-five me on the street. We were standing on George Street, about to cross the road. With his palm in the air, he said, 'Come on, don't leave me hanging!' But that was exactly what I did.

'I'm not going to high-five you. It's my policy,' I said.

*

In winter, something happened. Charles's emails to Sylvie stopped. The last thing he wrote was innocuous: *Hot day*. (It was summer there.) *I bought socks & an ice cream.*

This gave Sylvie no clues. Had he flown off in his micro-light and, like Icarus, gone too far? Sylvie nudged him: *miss ur updates! don't be a stranger.* But neither this nor other promptings drew any response. As the silence dragged on, Sylvie became short-tempered, then rude. She had always hated providing tap water to her diners, and had a bitchy way of saying 'the *lovely* tap water'. Now, though, she insisted that customers drink all the water they poured. She blocked the departure of one family from the cafe until they laughingly complied.

'We're in a drought, you know,' she told them, hand on hip. This wasn't true, but being city people, they did not know or care, and they went away saying what a character she was.

It was June, and Elise's solo show was a month away. Faced with the idea of sitting for a portrait, Sylvie blew hot and cold. She wanted to help Elise, and thought highly of her work, but sitting still and being scrutinised was her idea of hell.

'Who's going to want to look at an old wrinkled thing like me?' she said. Her trump card was the cold; she couldn't sit in the freezing garage Elise used as a studio. She held up her blotchy hands and claimed poor circulation. In the end I filled in for her, positioning a chair in front of a space heater.

I've since read that painters, like boxers, see more than other people. Instead of relying on the brain to fill in visual gaps, they train themselves to see what is actually before them. I can believe this after watching Elise's face as she painted. The gaze she turned on me was coolly appraising, a gaze of pure seeing, stripped of any judgement, and it made me realise why Sylvie stayed away. She had a secretive streak. She didn't completely trust anyone. Skilled at deflection, she hid her private self from view.

The truth was she was embarrassed about Charles's silence. She was mortified, dismayed. It was Elise who bore the brunt of her ever-worsening temper. When she broke one of the last of Erik's cups, Sylvie snapped, 'Stupid! You're so stupid!' She was rude to the building owner when he ordered a decaf. 'It's the worst for you, the worst,' she said with surprising force. 'Do you know the chemicals they use to strip the caffeine out?' She always regretted her sharp comments afterwards, and wished she could take them back. She renewed her offer to sit for Elise, but now it was too late, the works were already being hung. All that was left to her was to go to the private viewing and discreetly buy one of the paintings. To Elise, she said, 'Next show, I promise. Why am I such a wretch?'

In trying to get her to send a photo to Charles, what we didn't know was that she had sent one already, in an email just before the Great Silence. It was a perfectly nice photo, showing her standing by the counter. Not too close, she had told the customer who took it for her. Her dark hair was pulled back and her lips had a coral shine.

This was why she was upset. The Silver Fox hadn't written back. Sylvie had no option but to carry on regardless, as she had after their marriage, before finding happiness with Erik. He was older than her, forty-one when they met, and also separated. He owned a shop in Australia Square that sold souvenir ceramics. Sylvie, a new hire, noticed him hanging around. 'Excuse me, sir,' she said. 'I see you here but you never buy. Are you a spy or what?'

It was ironic that she'd said this, because in fact Erik had once engaged in a little light espionage. As a young man in

Czechoslovakia he had passed information on the communists to British Intelligence. That was until the day he walked into a restaurant and saw his face among others on a wanted poster. He got out of the country, leaving everything behind, and wound up in Sydney, where he had to start again.

So Erik became the story of the seventies. He and Sylvie lived next to his pottery among the factories of Marrickville, which was then still mostly industrial. Grit carried on the air from the trucks on Illawarra Road, but they had a swimming pool and two excitable Rottweilers. The business was successful. They wanted for nothing. Once, when the window of Erik's car jammed on a trip to Melbourne, he pulled in at Albury and bought a new car off the lot, leaving the old one by the kerb in front of the dealership.

Sylvie thought that a good thing could be good even if it ended. She parted from Erik when he met somebody else. Later, much later, he asked her to come back. By this time he was starting to suffer from dementia. She didn't go back but she helped him as best she could. When she went to the house, the surviving Rottweiler heard her car coming down past Newtown Station, and he would prick up his ears and whine excitedly. Sometimes Erik came to see her at the cafe, turning up in his dressing gown and drawing looks from the patrons. 'I walked from Marrickville,' he would say.

When I knew her, Sylvie had been living alone for years. She had a studio apartment at Rushcutters Bay. The boxiness of her main room might have been depressing if not for the water view and the extreme simplicity of her style. This required the banishing of clutter, the regifting of gifts, and a hardline approach to dealing with mementoes. She showed the same ruthlessness about Charles's correspondence. She claimed to have lost interest. She couldn't write emails all day.

'Some people have to work,' she said, setting out canapés. This was on a rainy evening at a catering job. She had asked me to come and help; someone had called in sick. When I arrived in my suit from work she said, 'You're great to me, Rowan. I know you don't need to do this.'

It wasn't her night: the job was an office party and she was cross with herself for having quoted too low. There were more people than there were meant to be and they fell on the trays of food. 'Like vultures!' she said. She was too proud to do what other caterers would have done, which was to serve cheaper food, fried things from the freezer. She tried to level the score by stealing whatever she could get her hands on in the office kitchenette. Taking handfuls of the popsicle sticks that were meant to be used as coffee stirrers, she shoved them down her pants.

'I'll use them to do my waxing,' she said defiantly.

She didn't care who saw as she left carrying her serving trays, with those popsicle sticks falling out of her trousers.

*

That July I saw (if you can believe it) a real live fox in Sydney. I honestly don't know how long it had been since I'd last seen one. You never saw them in the city. And yet here was this one, going about its business as I went about mine. It was maybe six o'clock and the Moreton Bay figs, those vast mouldering trees, were gathering darkness about them. The fox darted across the grass, keeping low to the ground, lower than you'd think. A streetlight made its eyes glow and illuminated its outline for several long seconds.

It was a winter fox. Thin and ratty-looking. There was a hunger in its features that I somehow recognised. A solitary creature, it knew how to be alone. It looked at me like it knew me, like I was no sort of surprise, just a regular customer, no biggie. Like it was seeing an old acquaintance. And maybe we did know each other, this fox and I. It regarded me with intent, as if willing me to remember some old, half-buried knowledge – some pact of long ago.

That twilight encounter left an impression on me. The experience was one of coming to my senses; it took me back to a part of myself I had almost forgotten. Maybe foxes can do this; this is part of their magic. Just like that, I was reminded of my pre-law-school self. What are you doing? I asked myself as it trotted out of sight. What are you doing with your life?

But as I went on my way again, I decided that the fox was a messenger for Sylvie, not me. If it was a portent of things to come, surely it had to do with her long-lost husband, the Silver Fox.

And sure enough, as if on cue, she received an email from him that same night. She told me about it the next day. All was explained. Charles hadn't gone cold on their correspondence at all: first, he had locked himself out of his phone, having confused his code with his bank card pin. Then he'd had his eyes lasered to correct his vision, and afterwards a troublesome infection had made it hard to look at a screen.

He wrote: *At last I am better. I am writing this without glasses. I am an entirely new man!* He loved the photo she had sent him. *Just wonderful to see you*, he wrote. *<3 <3 <3.* He remarked on the cafe, saying how charming it looked and how much he would like to see it.

It was just the thing to buoy her midwinter spirits. In the south of France, where it was summer, Charles flew his microlight over fields and towns, beaches and rocky coves. His messages arrived like warm drifts of air. They carried Sylvie through the bleak, cold days, bearing her along through the wind tunnels of the city and keeping her company at night when she went home to her flat. The email romance was back on, there had been nothing to fear, and all was well again in the garden of their affections.

'You know he's invited her to go over there,' Elise told me one day in her studio.

'What? Is she going to?'

'I don't know. I don't think she knows.' Elise took a sip of beer. We were sharing a Coopers longneck that she'd poured into glasses. She squinted at a painting that she had propped against the wall, and now, looking unhappy, she turned it the other way.

Sylvie hadn't said yes to Charles but nor had she refused. He had argued his case, describing the scenic flights they would take together, particular routes he liked at certain times of day. Elise could picture the two of them going flying, both in old-timey goggles and hats with furry flaps. Sylvie would dress like Katharine Hepburn in the film *Christopher Strong*, except she wouldn't have Hepburn's height, and hopefully she wouldn't fly to her death.

'Does he want to get back with her?' I asked.

'Who even knows? I don't care. She's always at me. I'm sick of it.'

Something was up with Elise. She had started doing collage using old books and magazines, and when we flicked through the latter to read our horoscopes, she made it very clear she only wanted the good bits. She said, 'Doom is for losers. Make it up if you have to.' Eventually she confessed that her most recent fling had ended. The worst thing, she said, was that she kept running into her ex, who lived nearby.

'I cry every day,' she said, 'but it's getting better. I get it over with quicker. It doesn't take me as long to stop, and then I'm like, tick, that's done, what's next?'

'I'm sorry. I didn't know.'

'Well, how could you? Anyway, tell me how David is.'

'Dave,' I said.

'Dave.' She was sceptical. She still maintained she could pick my type. 'Oh, is your name Dave?' she asked with mock politeness. 'Are you tall, intellectual and really pretentious?'

I could play that game as well. 'Oh, are you a shaggy-haired artist or musician? Do you like to go out with girls who are way too hot for you, but also like to make them feel like they're not good enough? Because you'd be perfect for my friend.'

Actually, I admitted then, things weren't perfect with Dave. We had fought on the phone the night before. We'd been arguing a lot recently. He said I wasn't any fun. That was probably true, but it was also true that he was drinking too much, staying out every night and getting recklessly messy while priding himself on his talent for hard living.

Elise said she spent most of her time alone, except when she worked at the cafe. Of an evening she was reading the novel *Infinite Jest*, which she acknowledged was maybe not ideal breakup reading. 'I basically read fiction to learn about life,' she said.

'Okay, but was David Foster Wallace all that good at life?'

To me, novels had ceased to seem like any sort of guide, at least not on relationships. I had arrived at the view that no one told the truth about love, that as a culture we peddled an assortment of wrong ideas. I had no idea how much it was reasonable to expect – how much any relationship, once it had been worn in, could deliver on the cliché of a romantic state.

Elise looked at her watch. 'Don't you have to go? It's almost six o'clock.'

I did. I was having dinner with Sylvie, and Sylvie being Sylvie we had agreed on an early time. I hurried to Darlinghurst and the cafe she'd chosen. She showed up walking her gliding walk, and we sat facing the street to eat the house spaghetti. She was in high spirits, and when she spoke about Charles and his offer to take her flying, she shuddered with pleasure. 'I'd be afraid of falling out,' she said. 'The whole thing is ridiculous.'

She was silent for a moment, gazing at the pedestrians. 'But what do I have to lose?' she asked. 'Do I want to make other people's lunches into my old age? Although, you know, Rowan, I worry. What if it's how it was with Erik? What if he wants a nurse?'

She had looked into it anyway, had seen her travel agent. She had a quote on a ticket from Sydney to Paris with a stopover in Ho Chi Minh City. 'You know,' she said, 'if I'd been a man, I would have had to go off to fight in Vietnam. They had that lottery for conscription. My birthday came up.'

She told me Charles had fought in Algeria, before she knew him. On night watch, he had been made to sit holding a grenade with the pin pulled out. If he'd fallen asleep and dropped it, it would have killed him. It was a form of torture, she said, shaking her head. She was sure it had played a part in his problems later on.

For a moment, she looked quite aged. Her eyeliner was smudged, her skin crepey under her tan. But her smile was valiant, her eyes peculiarly bright. She downed a glass of water, the *lovely tap water*. Changing the topic, she asked how I'd been. 'You're doing well, though, aren't you, Rowan?' She peered into my face.

'I'm doing great,' I said.

She was too preoccupied to dig further. Yet there was something I had been wanting to ask her. Feeling certain of nothing, and with no trustworthy guides, I wanted the opinion of a realist.

As we were leaving I came out with it on the street, asking if she thought I should go on with Dave.

'Is he good to you?' she asked, frowning with sudden concentration.

'Yes.'

'How is the sex?'

I was surprised. 'The sex is good.'

'Good,' she said. She flagged a taxi. 'You're fine. Stick with him, Rowan.' And with these words of wisdom she stepped into the cab.

*

Do as I say, not as I do. That was how it was with Sylvie. She wanted me to be happy and successful and secure. This was what she wanted in return for what she gave me, and it was what she hoped to see whenever she peered into my face. At times it made it hard to go to see her. It wasn't just that I was busy, occupied with other things. It was the effort of looking nice. If I hadn't done my hair I knew she would worry about me, would think I wasn't doing well. So, not wanting her to worry, I stayed away from the cafe.

In August, as she flew out, I was breaking things off with Dave. I had contradictory feelings. Desolation. Annoyance. I was more attached to him than I thought. It was all that dash and glitter. He raged and was petulant, and even then, at his most caustic, he had a way with a turn of phrase. Afterwards I was lonely, but I found an answering desolation in the city's wintry streets: the trees shedding their leaves and standing bare against the sky, the crystalline light when the sun shone, things stripped to their essentials.

As for Sylvie, she landed in Ho Chi Minh City. In the airport she moved among her fellow baby boomers. There were a lot of

Americans, a lot of Vietnam veterans, holding paperback histories like guidebooks to the past. By comparison to Sylvie they were large and slow-moving, shuffling in their sandals and glancing uncertainly about, and she ducked and wove between them, boarding pass in hand. She had not gone to any war, had never picked up a gun. As it was, she had bounced about without much consequence. It suited her to be the little person in history. She lived in the long stream of the present, but events and memories recurred. The past was always with her. Maybe this was why she decided she didn't need to search it out.

Because this was her decision, when it came down to it. She tucked her boarding pass in her pocket. At the time when they would have been calling her name at the gate, she was exiting the terminal, stepping onto a shuttle bus.

That night, she slept for an age in an airport hotel. The next day, she transferred to a resort town in the north. She let the second part of her air ticket go to waste; she did not fly on to France, did not rekindle things with Charles. Not that year or ever. That was it for the Silver Fox.

Don't think badly of me pls, she wrote in an email on her phone, biting her lower lip as she tapped the words. Whoosh. One more for old times' sake!

She knew he would read it over breakfast with his perfect lasered vision. His face was still dear to her, still tenderly familiar. Reclining by the pool, she pictured taking the flight he had planned for her visit: the two of them in helmets like a double-headed insect, lifting off from the small airfield of Fayence-Tourrettes, wafting over the orange roofs and all the patchwork fields, holding on for dear life and enjoying the joyride.

How is your great life?

At college, Dev Mishra had the room across from Ana's. At that time a devout boy with a liking for overalls, he possessed an unfailing sense of what was 'fishy' or 'fancy', these being the words he used to express his disapproval. At their university, which catered to foreigners in Tokyo, they were both scholarship kids among wealthier students. But when she called her old friend, three years after they graduated, he was living the high life in ritzy Azabu. He worked in IT for a Japanese bank and rented an apartment which cost, he was proud to say, more than Priya Vajpayee's whole monthly pay packet (Priya having been, at college, the benchmark for success).

It was a humid night in July, just past ten o'clock. 'So, Ana,' Dev boomed, 'how is your great life?' An hour and a half later, she fronted up to his building – a steel plate gave its name as the 'Imperial Satellite' – and took the lift up to the eighth floor. He opened the door in jeans and a T-shirt, his hair freshly combed back, and Ana was hit with a blast from the air-conditioning unit.

Inside, he gave her a key and a thick fold of yen. 'For groceries or whatever,' he said.

What could she do but take the money? She had no apartment and no job. She had fallen out with Shigeko, her former flatmate and friend, and was waiting to receive a renewed visa, without which she could not find gainful employment. She didn't really want to go on hostessing, which was how she had made her living since her final year at college. She had never had a problem with the work, but on recent dates with clients she had felt her smile grow wan and feeble, like a bulb about to blow. Worse, the greater her disaffection, the more some clients pursued her, attracted by what they took for an air of melancholy.

Dev was too tactful to ask awkward questions; it made it easier that his manner was brusque and businesslike. Pushing his hair back, he ran her through his week: on Tuesdays he fasted, on Wednesday nights he met friends for dinner, and on Fridays he went to the Den, a strip club in Roppongi. At least, that was what he'd done last Friday, he added. It was actually the first time he'd been to a place like that. Previously he'd always kept Friday evenings for cleaning and ironing. Now he was thinking of hiring a maid, a Filipina woman who would wash and iron his clothes and vacuum the apartment's fifteen tatami mats.

Ana looked around, twisting her hair on her finger. Her hair was as pale as combed flax, an unadulterated colour, and her fingers were long and thin, with raw, bitten-down nails. She still had her bag over her shoulder, and finally she dumped its dragging weight onto Dev's couch. She was relieved that he didn't try to entertain her. He offered her the bed but she opted to sleep in the main room, taking the foldout futon. When she rose the next morning, and on subsequent mornings, she packed the bedding away first thing, trying to keep the apartment neat.

She saw Dev in the evenings when he got home, usually late. He would pour himself some red wine, crank the air conditioning up to full, and settle on the couch in an expansive mood. He often spoke about his work and his colleagues at the bank.

'This is consumer banking,' he told her with a shrug. 'It's not a huge amount of money, a few million a branch. The technology is ancient. We're talking 1998, 1999. I was a schoolboy then. When the system goes down, most times it's the temperature. Some branches don't have dedicated server rooms. The idiots don't realise, they put their coffee cups on the servers, turn off the AC when they leave. These machines are like grandfathers. In the heat they fall asleep. *Oof.*'

He would also ask her opinion on all manner of things, such as whether it would hurt 'a great deal' if he waxed his chest. Eventually, though, his talk would turn to Sara, the Iranian beauty he had fallen for in college. He still spoke of her with wonder, and seemed compelled to go over the times he'd spent with her.

'Once, she came to see me on my break at work,' he recounted one night. 'The job was what we called grooming, which is brushing away cement. It was seven floors up. We worked without safety chains. I was the lowest of the workers, earning six hundred yen an hour and plucking chunks of cement from my nostrils every day. My skin was dust, my voice was hoarse. I got a fifteen-minute break, and I met Sara in a park. "I've never seen you like this," she said, her eyes brimming with sorrow. Oh Ana, if you could have seen those big doe eyes of hers!'

He shook his head. 'The jobs I worked. A summer labouring at a farm. A job in a factory crushing plastic in a furnace. My hair would change colour with the plastic in the air. The others left me their time cards and had me punch them out. Come on, they said. Let's go. But I would stay crushing that plastic until five pm exactly.'

Ana was shocked. She knew Dev had worked through college, she had done the same, but she never would have guessed at the conditions he described. On campus he had always been cleanly and crisply dressed. He was the student that their lecturer for Asia Pacific Trade, the jovial Professor Gupta, would single out to ask, 'And how is your great life?'

But those student jobs, Dev explained, were why he now took such pleasure, when coming home each night, in hearing his black Church's shoes strike the lobby's marble tiles. He was pleased that his couch was upholstered in fine-grained off-white leather and that his curtains were resistant to sunlight and heat. He was buying his parents a new house in India (it had four spacious bedrooms, and brass door handles throughout). He also planned to wire them ten thousand US dollars as a sort of apology for not going home for Diwali, the main Hindu holiday of the year. He couldn't leave Tokyo just now, he said, with how things were at work. Still, he toyed with the idea of going to the States. It was a dream of his to move there and work for a start-up, something fun. But then again, he said to Ana, what if Sara tried to call him, as perhaps she would one day?

He was always checking his phone – and he was always disappointed. Most of his calls were from colleagues or his mother. '"But Manu" – she calls me Manu – "how is your health?" she always asks.' Sitting back against white leather, Dev swigged his wine and grimaced. 'I'm tired of answering this question.'

*

In Tokyo that July, a series of typhoons threatened. Ana had never acclimatised to summers in Japan; back in Tallinn there

76

was nothing like this humidity. It made cowlicks in her hair, it made her top stick to her back, and worst of all, it made her feel sluggish and stupid. It was hard to reach anyone among her old group of friends, most of whom now worked in 'office flower' jobs – menial roles that meant long hours and low-level harassment. She whiled away the hours at the nearby Segafredo, listening idly to the talk of diplomats and bankers. After a long, lacklustre decade, Tokyo was booming again. It was a sign of the times that the hospital up the road was building a new unit for cocaine overdoses. 'But it's only another kind of bankruptcy in disguise,' she heard an American declare. 'Pouring money into Tokyo while the rest of the country is stagnating . . .'

A waiter was tipping a pail of water onto the footpath to cool the air. One table over, a man read Nanami Shiono's *Stories of the Romans*. The sky was a soft close grey; there never seemed to be a sun at this time of year. Checking her phone – it was near six – she saw a text from Shigeko: *I hope you are not ungry.* Did she mean hungry or angry? Angry, probably. Ana didn't answer, and just then the phone rang.

'So you'll be okay?' said Dev. 'With the eel guy, I mean?'

'Takuya? He's fine.'

She was still seeing a few clients, Takuya among them. Generous as Dev was, she had to earn some money. And Takuya, who made his living advising restaurants, liked to dine in the company of European women. That night he was taking her to eat *hamo*, a type of eel you could only get during the summer months.

Takuya was one of Shigeko's circle, like many of Ana's clients. The first such introduction had come soon after she moved in. Ana had answered Shigeko's notice on a board: 'Single Japanese woman seeks English-speaking flatmate.' It was a comfortable, large apartment not far from the college campus, and Shigeko did not ask for a lot of rent, although she did require key money of eighty thousand yen up front. She was in her early thirties, with a pale oval face and prominent teeth, and wore demure clothes. She was vague on what she did for work, but mentioned corporate events. When Ana moved in, Shigeko made her feel welcome by inviting her along to drinks and dinners out.

The first of these dinners was with a policeman named Akimoto. He was kind and unassuming, though Ana wasn't sure why he took them both to dinner. If he was dating Shigeko, why did he want Ana there? Perhaps it was just generosity to a student on a budget. Anyway, she ate the meal and swapped pleasantries. Afterwards, Shigeko gave her a slim white envelope containing twenty thousand yen. A gift from Akimoto, she said. 'For textbooks.' Uncomfortable, Ana refused the money, but Shigeko pressed it on her. 'Take it, it's a gift,' she said, smiling. 'What's wrong with keeping it?'

Now, just after six, Ana sat at the cafe, toying with her iced-coffee straw. Soon Takuya showed up wearing a blue basketball vest. His greeting came out oddly – 'Thank you for your cooperation' – but that was just his English. He always spoke to her in English, never in Japanese. As they walked towards Roppongi, he spoke about business.

'The Japanese food industry is very difficult,' he said. 'I have to persuade foreign investors to look at these businesses. Turnover is up but profitability is down. You have to work hard to make money.'

Takuya's steps were long and loping; Ana hurried to keep up. They passed the deep green sanctum of Arisugawa Park, several embassies and schools, and expensive apartments where heady-smelling jasmine flowed from iron-lace balconies. When they reached Roppongi Hills, a newish entertainment quarter, there was at least a tepid breeze waving the pond-grass in the courtyard. Early for their restaurant booking, they rode the elevator up to the viewing deck. Ana knew she was supposed to marvel at the view, to act like she hadn't been living in Tokyo for years, but when they stepped out of the lift she was genuinely staggered. The city stretched out before them in the dusk, a pastel metropolis. Dragonfly-like helicopters were sweeping the pink haze and the roads were arteries of neon, pulsing and converging. As Takuya led her to the glass, she was filled with a sharp dismay. This was a vertigo not of height but a huge and lateral whirling. How completely the city effaced the earth, she thought. Then she recalled the earthquakes that were a constant in Japan; they showed that the ground beneath the lights retained a violent will.

Down in the restaurant she ate the eel, which was suitably exquisite. All the while Takuya spoke in his stilted English, saying of the wasabi, 'Please do have some horseradish.' Ana nodded politely, but she felt somehow offended by the vest he wore; a few sizes too big, it gaped under his arms. Thankfully he released her once they'd finished eating; he got involved in talking business with the proprietor.

Outside, as she looked for a taxi, someone grabbed her shoulder. Turning, she saw a bouncer for the club next door, which by coincidence was the joint that Dev had mentioned. The Den, said a pulsing sign.

The bouncer gripped her shoulder and, as if playing a game, a game where you guessed the origins of passing women, shouted, 'You! Ukrainian!' and let out a harsh laugh.

Wrenching free, she hailed a cab. It slid to a halt beside her, wonderfully black. The taxi driver wore white gloves. God, she thought as they pulled away. She had seen the bouncer's face, his grin as hard as his grip had been.

*

The next night, she phoned her parents while taking a walk. Her father, when he picked up, asked about the weather, then said in his gravelly voice, 'That's one thing I don't miss, Tokyo summers. And your mother's asthma.'

He had retired four years ago from his import-export job. Working for a company that dealt in commercial ovens and catering equipment, he had been posted to Tokyo when Ana was in high school. He settled their family in a poky house in Chiba. Ana and her two brothers soon made new friends and thrived, but her mother felt out of place and socially isolated, and when the three-year posting ended, the rest of the family moved back to Estonia, while Ana stayed on for college.

'Hold on, your mother is saying something. She asks if you have a boyfriend.'

'She always asks if I have a boyfriend.'

'She worries you'll settle down and stay in Tokyo. Just like she worries Estonia will be reconquered by Russians.'

'And you, are you worried?'

'I am a fatalist, Ana. You'll do as you will.'

He passed the phone to her mother, and by the time Ana got off the call, she had reached the park. The air was velvety and soft and she sat on a bench to take it in. She thought of the boyfriends she'd had. Real boyfriends, not clients. She thought of Daisuke, too, though he hadn't been her boyfriend, only a friend. He knew what it was like to live in another country. He had done a high school exchange in Adelaide, Australia, and endured racist taunts from boys in his neighbourhood. Remarkably, the experience hadn't soured him on the West. As an adult, he preferred coffee to green tea, and read philosophers like Montesquieu and Bentham.

Daisuke – where was he now? Still in Tokyo, working for some company? In college he'd been impressed by *Made in Japan*, a book by Akio Morita, the co-founder of Sony Corporation. An account of Japan's rise in the postwar period, it made Daisuke want to work to better his country. He had also decided, as he told Ana, that it would be best if he married a Japanese woman, because of all the strictures of Japanese society. 'It would be too difficult for her,' he said, referring to a hypothetical non-Japanese wife. 'It's difficult enough for us Japanese.'

Some time after that, she had stopped seeing Daisuke. Not because of his supposed marriage plans, but because she didn't want him to know she was hostessing. It was a part of her life she kept separate from college, a world of nice restaurants and bars, of Shigeko and her friends, of drinking parties that went on until the men were shiny-faced and had trouble sitting upright. At college she had boyfriends who were students like her. She slept with some of them, but the sex was always awkward, experimental, as if she was mimicking a desire she did not really feel.

Once, she thought she was pregnant. She went to a clinic. She knew there were tests you bought in a box, the sticks you were meant to pee on, but she wanted to be sure, she wanted to see a doctor. At the clinic she was directed to undress in a room and sit in a chair with moulded stirrups for her legs. Their purpose became apparent when the assistant pressed a button and the chair tipped back and lifted her legs apart. A paper curtain was positioned to screen everything past her navel, so she was unable to see the doctor when he approached. He put his gloved hands on her stomach, pressing here and there, then poked two fingers into her vagina and felt about inside her.

It was all very impersonal, like being inspected in a spaceship by a faceless chieftain. Afterwards, when she had dressed, the assistant gave her to understand that she wasn't pregnant. She rode the bus home not knowing what to think or feel, but later that day her period started, as if triggered by relief.

Now, in the park, Ana stood and walked on a little. She was not afraid. She liked the dark. She liked the textures of the trees, the way the warm air seemed to swim. Deeper in, the small lake wobbled with dim reflections and she heard cicadas. She thought of the time she had gone to a summer festival with Daisuke, and on returning lain watching TV with him and drinking a bottle of white wine. She remembered the night clearly: a golf tournament was on, Tiger Woods was playing, and from the trees behind the house came the bleating of cicadas. She knew nothing about golf but was content to lie there watching. Then Daisuke, a little drunk, had said something unexpected.

'You're so free,' he told her, turning from the screen.

'No I'm not,' she said.

'It's because you're talented.'

The remark perplexed her. She did not feel talented. She did not know what he meant, but he didn't elaborate and she didn't press him on it. And nothing happened between them, though she would have liked it to. Nothing happened that night or ever.

Why hadn't it? she wondered now. She'd been too passive. Too damn passive. And a coward to boot.

To think that after this exchange they had just kept lying there, side by side, drinking wine and saying nothing, watching golfers hit golf balls on a golf course somewhere.

*

'Do you like men?' Priya asked as they drove. She swivelled to look at Ana, who was sitting in the back seat. Priya's likeable colleague Ken was driving them to a mountain onsen. By 'men' Priya meant noodles, but her tone was deliberately teasing. 'I love them,' she went on. 'Especially cool *men*, in the summer.'

Priya worked with Ken in the office of a big energy company, and she had organised the day trip, inviting Ana along. Priya was sociable and pretty, with glossy hair and a tinkly laugh. She flirted out of habit, even though she was now engaged. When they got to the spa and went through to the women's section, leaving Ken to go to the men's, her voice lost its sparkle, becoming flatter, merely pleasant. As they soaked in the outside pool she spoke about her fiancé.

She and Sanjeev had fallen in love while travelling in Europe – which was the storyline, as she said, of many Indian films. But then he had gone to Princeton and she had come to Tokyo. They had gradually grown distant, and Priya started dating Japanese men. After graduation and several failed relationships, she had gone home to ask her parents to start looking for a match. Deeply bemused, they had reasoned with her, 'Dear Priya, how do you expect us to find anyone better than Sanjeev?'

'I had to admit they were right,' she told Ana with a laugh.

They found Ken afterwards reading a newspaper on a bench. He was wearing the onsen's plastic slippers, and his hair, washed clean of styling wax, had gone silky and flat. They had to dash to the Nissan because of the pouring rain. They drove back through the wet, stopping off once at a service area for Ken to buy a can of coffee from a dispensing machine. Nearby, a stumbling drunk was startled to see Ana. '*Ara*!' he said, staring. '*Ningyo ka na to omotta*. I thought it was a doll!'

'You know what he said?' Ken asked.

'Yeah,' Ana said and they both laughed sheepishly. When Ken dropped her back at Dev's, she kissed each of his clean bright cheeks, causing him to blush.

Early the next morning, Ana met Takuya for breakfast. Walking through the fish market on their way to a sushi bar, he pointed out the best specimens on offer. Ana hurried past the shellfish, which were so mauve, so vagina-like they might give Takuya ideas. But he was busy explaining a new rule in the market, requiring visitors to keep a certain distance from the fish.

'There was an incident,' he said with a disappointed look. 'There were some foreigners. They tried to hug the tuna.'

At the tiny sushi diner, the chef put the sashimi portions directly onto the bar, which he wiped with a cloth between one round and the next. They ate several types of fish and some hacked-off squid, which was so recently alive that the pieces were still moving, puckering in protest on their beds of rice.

'By the way,' said Takuya as they left. He walked with a basketballer's gait, his feet splayed oddly wide as if to corner Ana. 'Miura-san sent a message,' he said, referring to Shigeko by her surname, Miura. 'She mentions her regards. Actually, she is feeling sad that you do not see her.'

Clearly he knew about their disagreement. Shigeko had been annoyed when Ana refused a client, and she won the argument by kicking Ana out. Shigeko had never profited from Ana's engagements – or not as far as Ana knew – but she liked being able to introduce her to her contacts. Having set the man up with Ana, and beset by a chronic need to please, Shigeko didn't want to have to explain the snub. Ana could still picture her face that evening, her smile fixed and brittle, her eyes strangely bright.

'She is worried about you,' Takuya went on. 'And this makes things difficult for her. Because, as you know, the role of a hostess is to bring happiness to people.'

'Is it,' she said tersely, irritated by the lecture.

He smiled indulgently, spread his hands and said, 'You should meet her. It's not too late. You can say sorry.'

'I'm not sorry.'

Taken aback, Takuya fell silent.

'Thanks for breakfast,' she said, and left him to his day. It was still early and she walked aimlessly, at length finding herself on Omotesandō-dori, an upmarket shopping street. She was looking in the Prada window when Dev telephoned.

'How was your date with eel-hands? Or whatever it is you call him.'

Ana laughed. 'Okay.'

'Are you going out tonight?'

'No. Unless you want me to be out.'

'Are you sure, Ana? You're not bringing some boy home?'

'No.' She snorted, laughed again. 'I'll see you at the apartment.'

*

That night and the coming nights, a typhoon swerved in close, dousing Tokyo with heavy rain. She and Dev went out anyway, defying the weather. One night Dev arranged to catch up with his friend Nitin and asked Ana to come. 'You need to meet new people,' he told her. 'No more of those idiots from before.' He meant Shigeko and her clique. 'You're so flat these days, Ana. It's as if you've got no *crackle*. No snap, crackle or pop.'

'Okay, I'll work on that,' she promised.

Ana had never met Nitin, which made her suspect Dev of trying to set her up. If this was the idea, it didn't work out.

Having organised the evening, Dev quickly became annoyed, starting with Nitin's choice of a budget Italian restaurant. 'Really, this is the place you pick?' It looked basic but okay, with plastic tablecloths.

Nitin rolled his eyes at Ana. He was delicately built and had a fine aquiline nose. A man on familiar terms with the city's night-life, it was he who'd taken Dev to the Den. Ana watched him carefully, wondering what he knew of other dens of iniquity. He worked in capital markets, where, Dev said, the guys took home the biggest pay packets in town. This was why it rankled Dev that he ate so cheaply.

Nitin, for his part, enjoyed needling Dev. 'Why don't you try the house bolognese?' he said. 'Oh, you don't eat beef? And why would that be, Dev?'

'Because, you know why. My family—'

'I don't know why.'

'Because I still adhere to some precepts.'

'You do?' Nitin faked surprise. He was like a cat with a stuffed toy, wanting to tease and tear. 'Which precepts are those again? When we go out clubbing?'

Ana waded in. 'Everyone draws a line for himself – or herself.'

'How true, Ana.' He grinned at her and she feared what he might say next, but he merely asked a waiter to take their order. Two bolognese, one parmigiana and, yes, the garlic bread to start. Then he resumed the conversation. 'How very true, Ana. I draw my own line. It moves as I do.'

Dev's mood was foul throughout dinner. When they had parted from Nitin and were walking home, he said he would take her out again to make up for the night. They would go somewhere fancy, a converted brewery on the harbour, a place he really loved.

True to his word, he made a booking there for the next evening, and met her beforehand at the closest station. She spotted him striding across the tiles in the cavernous hall. 'I love the space of it,' he said, waving a hand at the height above. 'Space for thinking big. I come here a lot, just to be near the water.' He had also been reading more, he added as they walked to the restaurant. He rattled off authors – Richard Branson, Barack Obama. 'A little Shakespeare too. I've been educating myself. I have the luxury of leisure.'

With relish he recited a couple of lines: '"Then imitate the action of the tiger; Stiffen the sinews, summon up the blood."'

At the brewery, they were seated at a table spread with a white cloth and gleaming silver. Soberly, Dev asked if she had noticed a change in him. It was true he looked different, as though his face was smoother, the set of his jaw more confident, but she couldn't put her finger on what it was.

'I had my tooth fixed today,' he said. 'See.' He bared his teeth at her. 'I can now afford to care about such shallow things.'

'Oh, yeah.'

Behind them, on the harbour, the rain was coming down heavily. It was the night when the typhoon was almost upon them, and it was there at the restaurant table that Dev told Ana what really happened with Sara.

'Her parents sent her to meet a man, a family friend in Tokyo. He was too old, she told them afterwards. Old and short. But they chatted online, all smiles. All flattery, you know? I had to go away for a while, I was working out of town. When I got back she called me. She was married, she announced. To the older guy, just like that.'

The lights of the harbour struggled bravely through the weather. Dev kept on with his story, how he had returned to

India after finishing his degree. Deciding he needed to become proficient in IT, with more hard skills than he'd acquired in his undergraduate studies, he had hired four computing experts to teach him one on one, in tailored sessions. He described rising early to work out before his first classes. Eating the lunch his worried mother prepared for him. Stopping for a nap and then studying again. For three months he had worked like this.

'Ana, do you know, my parents told me once that they'd rather I marry an Indian. But they said I was free to choose. I could bring home a Japanese girl, a Chinese girl, any girl as my wife. They would still be happy, they said, we would all be friends.

'Ana, Sara called me once. She was drunk. She slurred her speech. It was three months into her marriage. She told me her husband was sleeping with prostitutes. "He thinks he can do what he wants," she said. "I've caught him countless times but he doesn't care. I've made a mistake, I'm getting a divorce. I'll call you tomorrow." Yet the next day no call came. I called her parents, they hung up. I talked to her brother, who I'd met when he visited. I said I could fly to Tehran to talk to his parents. No, he told me, don't. He said Sara never thought of me as a possible husband. He said his family was broad-minded, they would have considered a foreigner if she had talked to them, if that was what she'd wanted.'

Holding his fork like a small trident in his fist, Dev stared unseeingly at the rain-smeared lights.

'You have to forget her,' Ana said. 'That's the worst story I've ever heard.'

'But there were times,' he said, ignoring her, 'I know she felt it. And if she could feel it then, she could feel it again. I could – I told myself – I could inculcate that love. After I saw that, I thought, okay, I'll wait.'

Then he described the time when he had last seen her, or rather the last two times, both soon after she married. After carefully composing her final college dissertation for her, he had met her away from prying eyes on a windswept Yokohama beach, handing over the finished essay in electronic and hard copies. Then he had seen her at graduation; she was there in a silver dress. On her arm was the man she had married instead of him. All the cameras, Dev said, sought her in that crowd, searching for her beauty, her white moon of a face.

*

The typhoon was predicted to hit Tokyo that night. But as often happened, it swooped away at the final hour, thanks to a quirk of topography that favoured the capital. Next morning when Ana woke, it was to the clearest day she had ever seen in the city. The air was dry and hot, drawing everyone outdoors. The park was full of pregnant women, children and their maids. This was also the day Ana's visa finally arrived, by mail, in an official-looking envelope that she tore at hastily. There it was in black and white, her permission to work.

She promptly celebrated by doing something she never did: sightseeing. Taking the train to Asakusa, she visited the temple and neighbouring laneways, where old people moved with tiny, precise steps. She ended the tour with an iced tea in a snack bar. She drank it looking into the storefront opposite, at a spinning mannequin that, 'Sale' sign notwithstanding, cocked its knee and posed with new-season confidence.

That night she and Dev fried gyoza in a pan. They ate the dumplings on the couch while talking of old times.

'Do you remember, Ana, when that friend of yours came to visit? You let her nap in my room without telling me. I came home to find her in my bed, this plump girl snuggled in the duvet, her big boob coming out a little. She woke up and said sorry. I said, no, no, don't worry, I'm about to get in with you.'

He laughed. 'I did not say that. I was very well behaved, very polite. In those days I was bright and young, not eating meat or drinking.' Recklessly he added, 'Now I'm a tiger.'

First the Den, the strip club, and now this talk of tigers – it was weird the way he always alluded to animals, she thought. What was the line he had recited, the one out of Shakespeare? *Imitate the action of the tiger.* He liked the idea of himself as a predator, but the truth was that he was never anything but kind. She was much more familiar than he was with the night side of the city, with men and women who behaved in predatory ways. She had come closer than she admitted to being swallowed up by that life. And if it hadn't been for Dev, she would have been, she thought.

Sitting back on the couch, Dev was flicking channels. Pausing at some CNN footage of floods in Romania, he was prompted to mention a Romanian girl he'd met at the Den with Nitin. 'She was working there. She was exhausted, you know? I keep thinking about her. I feel so sad for her.'

It suddenly occurred to Ana that he was talking about her. It was for her that he felt sad, equating her with the tired stripper.

'Dev,' she said firmly, muting the TV, 'I was a hostess.' On the screen, torrential rivers wrecked bridges and embankments. 'Are you listening to me? I was a hostess, not a stripper, not a sex worker. It isn't the same thing, which is what I told Shigeko.'

'I know, I know. I'm an ass.' He grinned, looking hugely relieved. Then his phone rang and he boomed, 'Priya-san, hello. And how is your great life? Oh, *ex*-cellent news.'

Priya had emailed photos of the ring and her fiancé. Bringing up the files afterwards, Dev said, 'They're nice pictures, aren't they, Ana? Look at them, so happy, smiling away. That rock on her finger, it looks like it's weighing down her hand. It suits her, of course. Very expensive, very nice.'

He was silent for a while, then frowned, prodding the last dumpling. 'Do you think it makes a difference? The material things, I mean.'

She now grasped his dilemma, which was that he needed both a yes and a no answer. Pining for Sara, he wished that his wealth and success would bring her back, while at the same time his idealistic self – the youth in overalls that Ana knew in college – hoped that love could not be bought. He looked at her trustingly, waiting.

'Sometimes,' she conceded. 'But I think more often not.'

He went out onto the balcony and looked up at the sky. His phone rang again, a work call this time. 'Kiran,' he said in answer, and coming inside, he opened his laptop and started speaking Hindi. A server had gone down; connecting remotely, he tried to bring it back up. It was almost midnight by then but he called all of his team. In an aside, he told Ana, 'If I'm not sleeping or having sex, neither will they.'

Leaving him to it, she stretched out on her futon. As he went on working she heard the odd word: 'Server! Ping! *Nankaimo. Tiga, tiga*, okay.' In between work calls, she heard him speaking to his parents. Yes, he told his mother, I'll book to come home for Diwali. Then it was back to his strange muddle of Hindi, English and Japanese. Ana went to sleep thinking of her plans for the next day. She would go back to the shops on Omotesandō-dori with her hair in a chignon and ask for a sales job. She would use her best Japanese, especially the honorific form that was used by shop girls just as it was by hostesses. She would keep going from store to store until someone said yes.

91

'*Nankaimo, nankaimo,*' Dev was saying.

She drifted off, comforted as if by a bedside story, one of servers like grandfathers in a subtropical summer. She did not know what time it was when he managed to fix the problem; it was as if he would be there always, tapping at his laptop. Then it was morning and he had gone to work already, and she rose to fold the futon neatly away.

Animal behaviour

Rose gave little thought to how she would be remembered.

Oh, she might cheerily reply if someone asked her, she hoped to be remembered in a small, footnote-in-a-textbook sort of way. Her work was in the field of animal behaviour. After a long and worthy if slightly dull career (this was what she pictured, looking down the decades), she'd maybe rate a mention in her old college newsletter, *CatzEye*. There would be no newspaper obit, not even in *The Oxford Times*.

But she was only twenty-nine, about to turn thirty. She didn't want to be famous for any reason, good or bad. Actually, she enjoyed being unobtrusive.

If people could be divided into foxes and hedgehogs, then Rose was a hedgehog. Someone said this to her once – not very charitably, she thought.

Foxes and hedgehogs.

The comparison was the kind of thing undergrads tossed into their essays in an effort to sound smart. It was lifted from the philosopher Isaiah Berlin, who had borrowed it in turn from the poet Archilochus. Rose used the quotation as a flourish in one of her papers in her first year at Oxford. A boy she was hanging around with then found her draft and read it aloud.

"The fox knows many things, but the hedgehog knows one big thing." He used an affected voice that suggested mockery of her work.

'That's like you,' he said, delighted. 'You're the hedgehog, prickly but faithful. I'm like the fox. That could be my motto: *Multa novit vulpes*, the fox knows many things.' He laughed.

Rose had long since forgotten what the essay was about, but in the months before her birthday she was taken back to that conversation by a series of events.

The first notable thing to happen was that she acquired a new boss. She started when she saw the name in the announcement email: Danny Coalcliff, renowned expert on animal welfare. And there was his photo. They didn't give his age but he looked youthful, early thirties. Appealingly shaggy-haired, like a layabout musician who'd grown up and made good. He was to be the pin-up boy for their shiny new centre. They were getting a whole new building, which didn't exactly thrill Rose. She loved the old centre. It was little more than a demountable classroom stuck in the middle of a field, with a few pigpens, chicken coops, and miscellaneous barns. It was a cosy place to work. Best of all, she was able to bring her dog to the office.

Rose was basically content with her life as it was. She wasn't looking for change. Each day she rode to work with Frank behind her in a trailer, leaving the narrow streets of Cowley for fields of frost or dew. At night, she came home to the small row house where she lived alone. She collected her veggie box if it had been left with a neighbour. She recycled and composted. At weekends she took long walks or did things around the house, with the TV on in the background for company.

Danny Coalcliff soon appeared in person. He turned up like a newly minted northern hero, charismatic, brilliant, friend to animals and man. Coming to Oxford, he was embraced by the faculty and staff as a breath of fresh air. He had been brought in to guide the centre towards a more commercial incarnation, no longer the dependent child of the faculty. He replaced a much older set of hands (Professor Booth was retiring).

Honestly, she guessed he would be good for the centre. He had an infectious passion for animal welfare, a passion she shared. In her early twenties, she had been very intense, even zealous, on the issue. She used to speak of wanting to punish humans for what they were doing to animals. These days, she worried about the meat content in the dog food she fed Frank, partly because of her stance against killing animals and partly because of the emissions footprint. But she was not as hard-line as she used to be, and more to the point, she loved Frank above all else.

He was a rescue. He had come to her unexpectedly – a little miraculously – after a friend at a shelter put out a Facebook call about a dog in need. He was a sheepdog mix, and he had committed the potentially fatal crime of biting a sheep. So they were both offenders of a sort, and both in need of a trusty friend, someone to love and be loved by, without question or judgement.

He was the love of her life. Unasked for. Undeserved. He saved her life, she sometimes thought. He got her through a rough patch, her early and mid twenties. She supposed they were difficult years for many people. Take any Oxford college, decant the students from its rooms and you would find many with eating disorders, anxiety, depression, you name it. Most people soldiered on, shouldering their burdens, or more likely suppressing them. That was her until Frank. And then, very gradually, bit by bit, she began to feel it was safe to take a breath and *feel* a little.

Encountering Danny Coalcliff in the office, she bravely took the lead. 'Rose,' she said. Conscious that her co-workers were looking on, she stuck out her hand. There was a suggestion of something Mick Jaggeresque in his features, with those deep horizontal lines that bracketed his mouth.

'Ah, yes,' he said carefully. Coolly, she might have said. But his next comment was genial. 'Saw your name. It's good to meet you.' And with this exchange the tone was set. They were amicable new colleagues.

As the new Executive Director of the Centre for Applied Studies in Animal Welfare, Danny had big ideas. He put up the architect's drawings of the new centre building on a whiteboard in the office. He served on the animal welfare councils of several large fast-food corporations, and at his first staff meeting he spoke of bringing clients on board with a new partnership model. Sitting at the long table, people listened and nodded, while several dogs lounged by the shelves of mud-covered wellies.

'It's a bit . . . corporate,' said Ravi, one of the older hands.

'Dirty word, I know.' Danny held up his hands. 'Mea culpa.' The room laughed, appeased. It was hard not to warm to him. He had kept his Manchester accent. This was something Rose noticed because she had smoothed hers out. It was now a little more RP, a little more priggish. She put more air in her vowels. No way to drop the habit now.

One thing worried Rose: whether dogs would be allowed at the new centre. 'Oh, definitely,' said Danny, when someone asked the question. He sounded confident yet vague. Perhaps he was distracted. Rose tried to catch his gaze, but he was looking around the room, and she supposed that it must be overwhelming for him, facing everyone at once.

Danny sought her out after the meeting and handed her a printout of some slides. 'Rose, take a look at this for me, will you? Just some ideas.' He gave her that careful look again. 'Your opinion matters to me. Always has.'

Was he testing her? She nodded. She understood that they had reached a tacit agreement: they would not disclose to others that they already knew each other, but alone they could be candid, in the manner of old friends. She gathered this was what he wanted, and it was what she wanted too. This private understanding, this secret, gave her a peculiar electric charge. It made her feel sneaky, as if she and Danny had once been in the secret service, except that neither of them was really that way inclined. Their interests lay elsewhere, it was fair to say.

She had no reason to doubt that he cared about what she thought. Over the years they had kept their distance, but he'd once liked a tweet in which she was mentioned. It was when a journal article she'd written, 'What is it like to be a chicken?', was garnering a lot of attention – or a lot of attention relatively speaking, within the particular circles of animal behaviour studies. It represented a fashionable new way of thinking about welfare, with an insistence on the recognition of animals' subjective conscious states. For chickens, this meant giving importance to perching, pecking and dust-bathing behaviours. At the time, she was startled to see Danny's handle among those who liked the tweet. She trawled his profile and feed, feeling oddly exposed and fearful.

In the weeks that followed the staff meeting, Danny's plans went live. Another broadcast email went out. Danny took the opportunity to announce an exciting new phase in the centre's work.

'It's a natural extension. Firms already look to CASAW for leading research and advisory services. Now they can access trusted auditing services under the one roof.'

It was the talk of the faculty and made ripples elsewhere. In coming days, there was more detail. A planning paper went out about the launch of a multi-step program for animal welfare in supply chains. From farm to fork, as the tagline went. Rose was heartened to read Step 3, Natural Behaviour, which stated that animals should be raised in environments that promote natural behaviour.

Step 6 was Accountability. This meant establishing third party audits to ensure supplier farms complied with the comprehensive standards. 'That's where we come in,' said Danny. Accountability was his niche.

Rose had the satisfaction of knowing that she knew all of this first, having seen Danny's slides. She felt distinctly proprietary towards the centre and its work. If the changes made her nervous in a way she couldn't shake, they also brought an undeniable sense of energy and momentum. Splashing out, she ordered herself a new pair of wellies she had been eyeing, a proper pair, not cheap, an early birthday present to herself.

There was a lot of media interest. Danny did well on the radio and in a *Guardian* interview. His unaffected style made him a good speaker; he always sounded very candid.

When Rose caught the tail end of a story on the BBC the next morning, she marvelled at how far they had come. What were the odds of the two of them ending up where they were, working together, no less? And for a split second – a nanosecond – she felt almost proud of them.

*

It was Danny who had told her she was a hedgehog. Where were they when he said it? Sitting by the river, inconspicuous, a couple of kids, that was the idea. His rucksack held the binoculars, hers had her tutorial paper in it, wedged in with a couple of books.

Isaiah Berlin had written that hedgehogs approach the world with a single, all-embracing idea, whereas foxes are fascinated by the infinite variety of things.

'And what variety there is!' said Danny, grinning.

She remembered the rowers on the river, the cox calling something. It was late spring or early summer, what should have been a time of possibility and promise. Evening. Or the gloaming, if you wanted to be fancy about it.

She remembered the way he looked then. Longer-haired. Full-cheeked. He was visiting Oxford, down for a couple of days. She knew him not from uni but from a demo in Manchester – or really, the demo afterparty back at Garrett's house. They had both helped out with the guerrilla projection of footage onto the shopping centre wall, then put on masks and walked about handing out leaflets.

That was a world away from Oxford, as Danny remarked on the riverbank. He was studying at Manchester but liked to play the working man. Very faintly they could hear the bells tolling in town. As they lay by the gentle river, he snatched and read her paper. She focused at the time on the fact that he called her a hedgehog, which she took to be a slight. It was not very flattering, to say the least. But perhaps she should have heeded the other thing he said, about him being a fox.

This time around, too, there were signs of the differences in their natures. One was revealed at the dinner at high table. Danny was being feted by the faculty, who held a dinner to toast his plans for the revamped centre. It was hosted by the chair of the zoology department, a fellow of Halsbury College. Rose arrived at the college a half-step behind Danny and the sprightly professor.

'Evening, mate,' Danny said to the porter as he entered. Very familiar, very likeable. As if he was Brian bloody Cox.

Rose stopped a moment longer. A fixture in the college lodge, the porter knew everyone's comings and goings. 'Hello, Red,' she said, greeting his elderly staffy, who wore a jaunty red bandana for a collar.

'Hello, Mrs Frank,' the porter said. He didn't know Rose's name, but had seen her out walking her dog. She was touched that he recognised her in a different context. She didn't normally come to this college, which was very big and grand, one of the grandest in Oxford. 'And how is Frank himself?'

'Oh, he's exceptionally well.'

Patting Red, she noticed just how old he was, and the thought of how his death would devastate his owner made her feel suddenly like crying. Not normally prone to tears, she wondered if she was starting her period. Walking at the heels of two other dinner guests as she entered the hall, she realised they were talking about the porter.

'It was his son who died. Doing the rounds.'

'Was it? Christ, I didn't know.'

'Terrible business.'

Inside, she sought Danny's eyes. She was rattled now, and she wanted to know whether their secret was having the same effect on him, making him feel permeable and exposed. If so, he showed no sign of it.

At dinner he was in good form, conversing easily with the dons at the long table. It was the whole Harry Potter extravaganza: little lamps on the table, vaulted stonework high above. Sitting diagonally opposite Rose, he didn't draw her in or introduce her. He seemed not to be aware of her turmoil.

(What is it like to be Rose Dawson?

'We must consider whether any method will permit us to extrapolate the inner life of a Rose Dawson from our own case, and if not, what alternative methods there may be for understanding the notion. Our own experience provides the basic material for our imagination, whose range is therefore limited.')

The dinner should have been a triumph and outwardly it was. Back at home, she cried and cried. Her despair threatened to pull her under. Frank found her on her bed, sniffed at her and whined. He put his warm nose into her hand and she felt his breath on her skin, in and out, in and out, on the heart line of her palm. They stayed in that pose for ages, until both of them calmed down and Frank settled on the floor with a weary groan.

*

Soon the snow melted. The meadows flooded. The days were grey and indistinct. On Valentine's Day she spent the evening with friends in a house off Cowley Road. It was a curry night for singles. Her bike was in for repair, so she walked from her place, passing the co-op and then, after turning onto Magdalen Road, the halal minimarket and the Magic Cafe.

The gathering was more town than gown. It was hosted by Liz, who used to pull beers with Rose at the Half Moon in St Clement's. Her housemate, Gary, a DJ (he was doing a set later at the Oxford Academy down the road), was there, and his soon-to-be-copper friend, a guy by the name of Dale.

They sat in the lounge, balancing plates on their laps, drinking wine and telling stories of exes. There was the ex-boyfriend of

Liz's who, after getting her pregnant years back in Glasgow, came around to see her with a cheque for a thousand pounds and the message that the baby wasn't his but he had a friend with a clinic . . . And Liz's mum, who caught him making this pompous little speech, was so enraged that her brother had to pin her to the kitchen floor to keep her from attacking the guy.

There was Gary's ex-girlfriend, a tiny little thing, he said, who used to punch him with great hatred.

'My current ex-girlfriend,' said Dale, 'I mean, the one I broke up with today and who I'll start up with again tomorrow . . .'

'What did she do?' Liz asked.

'I sat around all day trying to come up with bitter things to say about her, and I decided to say that she kicked my dog. And it died.'

'Yeah,' said Gary. 'What a bitch.'

Rose kept quiet about her exes. What could she say?

'Bet you've a story or two, Rose,' Gary said.

'You'd be right there,' she said, laughing, but in the end she came out with something trivial and silly. One ex-boyfriend, she told them, a yoga teacher with dreadlocks, kept her bike when they broke up. 'And sold it,' she said.

'He *sold* it?'

'For a tenner. That was the worst part.'

It was a feeble offering, but they didn't press her, thank god. Clearing away the remains of dinner and opening another bottle, they carried on swapping stories about disastrous hook-ups. Eventually Rose slipped away. She was very aware, as she said goodnight, of Dale studying her with his soon-to-be-copper eyes. Did he know something? No, he couldn't, she told herself firmly. She took herself home to bed, giddy and nauseous with the feeling of having gotten away with something.

The following week at work, she had to defend Danny against naysayers. The forces of opposition were definitely gathering. People didn't like his talk of monetising the business model, *or in our case the science model*. There was talk about his directorships on boards and dubious side contracts – it was all layers of intrigue, rumour and suspicion. The words *conflict of interest* were uttered in low tones. Rose didn't know it at the time, but two of her co-workers, Ravi Anand and David Kostowicz, were preparing an anonymous dossier, which they would later photocopy and slide under people's doors.

'He doesn't accept payment for his directorships,' Rose said at lunchtime on Tuesday. She was outside smoking with some of the others, puffing in annoyance on her once-in-a-blue-moon cigarette.

'Is that a fact?' asked Ravi, who was doing his best to look cynical despite his cheerful yellow mac.

She didn't know why she bothered. No, she did know why. She spoke up not out of any loyalty to Danny, but because of a certain pesky fidelity to the facts. Also, she felt a lingering childhood sense of justice – something she shared with Danny, she supposed.

Later, she kicked herself for drawing attention to herself. What did she owe him? Nothing. She wondered whether Danny dwelt much on their uni years. It didn't seem like it, and it grated on her that he was able to put those events behind him. At times like this, she wished she could talk to him openly. What a relief that would be, to talk about what had happened!

For so long, she had tried not to think of that time. Mostly she had succeeded. It was only occasionally that something brought it all up again, like the time not long ago when, coming back from a long walk to Port Meadow with Frank, she took a shortcut along a passage from St Giles and came out without meaning to near the science campus on South Parks Road. There she was confronted with the Biomedical Sciences Building, a horrifyingly hard-edged edifice of stone and glass with opaque turquoise-coloured windows so you couldn't see inside. There was a reason for that, she knew. She hurried on, saying, 'Come on, Frank,' and ducked into the green relief of the University Parks.

Try to think of the good times, she reminded herself. The evening after her exchange with Ravi, she was tracing the reedy Cherwell River with Frank when she saw the tied-up punts waiting for warmer weather. They made her think of something Danny had said on a trip to Oxford once. He used to be sceptical of the city's charms and was always mocking her for being susceptible to them. 'What is a punt, really – except a shit kind of gondola?'

She took the risk, the next day, when they were alone in the kitchenette at the centre, of reminding him of this. She expected he'd be amused. I never said that, he might say. I would've said shite, not shit. That's far more likely, Rose.

Instead, he reacted badly. Spectacularly badly. He spun around to check whether anyone could have heard, then leaned over her, gripped the back of her neck and squeezed. He hissed, close to her ear (it was almost intimate, this closeness), 'Do you think this is funny? We're both on the line here, Rose. If you say anything about us, you're dead. You hear me? Dead.'

Rose twisted in his grip. Grimacing, she said, 'Alright, Danny, I'm sorry. It's okay. Let me go.'

He laughed in a strangled way then told her, 'Go on, you're alright.' He dug his elbow into her ribs, making her slop her builder's tea. 'Careful, now,' he added and left her to wipe it up.

It took her some time to recover from the shock of his response. But the more she thought about it, the more she felt strangely appeased. At least she'd got a reaction from him, something to show that things weren't all fine and dandy. He too felt fearful and exposed, despite his proficiency at hiding this at work.

For a couple of days he was extra-nice. Typical, she thought. Then, on the Friday, he called her into a meeting room. The centre's senior consultant, Barnsley Avery, was there too. The two of them proceeded to grill her about her work. Barnsley's manner was faux-casual, but it felt like an ambush. 'So what's on your slate?' he asked.

She listed several research projects before Danny interrupted, saying with devastating coolness, 'That's just it, we see your strengths as suited to academia proper. We're moving away from that, as you know. We want you to think about your plans.'

'My plans?' she repeated dully.

'Yes, your aspirations.'

Rose looked away. What were her aspirations, if not to do what she was already doing?

'I knew you'd understand,' Danny said, in that same smooth tone. 'We'll be advertising new positions but they'll be different roles, more on the consulting side of things. They'd be beneath you, to be honest.'

Rose felt her stomach drop away. She couldn't believe he didn't mean to take her along with him. He ended the meeting quickly, saying, 'Think on it, then we'll talk.'

She left dazed, wondering if this was Danny's ploy to be rid of her. Then, picking up on the chatter in the office, she learned that she was not the only one being cut. All the postdoc research-ers had been told they could apply for the new jobs. She felt sorry for them, but not too sorry. A couple of them were dead weight, ineffectual sorts she would be glad to see the back of. There was sense in doing a spill and fill; she simply thought she should be exempt.

Think on it, then we'll talk, Danny had said. He had to be seen to be impartial, of course. Treat her no differently from the others. That she could understand. Well, she would look at the new roles. Map out her application, get ready to make her case. She wouldn't curl up like a hedgehog, as much as she might want to.

She gave herself this pep talk as she walked Frank that afternoon, having slipped away from the office early. At the Isis, she was reminded by the number of rowers making a ruckus that it was Torpids week. Supporters had gathered at the boathouse on the southern side of the river. It was the fancy new one, architect-designed, quite minimalist and boxy. She remembered the hoo-ha when it was finished. It was put up to replace the boathouse that had burned down. Someone had died in the fire, a security guard. There was an inquest, a verdict, but no one was ever charged. It hadn't taken the college long to find some old boy with money to stump up for the new boathouse. An American, apparently. A saviour with deep pockets.

For several long minutes, maybe more, she stared blankly at the boathouse. She only snapped out of this state when she heard Frank give a worried whine. He was picking up her vibes and trying to console her, pushing his warm snout into the palm of her hand. 'Come on then, you,' she said. 'It's like rush hour here today.' She wasn't keen on rowers. They disturbed the tranquillity of the river, especially of a morning when they came shooting out of the mist. The cox was always yelling something nonsensical. 'Power ten!' 'Easy on port!' 'Way enough!' 'Set it up!'

She passed a gaggle of guys wearing colourful patterned skins, some with shorts over the top for modesty's sake, some proudly without. Ridiculous, she thought. Put it away, boys.

She caught herself being cross. She was out of sorts after her day, her meeting with Danny.

Power ten, she told herself. Change could be a good thing. She needed a kick in the pants, and if the kick came from Danny, then so be it. Well, she could do what needed doing. She believed in the power of transformation; she wasn't the sort of person who said a leopard couldn't change its spots. Actually, lots of species went through transformations in order to survive. There was the pepper moth, which originally had very pale, mottled wings that camouflaged with tree trunks and whitewashed cottage walls. When the country turned black with soot during the Industrial Revolution, darker pepper moths prevailed, thanks to natural selection. Later, with the clean-air laws, the pale moths came back.

She loved this story, loved its message, or what she took to be its message. It said that damage could be reversed, the world could be made clean again. It was downright redemptive. The idea gave her a spurt of hope.

At home that evening, she sat down with a glass of wine and a notepad and began building the case for her defence. Doodling at the margins, she drew a building, a door, a lock, then hastily scrubbed them out, black ink effacing ink. She had a message from Liz asking about her birthday plans. *You're not dodging this one, I hope you know.*

Preoccupied, she did not reply. She had a job to keep. When she'd roughed out the main points, she decided she was ready to speak to Danny. She would issue an invitation.

She went to bed excited rather than despondent. She had done it before, remaking herself from the ground up, becoming the good student, butter wouldn't melt, et cetera. No one had sniffed her out; no one had held her to her past. If she had managed to do it then, why shouldn't she do it now?

*

It falls to researchers to ask: what does Rose Dawson know? What does she experience?

Certainly it is possible to believe that there are facts which humans will never possess the requisite concepts to represent or comprehend.

Rose did not know certain facts when she asked Danny to visit. She did not know that her colleagues David and Ravi had distributed their photocopied bundles of papers overnight, sliding them under doors and leaving them nestled in in-trays. Everyone was meant to get a copy at more or less the same time on Monday morning. They hadn't counted on Danny going in to work on Saturday morning and discovering the papers sooner, by himself.

Rose had one thing in mind when she asked Danny to stop by: to persuade him to see things as she saw them, especially as to why she should stay on at the centre and keep doing the work she loved. She would show him she could contribute to the 'farm to fork' welfare vision.

'*We need to talk about work*,' she tapped, and hit send on the text. She was pleased and a bit surprised when he messaged back soon after to say yes, he would drop in. He came soon afterwards, at lunchtime, but he said he wasn't hungry. He looked rattled, hollow-eyed, as if he had slept poorly. He glanced distractedly at the football game that was playing on the TV in the corner, but his gaze didn't settle.

'Is something wrong?' she asked, handing him a beer.

'Yes,' he snapped. 'I'm being threatened.'

'What?'

'It's petty stuff, unbelievably petty. The worst sort of jealousy. It's sabotage really. It only looks bad, that's the thing. Of course all my dealings have been completely legitimate.' He opened his satchel, took something out and threw it on the table. It was a packet of papers. Rose saw Danny's name and the words 'charlatan' and 'corrupt'. There were photocopied pages, parts of company reports, some contracts regarding directorships and so on. Rose had never seen the papers before. There was also an old report from a disciplinary panel. Surprised and incredulous, she tried to skim the findings.

Danny stood at her elbow, radiating fury. He downed his beer quickly, setting the bottle on the table with a jarring impact. With him standing there like that, it was hard to focus enough to read, but phrases leapt out from the text, a litany of accusations: 'aggressive behaviour', 'anger management', 'ruthless'.

She looked up at him and grimaced. 'Well, you do have a history.'

'What do you mean, a history?'

'Nothing.' She backed off, raised her hands, gestured at the papers. 'Just all this.'

He glared. 'Do you know why I came here, Rose? You're the one person I can trust not to squeal about this rubbish.' Narrowing his eyes, he asked, 'Why did you want to see me?'

'To talk about my job, my ideas for the centre!' This was sounding like a plea, not the pitch she had in mind. There was a tremor in her voice.

'And what were you planning to tell me? Out with it, then. I'm listening.'

This meeting wasn't going how she wanted it to go. Danny's attitude was hostile, but she launched into her spiel about researching poultry stress. 'Think about it,' she said. 'The UK has twenty million hens in modified cages. This is what we're about, addressing suffering, Danny. It's what we've always been about.'

He looked at her with suspicion. She was veering off-script, making things personal.

'You can't forget the past,' she said. 'What we have is hard to come by. It's about trust, about loyalty . . .'

'What are you saying?'

'I didn't want to say this. Are you going to make me spell it out?' She let out an awkward laugh then continued, using simple words as if she was speaking to a child. 'We know things about each other. I know things about you, and you know things about me. That's why you can't push me. It's why I won't be pushed.'

Danny stared, astonished. He seemed to be blindsided by this message. Reeling, he said after some moments, 'And these papers – are they your doing? I didn't think it would be you.'

'It's not. Of course it's not.'

'You're the one talking about the past!'

This was becoming a proper row. Frank growled and started barking, and Rose had to put him out in the garden and shut the door. She was indignant at this point, feeling wrongly accused.

When she returned to the room, Danny nodded very slowly, as if the truth were dawning on him. In a slightly disembodied way, she watched his changing expression. He'd always had a tremendously mobile, expressive face, and now it was remarkable to see the way his anger took a physical hold of him. He blinked his eyes rapidly. The full lips stretched into a smirk and then his face contorted further, becoming a mask of loathing.

'I can't fucking believe it. You of all people. I wouldn't have thought you capable of it, spreading that muck, but I should have known better. Of course you are, you obstinate little . . .'

In the back garden, Frank – her Frank – kept up his frenzied barking. At this point, she cut Danny off. She had been sitting on her ace card. She didn't think she would need to use it. She had barely allowed herself to think about using it.

'You think I'm talking about directorships? About probity, independence, your management practices? When it comes to what I know, that's the least of your problems!'

Danny lowered his brow and stared at her angrily, like a bull. 'What are you talking about, the fire?'

'Yes, the fire,' she said.

*

To be fair, he had not been the leader. They were both only students. The other two activists were older and battle-hardened; they knew about tactics and homemade explosives. Danny and Rose formed what Garrett called the smarty-pants division. He said this sarcastically, resenting them for being cosseted university students, all the more so because he knew he needed them.

Rose was never involved with Danny, not in the romantic sense. What they had was something greater: a cause, a union of conspirators, a sacrament of the just. Plus, if she were honest, they were both under Garrett's spell. Garrett Freeland was older, edgier, magnetic. Which made it easier for her to feel, after the fact, that they had both been in some way victims of his powers of persuasion. He had a notebook full of targets and information he had gathered. He had grown up in the movement, was a bit of a hero really. He came of age guarding osprey nests with his parents up in Scotland. She didn't know what happened to him afterwards; she had refrained from looking him up with any of the methods that were now available.

He gave her her first job, which was to steal a security pass. He said in his soft, coaxing voice, 'You can do that, can't you, Rose? Good girl. Course you can.' He had lovely green-flecked eyes. There was nobody like Garrett for making you feel extraordinary.

He was her first true love, even if it was a one-sided love. He spoke like a tutor or a priest, all patience and understanding. She pushed herself on him, if the truth be told. He could probably have done without a nineteen-year-old girlfriend, given the other matters at hand.

They set fire to the boathouse during the summer recess. More than any other university building, the boathouse was vulnerable, unguarded, on the south bank of the river. An easy target. It was early July, warm and damp. The night closed in around them, intimate and cloying, as they made their way to the timber-framed two-storey building. Downstairs were the rowing boats, about two dozen or so. Upstairs were the social rooms, full of old photos and mementoes, but they left those alone. The guys carried a gallon of petrol each in square blue plastic bottles. Rose was let off this duty; Garrett claimed the weight would slow her down. He had the incendiary device, which had a fuse he'd made out of sparklers, the kind you put on birthday cakes, with the sulphurous smell that Rose always rather loved.

He set the device between two boats in the Eights bays. They moved efficiently, quietly, without speaking to each other beyond Garrett's 'Okay, let's go.' Before they left, he re-padlocked the door and glued the locks, to stop anyone entering and getting in the way before the device ignited.

He didn't mean – none of them had meant – to stop someone getting out. They had no idea anyone was inside. He must have been upstairs, checking the premises. The porter's son. The son of Mr Red.

Oh, Rose knew his name, of course. It was etched on her mind. As was his face, from all the newspaper stories, the TV reports. All those times she used to speak of wanting to punish humans for what they were doing to animals, she'd never thought of that punishment landing on one person in particular, out of all of the billions of humans on Earth. She never thought of a single person bearing that suffering, as distinct from the mass of greedy, grasping humanity.

He was nineteen – the same age as her. He had picked up work from the college doing night patrols at off-site buildings. He had a habit of going everywhere with his earphones in, but as the porter's son he was trusted and liked. 'A good sort of lad, never a trouble to anyone.' That kind of thing was said. But for all they knew, argued Garrett, he was dealing drugs and screwing thirteen-year-olds.

She believed it for a time. She had the zealotry of the young. Then she found a way to rationalise it as the fault of the college. They had sent him out to patrol the building, having received reports of kids hanging around, kids who were not from Halsbury College. God forbid anyone should trespass on hallowed college property.

To make everything worse, the fire did not stop anything. It only slowed things down. The police knew an animal rights group was probably to blame: the fire came after bitter protests against the university's plan for a new animal-testing laboratory. Undaunted, the university opened the facility several years later, in the specially built, secure Biomedical Sciences Building. Mice, ferrets and primates – they did the full spectrum of vivisection. The government stepped in to pick up the bill for the extra security that was needed. The college put up the new boathouse, this time with student accommodation on the second storey, using the students as human shields to deter future arson attacks.

Not that they would have tried it again. They were already scared off after what had happened to the watchman, after what they had done. The group broke up and its members scattered, all except for Rose, who stayed exactly where she was, suspected by no one. There was the inquest, the verdict of probable manslaughter.

What is it like to be Rose Dawson?

For all her sensitivity to animals and the natural world, and despite everything she'd learned about animal behaviour, she was insufficiently attuned to specifically human perils.

The harm they could do and the harm that could come to them.

*

The game was on, Nottingham Forest and Swansea City, red- and white-clad players darting here and there onscreen. At the back door, the dog was barking, going mental, the neighbours said.

Humans were good at forgetting. But Rose did not forget. She wanted Danny to know it. She would make him remember too. Maybe after all she was a little bit animal. The hedgehog, as he said.

This was what she wanted to tell him, before he lost control, before his hands went to her throat. It was the line from Archilochus.

'The fox knows many things, but the hedgehog knows one big thing.'

The best left in Europe

Damien didn't go alone. Maybe that's where he went wrong. He roped in his Italian cousin Max, who lived in France. It was a warm afternoon in late September when they drove into the Basque valley – both in their twenties, both windswept and dark-haired, looking like they belonged to the same genre of person, a genre of dark-haired surfers with hopes of the perfect wave.

'This is it,' he said. 'You'd better be ready, Max. It's going to be sick. An amazing left-hander.' Damien was already in board-shorts, ready to leap out of the car without wasting a millisecond.

'I'm ready, don't worry.' At the wheel, Max smiled broadly as he rested his elbow on the sill, shirt cuffs flapping freely in the wind. Although it wasn't great for a surfing trip, the near-vintage soft-top Mercedes was his pride and joy. Behind them, the surfboards stuck up in the back seat, their bags and rolled-up towels jammed around the fins.

They pulled into an old fishing village. Narrow streets, stone buildings, guesthouses, a church. A river sliding out from between the hills, widening into an estuary, emptying over a sandy bar into the ocean.

It was a dream of a river mouth, the best left-breaking wave in Europe. Damien had fantasised about it. He and this wave were meant to be. The swell charged around a headland and arrived in long straight lines, creating barrels that could last for more than a hundred metres.

But not today. There was no swell. All that was out there was the flat blue Atlantic.

'Is this the place?' Max asked. 'I have to say I'm not seeing it.'

Damien frowned his disapproval at the vast, untroubled ocean. At a family get-together in Italy the previous April, he and Max had agreed they were long overdue to catch some waves together. Damien was already flirting with the idea of Spain, and he sold Max on the idea. 'You won't want to miss it, I'm telling you.' He had been planning this trip for more than a year, and had come through three different airports to get here, lugging his surfboard in a padded foil bag.

He had come here for one reason, which was that water obsessed him. Not water in all its forms. Only saltwater, and only saltwater shaped just so, *sculpted* just so. Hollowed out by an offshore wind, smooth and green and glassy. The sort of wave he hoped he'd find at the river mouth. There was no shortage of footage on YouTube and elsewhere, a lot of it from the WCT – the World Championship Tour – which used to take over the small town for a week or two every year. That was until a few years ago, when a disastrous bit of dredging for the sake of shipping traffic extracted too much sand and gutted the wave.

After that, the professionals had stopped coming, leaving the town to its slow rhythms and fishing trawlers. But Damien had heard from a friend, who'd heard it from someone else, that the sandbank was gradually taking shape again.

'The autumn swell should be on its way,' he told his cousin with more confidence than he felt. 'We'll intercept it in a few days when we come back.'

'Better too early than too late,' Max said, to be cheerful.

'Not really.' Damien couldn't entirely master his disappointment. 'But so be it. We couldn't do much about the dates. You have to be back in Paris at the end of next week.'

There was (and this was something) at least a cool note in the air. Damien felt it in the brisk nor'-easter blowing onshore. He hoped he was right that the waves were on their way. Their plan was to drive southwest, roughly tracking the pilgrimage trail of the Camino de Santiago, and then work their way back more slowly.

'There's another place near here,' said Max, studying his phone. He was in his mid-twenties, the younger of the two. Damien had always thought him a bit indulged. Their fathers were eight years apart, and Damien's had left Italy for Australia before Max's was out of primary school. Max was a natural linguist, and the names of towns on roadside signs rolled easily off his tongue. He pointed to the map he'd found, then read out the description like an excitable tour guide, a blurb about a hermitage, a cave, Knights Templar and treasure.

The river mouth would keep, Damien consoled himself. Max's cove could be a good vantage point to see surf spots further on. Driving northwest to reach it, they found a beach with steeply raked dark sand. It was windy and exposed, even desolate in the chill of late afternoon. The only colour came from Damien's board-shorts, which were the same eye-watering orange as the high-vis vests he wore at work. He had felt self-conscious in the shorts when they stopped at Guernica to take a look at the Peace Park earlier that day. Could you stand around reflecting on wartime devastation while wearing a pair of fluoro boardshorts on your way to the surf? he'd wondered aloud.

'Why not?' Max asked. He shook his fist in the air. 'This is how we show the fascists!'

By this point in the day, Max had lost some of that defiance. Goose-pimpling in the wind, he dumped his wallet, keys and phone.

'*This* is an ocean,' Damien said with appreciation, trying to console himself for the lack of surf. It was true, though: this was his idea of what a coast should be – wild and rocky, with strong currents. Forces beyond human control, with enough power to pummel you into insignificance. The Atlantic coast of Spain was nothing like the Med, which he thought of with disdain as a cut-rate paddling pool.

'Like the beaches at home. Awesome natural beauty.'

'Natural beauty, huh?' Max grinned. 'You're digging it up out of the ground. A mine with a beach, isn't that what people call Australia?'

Damien returned the grin. 'We don't mine everywhere,' he said.

He felt defensive at the dig, but he wasn't about to let Max see this. This early in the trip, they were still testing each other, re-establishing their dynamic. Max was affectionate, but also deeply competitive, going in for one-upmanship.

Later, Damien realised that they should have paid more heed to the movement of the water, but other things vied for their attention. For Max, it was the bridge out to the island with the old hermitage. He said the path was marked with the stations of the cross, probably for the use of villagers when they held processions. 'But their faith has weakened!' he declared, shaking his fist again, this time in mock-disapproval at the failings of Christendom in general.

For Damien, who knew something about geology, it was the dramatic striations in the causeway and the cliffs. These were shale bed deposits that ran seam-like through the rock, signs of the long-ago rift that had caused the continents to separate, allowing water to rush in and fill the breach. Waves had been pounding on the cliffs for millions of years since.

And for both of them, it was the shock of cold when they leapt in. It was even more intense than Damien expected, heart-thumpingly brisk. There was nothing you could do to prepare yourself for cold water. Pushing off from the rock ledge, they made for the island and the cave that yawned darkly on one side.

'The cave's where the treasure is!' said Max, putting his head down to plough forward. He swam with choppy strokes and Damien followed, then overtook. He kept being shunted off course, and it was only after a third readjustment that he realised how powerful the current was. As they neared the cave he felt himself being sucked towards the deep opening in the rock – he figured the cave must run all the way through to the other side of the island. Swimming through it would be a worthy challenge, an adventure in lieu of the surf they'd missed.

But when he turned to check where Max was he knew they could not go on. His cousin was struggling – no, flailing. His face had a glazed expression. Damien could see he was about to start panicking.

'Abort!' he called out. The wind tossed his words away. He knew they had to move, and fast. If Max went into a full-blown freak-out, he'd be impossible to help. He was bigger than Damien, tall and broad-chested, and a panicking man was dangerous. Damien knew stories of ocean rescues gone wrong, when the person in trouble drowned his would-be rescuer. It was a primal response to flail about or fight.

Damien drew a finger across his neck in a cutting movement. 'Abort!' he yelled again. 'We're going back!' And without waiting he started swimming to shore, giving Max no choice but to follow.

*

This was at a time in Damien's life when he lived for surf trips, saving everything he earned so he could spend it chasing waves. Missing the surf that afternoon had made him push their luck, or at least blinded him to the risks of swimming to the cave. At some level he imagined the ocean owed him something – a different thrill in recompense.

Of course, he never imagined Max would get into trouble. Damien knew he was by far the better surfer, but he hadn't questioned – should he have? – his cousin's ocean fitness. In Wollongong, where Damien grew up, you either surfed or skated; those were the only options on offer. Having surfed his entire life, he was used to being in the ocean. It took a lot to spook him.

Max had started surfing later, at eighteen, on a year-long working holiday in Australia after high school. For the first couple of months he stayed with Damien's family, and Damien took him out on a second-hand foam board, giving him lessons on how to paddle, how to stand up. He was at university then, doing an engineering degree, and could afford the time. Then, on moving to the UK for his undergraduate studies, Max had kept it up, surfing in Cornwall, different parts of France, and elsewhere. Perhaps he'd talked his exploits up, Damien thought now, given them a bit of spit and polish.

'That was hairy,' said Damien, when they eventually made it back to shore.

'I'm fine,' Max told him. 'Fine.'

But he wasn't fine. He wore a long scrape on his arm, violent and red, from scrabbling up the rocks to get out of the water. And he was defensive; there was none of his usual easy bonhomie. He clearly wasn't happy that Damien had swum away and left him.

Damien wanted to say, but couldn't: *I saw you were afraid, that's why I did what I did.* But not knowing how to talk about it, he tried to make light of things. He did a Ferris Bueller jump into the car without opening the door, vaulting himself in with one hand on the sill. He actually made the jump (and was proud of himself for this), but in doing so wrenched off a piece of the window seal, a length of several inches.

'Sorry,' he said, holding out the piece of rubber with exaggerated contrition, before stowing it in the glove box. After the first stab of guilt, Damien felt strangely better. Now something was actually broken, a small thing, easy to fix and get over.

But Max's face had darkened. He stared blankly at Damien – whether in anger or exhaustion or indifference, he couldn't tell. Setting off, they drove in silence for half an hour, passing through villages and towns. The newspapers spoke of a new normalcy in the Basque regions, yet the towns through which they passed had a guarded air about them.

At dusk they reached Bilbao, spread out by an even bigger tidal river than the one at the fishing village. They were meant to be meeting somebody here, a friend of Max's, a girl. He knew her from INSEAD, the graduate business school he'd attended in France. Damien had been wary of this stop on the itinerary, and frankly a bit annoyed. In his world, a surf trip should be like a

Corona beer commercial: an empty beach somewhere at sunset, no hordes or restaurants or bars, just a campfire to tell stories around. Now, though, he hoped the catch-up would reboot Max's mood. Maybe the presence of another person would be good for both of them.

They found the bar, the sort of place that served pintxos and wine. 'Very *typique*,' said Max, using the French word for no reason.

The friend, mercifully, turned out to be good value: Laura was Spanish, smiled a lot, and had a forthright way of speaking. On arriving, she beat a path to their table with a bow-legged stride and Max's foul mood disappeared. He kissed her on both cheeks, ordered drinks for them all, asked what she'd been up to. He was his business school self, full of warmth and wit, enquiring about their mutual friends and describing the drive on the way down. He didn't flinch when Laura asked how the surfing was. 'We haven't been yet,' he said smoothly, without a glance at Damien.

After peppering them with questions about their plans, Laura talked about the consulting work that had brought her to Bilbao. She was writing a case study on the city's regeneration model.

'It was an industrial city,' she said, putting down her glass of Rioja. 'You used to have steel mills, shipyards, all along the river. For years it was the usual story, decline and unemployment.'

Now it was Damien's turn. He knew about industrial towns. He told her about Port Kembla, in Wollongong, with its steelworks, coal port and hilltop copper smelter. There was talk of a cancer cluster at the primary school. To his mild surprise, Laura gave every appearance of listening intently.

Also, she was attractive. She had an angular chin and a wide, expressive mouth, which meant that when she smiled her whole face was transformed. She was all curves under her loose, peasant-style blouse. They were getting along well, something Max seemed to size up when he came back with another round of drinks. He set about turning on the full force of his charm – Damien thought he could almost see the mental rolling up of his sleeves for the task. He began his counter-flirtation by shifting the conversation to the MBA he and Laura had recently finished. He teased her for being just as conservative as the rest of the class.

'I was the token lefty,' he boasted.

Damien wanted to scoff. Token was right. He was confident that Max had never been a member of a union. His politics were sincere but entirely theoretical. As the youngest in his family, Max had been given licence to skip out on his father's construction business. After good schools in Italy and then an economics degree in London, he had ended up at INSEAD. In Instagram photos that Damien had seen of the campus, the college was housed in what looked like, and maybe was, a huge chateau. Perhaps in that context Max *was* a lefty.

Laura laughed indulgently. She started to lecture him on the need for labour market reforms, while he threw up his hands and pulled faces in response. For most of the evening Max kept the conversation outside Damien's comfort zone, so he sat back, sipped his beer and let his cousin have the floor. He had the feeling of being used, of being made to witness this display. Watching Max, he had a vision of the cave that afternoon, and Max's face as he was swimming, his slack mouth and glassy eyes. He was nothing like that now; he literally looked like a different person. The scratches on his arm were hidden inside his cashmere jumper, which was softer than any jumper Damien had seen on a man before. It fitted his chest snugly, making him look manly and refined at the same time. Damien realised that his cousin wasn't just good-looking, he was good-looking in a way that registered with Laura.

In full flight, Max begged her to tell them about the time she danced with the king of Spain. It didn't sound to Damien like a thing that could really happen.

'He was only the prince then,' Laura said, turning red with embarrassment. 'Your cousin doesn't want to hear this.'

'Yes, in fact I do,' said Damien, speaking up.

'There, you see.' Max slapped the table gleefully.

So Laura relented. As she told the story, Max looked on as if this, too, was a minor strategic triumph of his, but Damien was interested enough not to care about his cousin.

Laura had grown up in a small city in Galicia. It was Franco's hometown and a nationalist stronghold. Her family had split during the war along political lines. Afterwards they neither flourished nor fell into ruin; theirs was a middling fate in the long years after the conflict. The city was a church-going place where men went to sea with the navy and the women stayed home.

'Like good wives,' she said, rolling her eyes.

The town was so old-fashioned that it still held dances even when Laura was growing up. Mothers told their daughters who they were allowed to dance with, a partner being eligible or not according to his father's rank.

'But I could never stand the business with the dancing. At that time in my life I thought boys were idiots.' She smiled disarmingly at Damien. 'I had my books and music. I studied classical guitar. Then one day, a reception was held for the prince, who was serving with the forces in Galicia. A ball.'

Damien listened, fascinated. He had never heard of anyone he knew meeting a prince. The idea was completely foreign. Laura looked pained as she described how her father, a low-ranking naval officer, insisted that she go to the ball. In an act of resistance, though, she flatly refused to attend the preparatory dance classes, making him stamp her attendance form nonetheless. When it came to the night of the reception, she tried to slip away down a side corridor, only to bump into the prince as he came out of the toilets.

'*Mierda*. There he was. I said, "You're supposed to be inside." "Well, I'm not," he replied. "They're not ready for me yet. They – you – have to assemble to do the curtseying. And I have to do the choosing." He looked at me and said, "I can do the dance with you."

'I can't, I told him, and he said of course I could. I argued with him. I said, "I really can't. I don't know how."

'"Yes, you do. You did the course."

'"I didn't."

'"But you got the stamp, the certificate."

'He must have known you had to get the certificate to come to the reception. He looked around at some waiting officials and said, "Somebody teach her. We have time." And so someone had to teach me while everyone waited in the hall.'

Laura shook her head, horrified by the memory. 'When I walked in with the prince, I saw my friends' faces. I could see they were thinking, What the fuck is she doing? The prince whispered to me, "Your smile, you look frozen. You need to relax the muscles in your face." I told him, You're not helping. Then we did the waltz to open the ball. Luckily I knew the basics because my friends had been practising the stupid dance at school for months.'

By this time Damien felt mortified on her behalf. Not Max, who was laughing. His face lit up with delight, as if it was his story, as if he could claim the credit for it.

'Later my father was furious with me. He was sure he would be punished. Then the prince wrote a letter to the naval command.'

'Saying what?' Damien asked. He put aside his irritation at Max and his games. He needed to know how the story ended, and Laura gave him a grin, all teeth, a hundred thousand watts.

'Saying that Laura Álvares acquitted herself well.'

*

The next day, Sunday, they drove on, leaving Laura and Bilbao. With every mile they drove further from the river mouth of the day before, turning their backs on the small town with the famous break. The route had seemed to Damien like a good idea when he planned it, but now he couldn't help but feel they were heading in the wrong direction, going further from the break that was the whole reason they were here.

He was driving for a change. This suited them both. Max was cheerful enough today, tying a scarf around his neck and letting it fly about in the wind. Damien decided that whatever had happened yesterday between him and Max, it had now passed. There was nothing wrong between them. Everything was fine. At one point they stopped for fuel and a bag of *pipas*, sunflower seeds, which they devoured in the car as a substitute for breakfast.

'We're like birds,' Max announced, nibbling a husk. He toyed with his phone and looked pleased with himself in general. 'Laura says hi,' he said, keeping his voice light.

'Oh?'

'She thought you were smart.' He turned down the volume of the song that was playing on the iPod. Before the trip, Damien had loaded it with classic surf film soundtracks – *Morning of the Earth*, *Green Iguana* and others. 'She says it's just a pity you have terrible taste in music.'

Damien laughed. He didn't take the bait about the playlist. He did, however, think of Laura and their conversation. She had told him all about Bilbao: the rehabilitation of the river, which used to be heavily polluted, and then the construction of the Guggenheim Museum on its banks. She said: *It all started with water,* everything else followed the clean-up of the river. Investment, the art museum, visitors from all over.

'You can't build an art museum in every town,' he had told her, speaking frankly. It was all well and good for Bilbao, but it was hard to see the city as a template for down-at-heel cities elsewhere. Laura was an idealist, while he was a realist, he decided. Or simply a pessimist. Still, there was something extraordinary in the way they clicked, he thought. He had a sense that Laura (how could he know this?) would never go down in his esteem; she was someone who was worth getting to know better.

He didn't delude himself – he remembered the other part as well. How Max was with Laura – and how Laura was with Max. How, as they left the bar, Max pulled her into a sort of huddle, putting his arm around her shoulders and giving her his jacket. Damien knew from her reaction, an expression of pleased surprise, that Max hadn't paid this much attention to her before.

'You want to know what she says?'

'I'm sure you want to tell me.'

'Funny. I thought you liked her.'

'She's not really my type.'

'Sounds like sour grapes, my friend.'

Speak for yourself, Damien thought.

And Max, because he was Max, kept checking his phone. He should have been navigating. The roads were complicated, with long identifying numbers. The road they were taking must have diverged from the pilgrimage trail, because they did not see anyone on foot, pilgrims or otherwise. They passed into Cantabria and a stretch of wooded hills. They were taking the shorter inland route because of the lack of swell, and Damien was very conscious of missing out on a stretch of coast. On the way back, he told himself. We'll see it coming back.

'We can catch up with Laura on Wednesday night,' Max said.

'Will we be back then?'

'We can be.'

'I don't know if the timing works.'

Max adopted a vague expression, as if questions of time and space were beneath his notice.

'You'd better not say yes. I don't want to be locked in.'

'Locked in! Listen to you. It's so hard to be Damien.'

'Aren't you seeing someone in Paris?'

'In Fontainebleau, you mean. Alice. It's on and off.' He did his best to look forlorn. Scrabbling in the glove box, he asked if Damien had seen his Bob Dylan cassette tape. He'd brought his own music for the trip, mostly vintage Americana. He bought the cassettes on eBay – Bob Dylan, The Doors, Creedence Clearwater Revival – as if he found the tapes themselves appealingly retro.

'Have you checked under the seats?'

'Of course I've checked under the seats.'

There was hostility in his voice, a lingering note of blame. That note had been there all morning – and all last evening, in fact.

Ah, so that's what this is, Damien thought. It's about what happened at the cave. Max blamed him for leaving him, swimming off. Now he was retaliating, finding things to get angry at or trying to show him up. That's why he was making the thing with Laura into a stupid competition.

Good luck with that, buddy. Damien shrugged and ignored Max's accusatory tone. For a minute, he half-wished he'd come on this trip alone. He could have rented his own car, one that actually fitted his board. That way he could suit himself, without any of this shit, all the game-playing and blame from his spoiled younger cousin.

*

Santander was a jewel. It nestled against a verdant cape. The ocean that lay beyond was placid, unrippled, like a bolt of cloth unfurled to the horizon. There was nothing here to raise Damien's hopes, nothing to spell trouble for Max.

Letting Max take the first swim at the busy city beach, Damien stood guarding the surfboards. There was no way to lock them in the car; they poked up in the way of the retractable roof. He hadn't had a reason to take his board out of its foil bag or the inside layers of bubble wrap and foam. Inside all the wrapping was a beautiful six-foot thruster, with a rounded tail and slender rails, hand-made to order by a shaper on Sydney's northern beaches. He ran a hand over Max's board, a chunky older model, and shook his head at the thought of how it would handle in big surf. The bulk of it would make it easy for his cousin to get a wave, but it would be hard to duck-dive under waves of any size.

The day cooled as a breeze picked up, flapping the shade cloths on the sand. At the sight of rainclouds in the distance, Damien skipped his swim so they could get going again. With Max back driving, they tried to find common ground on music and finally, giving up, settled on the radio. The station played recent pop interspersed by the sputtering commentary of the local announcers, who spoke with so much excitement that to Damien's ears they sounded like they were hyperventilating.

'This research contract you mentioned,' he said, talking over the sound. 'Back in France next week. Is that what you're doing, now you're done with business school?'

Max kept his eyes on the road. 'I've applied for positions with some companies,' he said. He added that he had spent most of the summer doing an internship for a ratings agency, and he had lined up some research work on contract for an EU business unit that would tide him over for a few months. 'Papa EU will provide,' he joked with affection. 'What about you? How's work?'

Damien shut his eyes a moment, thinking of what to say. His work was mapping gradients using computer models, not the easiest thing to explain. A lot of the time, he spent his days at huge open-cut mines. Their scale was impossible to convey to anyone who hadn't seen them: the open-bellied earth, the trucks with tyres the size of an ordinary car. At work, he stayed in a cabin like a shipping container, airtight and self-contained, marooned in the desert as if by a giant tide. They (or we: he was part of it) were digging out iron ore. It mostly went to China. It went into furnaces there and came out as bright new steel for construction, factories, new cars off the lot.

It was only recently that he'd started to think about all this. Even as a surfer, with an affinity for nature, he hadn't seen a reason not to go into mining. In Wollongong, these worlds had coexisted – mining and industry on one hand, surfing on the other. That is, they *seemed* to go together, until they didn't. Industries failed, plants were abandoned and decayed, and pollutants seeped into the groundwater.

Max took advantage of the pause. 'Usually people want an education so they don't have to go down the mines!' he said. 'In Australia it's the opposite. *Everyone* wants to go down the mines.'

'I have an education. I have a degree in engineering.'

'And what about philosophy, the humanities, the arts? Is there a place for those underground?'

'Says the guy with the MBA.' Max chuckled, but Damien shook his head and checked the map again.

By now it was dark, which was worse than looking at the clouds because he couldn't tell how close they were getting to the rain. If they hit rain, things would be tricky. With the surfboards in the back there was no way to close the roof. There was also the problem of the damaged window seal, which was no longer watertight thanks to his Ferris Bueller stunt. They hadn't come far on the A-67 but, deciding they'd better stop, they picked the town of Santillana del Mar to stay in for the night.

'Santillana,' said Max. 'Like *Gil Blas de Santillane*. I wonder if it's the same.'

'What?'

'It's a book.' He could hear the glee in Max's voice. 'Literature!'

Damien's reply had all the grace of the last swing in a pub brawl. 'Maybe you should ask your father about who understands the value of education.'

'What do you mean?'

He wanted to get under Max's guard. 'Oh, come on. You don't know? Dad sent money back to the family for years.'

His father and Max's had lived very different lives. After leaving for Australia, Damien's dad got a job as a coal miner, the sort who really did work underground. Literature was of no more use to him in the Illawarra than it was in the fields of Veneto, where the rest of the family remained. Then he got a better-paid job in a packing yard, which meant that he could send money back home, and eventually buy his own home in Dapto when he married Damien's mother.

Max looked genuinely surprised. He was actually lost for words. But just then, with a flash of lights, they were waved to a stop by the police, the Guardia Civil. The car must have been waiting by the road in darkness.

'I wasn't speeding!' Max protested as he pulled onto the verge.

But the cop who walked up beside them fined them a hundred and five euro anyway. He said they had been spotted further back on the highway, driving with their high beams on. This was apparently an infraction. He casually rested his hand on the holster of his gun.

It was an unpleasant transaction. They didn't argue. It was hard to be sure the lights didn't malfunction, and it didn't seem the time to get into a dispute. Damien was the one who had the cash to hand, but afterwards Max was the most put out. He thought he deserved better as a visitor to the country – it had been Spain's sovereign credit rating he'd helped to review in his summer job.

'Okay, so we didn't raise the rating, but we didn't drop it either, which was frankly a good outcome in the circumstances.'

But to the Spanish, they were just two guys with surfboards in a car with foreign plates. At least the rain held off, and the education argument was forgotten, or put to one side for the time being.

At their lodgings for the night, they wrestled their boards inside. The middle-aged owner of the guesthouse watched them with sharp eyes, making sure they didn't mark her walls as they climbed the stairs. The rooms were thirty-five euro, and they each had an attic room with goat-hide rugs and heavy linens. Their hostess sent them to a restaurant where an old woman cooked their dinner and Damien paid in an attempt to cheer his cousin up.

Damien slept fitfully that night, waking from a strangely vivid dream. He was walking uphill on a stony road. Walking up and around, and hearing a bell tolling, he passed some kind of building made of the same stone as the road. He woke from the dream unsettled. It had felt so real, so vivid, and yet he was sure he'd never seen the place in the dream. In the morning he was unnerved to hear that Max had a dream like it. He felt as if they'd dreamt someone else's dreams – as if, in those heavy old bedlinens, they dreamt the dreams of pilgrims. Which was not what he signed up for, he thought, feeling out of sorts.

It was Monday, but the days of the week had lost their meaning. This is how you know you are on holiday, said Max. As they set out, they found that another cassette tape had gone missing.

'Seriously, this is fucked up.'

'They're probably under something.'

Max rummaged, frustrated. 'I can't believe we got that ticket. The guy was targeting us as tourists.'

'So? That's cops the world over.'

'It's the principle,' he said.

'You and your principles.' Damien had to laugh. 'How do your principles sit with your plans of working for a big international corporation?'

He asked this partly to needle Max, partly genuinely wanting to know how he justified his choices. This question had been on Damien's mind of late. He wished he could be as blithe as Max, as cheerfully unconcerned.

Max didn't take offence; he was eager to explain. He launched into a long and complicated speech about why he couldn't work in Italy if he tried. He knew so many people his age who were struggling to find jobs. 'It's not just the economy, it's politics, everything.' He went on to talk in a world-weary tone about how graft and corruption 'corrode the civic fabric'.

'Graft, huh,' said Damien, if only to stop him going on. 'Is that like fixing up your house with money from an earthquake fund?'

His cousin shot him daggers. 'There was earthquake damage to the house.'

Damien, mischievous, grinned and raised an eyebrow. 'Significant damage, was it?'

They were talking about their grandparents' house. It was in a small, neglected village in the Italian countryside, some distance from Treviso. Thanks to a grant from an earthquake recovery fund, it had a new front facade and driveway. Damien was sure the earthquake damage was minor, the worst effects of the quake having been felt in other regions. He figured the grant application was opportunistic at best. It would be like his uncle to make the most of the situation.

'Look, I was there,' Max protested. 'I went up there with Dad. What would you know? I didn't see you there at weekends trying to fix the place.'

'It's his house now. Your dad's.'

'Do you have a problem with that?'

'No.'

'Your dad does, though, I hear.'

'What would he want with it? He's old.'

'He could give it to you.' He said this lightly but with intent.

'That's what's worrying you, is it?'

With impeccable timing, they came to their surf spot of the day, or supposed surf spot. The Playa del Silencio – or Beach of Silence – in Asturias. The silence part was apt, since they weren't talking to each other. It was another amphitheatre cove, ridiculously steep, with a rim of dark grey sand. The surf was still non-existent, to Damien's chagrin, but he felt sure the swell was coming because the water was cold, properly cold.

To hell with Max, he thought. I am not my cousin's keeper.

He swam out a long way, alone, floated on his back, spouted water. Then he stared at the horizon and willed the swell to come.

*

Maybe he did it wrong, the whole manifesting thing. What they got was not swell but rain. They had to run back to the car. The rain wouldn't harm the boards, but the car interiors and their bags would cop it.

Driving with the top down in the wet was a new low. Or it should have been. They held towels over their heads, wrapped themselves like nuns. Max took a sideways look at Damien and started to laugh, and soon they were both laughing – at each other and at themselves. What else could they do? They were stuck with the rain and with each other.

'God help us,' Max declared as he pulled out onto the main road, indicating and speeding up to merge with the other cars. They had to get to Santiago de Compostela, where they had a booking and where they could, at least, be sure of finding a covered parking station. It pissed down for three hours, all the way there. They spent the night in a rental apartment in the centre of town, relieved to be out of the weather. Dinner was two greasy pizzas eaten out of cardboard boxes. It tasted better than anything that Damien could remember, and they toasted their journey with cans of beer from the convenience store downstairs.

The next day, they woke to the light of morning. Or a grey drizzly almost-light. The weather hadn't cleared, though at least it wasn't pouring. They left the wet contents of their bags strung over chairs and tables, airing. Walking to the cathedral, they fell in with sodden pilgrims. Seeing them trudging with their packs, Damien felt humbled and impressed. They had slogged it out on foot while he and Max sped here in a car. In a convertible, no less. And arguing non-stop.

At the entry to the cathedral, more pilgrims milled about. Damien had to wait for Max, who went looking for a toilet. He shivered in his clothes, which were damp from the day before, until his cousin at last came to join him in the line. This meant cutting in front of most of the waiting pilgrims, which he did by hurrying past them, calling, 'Forgiveness! Forgiveness!'

His manner was apologetic, hapless and silly. Everything about him meant you had to forgive him, and also they were pilgrims so they couldn't reasonably refuse. Damien felt bad that he'd goaded Max on the drive here. He should have taken the higher ground, been more tolerant of his shit-stirring. He'd given him a hard time about the house – not just about the earthquake damage, but about the ownership question too. In truth, he had no intention of trying to claim the place, but he hadn't told Max that, wanting to let him sweat it.

Inside the cathedral, he stared, craning his neck, seeing bell-towers, tiers of stone, some arches here and there. He found it all too ornate, too overwhelming to take in, and as he wandered, looking around, his thoughts strayed back to the time his cousin visited Australia. He was eighteen and alone, fresh out of school, wide-eyed and trusting and impressionable. After they'd spent a couple of months surfing in Wollongong, Damien had taken him on a surf trip down the coast, to Mollymook, Narooma, Merimbula, Green Cape – places with names that sounded exotic to Max's ears. Paradise, he called it. A garden of Eden. The world *ab initio*, unspoiled. As if, unlike Europe, it existed outside of the troubles of history. You could shoot that idea down in a thousand different ways, but his enjoyment was so childlike that Damien didn't want to spoil it.

After the cathedral, they hit the road, going back the way they'd come.

Hello I love you sang The Doors.

'When do you think we'll reach Bilbao?' This was Max, checking his phone. 'We could get back in a day.'

'Two days.'

Laura was the third presence in the car, present in absentia.

'Don't you want to stop?' Damien prodded his cousin. 'Take a look at some surf spots along the coast?'

'Yeah, I'm not super keen.'

'You're a pain, you know that, right?'

'Yes, of course I know. How could I not know? It takes a lot of effort to be this much of a pain.'

Damien laughed. Alright. They could skip some beaches. He had his own reason for agreeing: he'd read the forecast that morning, and he wanted to get back to the river mouth, just past Bilbao.

He pushed the limit on the highway, nudging the needle. They kept the rainclouds behind them, low formations in the mirror, marshmallow turning into steel. The sight made him think of something Laura said, that he had to see a show at the Guggenheim. A Richard Serra exhibition, all steel, in great big arcs. You'll love it, she said. I promise. Leaving the impression that she might take him to see it.

Laura, who he suspected of being remarkable. The only person he knew who had danced with a prince – and hated it.

In the evening, when they stopped, he called his dad at home. He wandered away from the guesthouse and along the darkening street. Trip's going well, he told him. How is everything at home? Then, when the call ended, he risked making another call, dialling the number in the soft night air.

*

The next day was Wednesday. The sky was grey but it didn't rain. The forecast was for swells of four to five foot. 'We're in business,' Damien said.

'How much business?'

'Big business.' Deciding he could afford to go easier on Max, he dug out the cassettes he had hidden in the back.

'What do you know,' Max said, giving him a naked stare.

'You're lucky I didn't bin them at a service station.'

They stuck to the highways now, no detours.

Checking the chart again, Damien said, 'I bet the water will be freezing.'

'It's already freezing,' Max complained. 'Why do you think I didn't want to come here in October?'

'What?'

'No, actually. I admit it! I wanted to come while it was still warm. Is that so terrible, Damien? Do we have to act like martyrs?'

'The trip is about the *waves*.'

Damien had pushed for them to come a couple of weeks later, in October rather than September, to be sure of getting the autumn swell. But Max, pleading work, insisted on the September dates.

'I didn't think it would make a difference.'

'So the research, the contract?'

Silence. He could not believe it. 'You mean you made that up because you wanted it to be warm.'

He was the worst. The actual worst. They passed more time in silence while Damien simmered. *Do we have to act like martyrs?* He pondered the question. If acting like martyrs meant dealing with cold water, then yes, the answer was yes. He took this as a given. At the same time, Damien got that he could be severe at times. This severity was a quality he cultivated in himself.

He lived a stripped-back existence, a life of withholding and denial. Of desolate extremes, desert and ocean. And why? To what end?

He knew the answer, of course. It was always the same, the one all-encompassing pursuit that gave his life its shape. Could you revise the list of things you lived for? He didn't think it was possible. What if there was only one thing on the list?

All the while they were driving east, tracking along the coast. As they neared the Basque coast, their destination, Max looked increasingly rattled. He was nervous about the surf. More than nervous. He was afraid. He's right to be, Damien thought. Only fools do not fear the ocean.

'If you're not feeling it, you know you don't have to go out.'

'If you're talking about Saturday, that was because of the undercurrent. That thing was fucking lethal.' Max tried to buzz his window down, but it went so far and then stuck.

'The worst thing is to panic.'

'I know that.' His eyes glittered, each one a miniature abyss. His anger hadn't dissipated; he had sharpened it to a point. It was audible in his voice, visible in his bearing: he carried the shock of having faced his own mortality and weakness. Raising his voice over the wind, he said, 'I'm not like you, Damien. I'm not obsessed with surfing. There are other things in my life. It's the most useless thing in the world to try to be good at!'

'There are other things in my life.'

'Are there? Like what?'

It was galling to realise he didn't have a comeback.

*

When they came over the hill at last, Damien caught his breath. Magnificent lines of swell rolled in to the rocky coast. The tide was fairly low, an incoming tide by the looks of it, while out beyond the breakwall the waves were gathering strength.

They had to check into a guesthouse. There was only one twin room vacant. In the room, Max kicked off his shoes, collapsed on a bed, and hung his big paddle-like feet over the end. Damien came out of the bathroom to find him like that, asleep, looking tender and angelic. Taking his chance to slip away, he grabbed all the sugar sachets from the shelf next to the kettle, tore the corners open and tipped the sugar into his mouth. He went out carrying his surfboard, crunching the crystals for energy.

He let his cousin off the hook, went for the surf without him. A determined wind blew from the south and funnelled through the valley. This turned the wind offshore, perfect for hollowing out the waves. Sure enough, as he ran downhill to the breakwall, a barrel formed on the sandbar, forced into being as the swell hit the shallow water. It thickened into a wedge-shaped wave, and then peeled neatly northwards. He could see a small group of surfers jockeying in the lineup. Jumping off the wall with his board, he paddled out through the breakers and took an uncrowded spot.

Swivelling to look back, he was surprised to see Max. There he was on the rock wall, a seal-black figure in his wetsuit. He jumped off with his board. He paddled, copped a wave, got dumped and was plunged under. His big old surfboard was a shocker of a thing to have to duck-dive in this surf. He surfaced and was thrown about as Damien watched. Even from this distance he could see he was having trouble. Another set of waves approached and Max tried to duck-dive the first, but it deftly flipped him over and pounded him in the wash.

Come on. Damien cringed. But Max righted himself, kept paddling, came back for more.

By this time Damien was in position for the next wave in the set. Distracted by watching Max, he found it was almost upon him, and had to paddle fast to catch it. The takeoff was difficult, steep and unforgiving. He tilted a little, kept his footing, and managed to land the drop. Sliding down the perpetual face, he made it through to the barrel section, where the wave curled over and almost enclosed him. And there he was: in a green glass cavern, a cathedral outside time. His world became the booming of the wave and the rushing of air.

Except that here the wave closed out. It dumped him and held him under, pummelling him hard. He felt the yank and release of his leg rope and knew it had snapped clean. Coming up gasping, he looked around. In time to see the board bounce against the breakwall, hard and white and brittle like a piece of old cuttlefish.

Just like that, it broke in two, his beautiful prized board. One half bobbed on the surface; the other tumbled out of sight. So that was it: wipeout. What a comprehensive fuck-up. He swam to retrieve what was left, the piece of board he could see. By this point, the tide was getting fuller. Behind him, over the sandbar, the waves fattened as they formed. Without the tempering effect of the incoming tide, the outgoing rip was stronger. It was dangerous, this rip.

Forgetting his board, he looked for Max, raking the lineup with his gaze. When he spotted him, out the back, he was catching his own wave. He made the steep takeoff, a small miracle in itself. He survived the sticky middle section where the wave looked like it could crumble. It almost closed out too, then didn't. It barrelled along the bar. Damien saw him in the barrel – he was crouching, holding on.

This is the wave, Damien thought, that should have been his, the best left in Europe. It was the wave of the day, a glorious thing they would remember, Damien with a tinge of envy, but also with a shot of pride. Because despite being sick of Max, he was also somehow thrilled. 'Go, Max, go!' he shouted, giving a hoarse, yodelling whoop.

It was beautiful to watch him. It was a useless, beautiful pursuit, the act of riding waves. He figured Max should come away from this triumphant, and it looked like he did at first. He scudded in on the wash and clambered out after Damien. He grinned as he approached, flicked the water from his hair and laid his board flat on the grass.

'Thought you'd go without me, did you?'

'You snooze, you lose, my friend.'

'You shouldn't have left me. You shouldn't have gone without me.' He was still grinning when he said this but he was serious all the same, serious enough to make Damien look twice.

You shouldn't have left me. Here at last was the accusation. It was what he'd wanted to say out loud since they swam back from that cave. The next thing Damien knew, his cousin moved to trip him, wrenching him by the shoulders and sticking his leg out behind his. Damien spun about on instinct and seized his shoulders in return.

'You want to go?' he asked. He turned the tables and unbalanced him. Max fell back on the grass, pulling Damien with him. They grunted and fake-wrestled, and then the fake wrestling became real. People watched from the promenade. Max gave a laugh for show.

'Tap out if you want.'

'Fuck off.'

Alright. So he pinned him, got him, held him. He put Max in a headlock. 'Tap.'

'I'm tapping.'

Damien let him go.

'Jesus.' Max rubbed his neck. It was over. He'd made his feelings known. He got up, dusted himself off, bowed like a clown to the onlookers.

'Are we good?' Damien asked. 'Because I have somewhere to be.' He turned to walk up the embankment. 'I've got to go meet Laura.'

'What?' Max stopped. 'Since when? You're a sly one, Damien.'

Standing there, he started to laugh. He laughed so hard he doubled over, but then he suddenly reared back, jerking his head like he was injured. An alarming stream of liquid poured from his nostrils – from his sinuses, from somewhere, the deep recesses of his head. The liquid coursed from him. Gushed out. It spattered on the earth.

Blood, or so you'd think. Anyone would think so. Damien was with him in two strides. He put his hand on his shoulder.

'It's only water,' he said. And meant it.

It was only water, after all.

The understudy

'Worse things happen at sea,' said Ben. It was one of his sayings. He came from a sea-going Southampton family, boats and the navy and all that. He said it to Holly the day Genevieve avoided her by the river.

The meeting (or non-meeting) happened near the Chiswick lifeboat station. Holly had come down after rehearsals to pace along, learning her lines, script in hand, while Ben finished his shift. He volunteered on the lifeboats; this was one of the things he made a part of his post-acting life. He was normally at the Tower station, but he was covering someone's shift at Chiswick, on the higher section of river where the little wild-looking islands started, funny mounds of ill-kempt green that popped up from the water, at odds with the general sense of groomed propriety onshore.

It was a novelty to be able to walk down from Hammersmith to meet him. It was right on dusk, and the light, already soft, was turning fuzzy. Even so, Holly was sure it was Genevieve she spotted. She was walking towards her, a solitary figure in boots and a khaki jacket. Then the figure turned back and left the Thames path pretty smartly, disappearing into a side street.

'I think she was avoiding me,' Holly told Ben when he showed up. 'Why would she do that?'

'Because you smell.'

She barged him with her shoulder. 'She saw me. Then she split.'

'Maybe,' he said. 'Worse things happen at sea.'

And out in the open, by the river, with the sky turning purple and birds flitting overhead, it was possible not to mind or even care all that much. She understood why Ben was doing what he was doing, making room for himself to live in a different way, removed from the all-consuming nonsense of an actor's life, the constant jockeying and fruitless auditions. She admired it, in fact. It was as if he'd flung open a window to let in a fresh breeze.

But she, unlike Ben, was still in the acting game. Very much still in. There was no way to do this job that was not a headlong tilt. Anyway, she loved it. She loved almost everything about it. Even – yes – auditions, making the rounds in her sneakers. Acting was the thing she was meant to be doing; this was an article of faith around which she had built her world. It justified every effort. It justified obsession and sheer bloody-mindedness. It justified everything and more – and then more, and more, and more.

But still, the sighting of Genevieve by the river – this bugged her.

Genevieve was Genevieve Wishart. Holly regarded Genevieve as her nemesis, partly because she thought it was funny to have a nemesis, and if she was going to have one then Genevieve seemed made to order. She was more than usually beautiful, in an actressy sort of way, and she had an artlessness about her that won people over. She was artlessly *nice*. Unbearably, supremely nice. Holly found this irritating; she liked people who had more personality, more bite.

She had known Genevieve since Guildford, the drama school. Straight off, she had come across as precious, a rarefied creature from the leafy depths of southwest London, the banker-and-broker belt that stretched away to Surrey. Since then she had gone on to become the breakthrough actress of their year, effectively cornering the market in playing the ingénue. One year she was Cécile in *Les Liaisons dangereuses*, the next she was Hero in *Much Ado About Nothing*. She had done plays at the Donmar, the Barbican and the National Theatre. Holly had once stood in for her as understudy, in a production of *Miss Julie* at the Young Vic. Genevieve hadn't done as much work of late, or not that Holly was aware, but this probably just meant she had big things in the pipeline.

Casting the two of them in the play was Miles Ajayi's idea. Miles was the director, just back from Berlin and a stint at the Schaubühne, and excited to be staging a work of Chekhov's. He was full of brilliant ideas, not all of them practical.

'I know you and Genevieve would be great on stage together,' he said.

'Really?' Holly asked. 'Why?'

'It's the mismatch, isn't it,' he said. He grinned wickedly, showing his teeth, and he laughed, a belly laugh.

'You're a mischief-maker, you.'

'I'm a director.'

Later, she realised he knew more than he was letting on. He was the architect of the thing, in more ways than one.

*

Miles sold Holly on the part. He praised her performance in *Miss Julie*. 'I've never forgotten it,' he said. 'And it would be amazing if you could bring some of that, what would you call it, that *epic disastrousness* to this role. Like, this estate is going down, the whole gentry is going down, so let's put everything on the line.'

Miles favoured minimalist staging and a free hand with adaptations. Holly had worked with him before, so she knew what she was in for. Or she thought she did.

I'm doing Chekhov, baby, she messaged Ben when she accepted the part. *She's a glamorous widow, but a widow. Do I look like a widow?*

Yes. In a good way. You would look great in a black veil.

But things got off to a rocky start. She was late for the read-through, the first gathering of the cast, because on leaving the flat, she spotted her pet rabbit – or a part of him – by the gate. At first she didn't know what she was looking at. She saw a section of fur, very neat and precisely cut, like something that belonged on a furrier's worktable. Picking it up, she saw the underside and recoiled. It was still warm and wet with blood but all the flesh had been stripped away, cleanly and surgically, as if with a scalpel.

'God damn it,' she said, dismayed.

It had to be a fox. She knew they were about. They loped at night across Weavers Fields, and nosed around the bins at the back of the chicken shop. The rabbit must have got out the night before, probably when Ben stepped outside for a joint. Pickles had a way of scampering out when you weren't looking; he loved moseying about in the weedy courtyard.

Poor defenceless Pickles! He was so lovely, so rotund. Where was the rest of him? She couldn't hunt for the body now. Not knowing what to do with the pelt, she laid it on the outside sill. Then, darting inside, she washed her hands and left again.

The violent fact of the rabbit's death punctured the morning. Arriving at the theatre in Hammersmith with a sheen of perspiration, she found the others in a back room on mismatched chairs. She dumped her bag and took a seat, saying, 'Sorry, sorry, hi.' She chose not to volunteer the reason for her lateness, feeling that it did not reflect well on her as a pet owner.

Miles beamed at her in welcome. 'Everyone, this is Holly.' The others chorused their greetings, looking bemused at her arrival. 'And we have Genevieve via Skype.' He gestured at a laptop propped up on a stool. There on the screen was Genevieve, looking effortlessly lovely. She appeared to be sitting on a couch in some kind of *House & Garden* heaven.

'Sorry not to be there,' she said. 'I'm dialling in to save you all from this rubbish cold.'

Dialling in? Could you do that? Since when was that an option? It was just like Genevieve to think she was too good to come to a reading. She had been sick when Holly had been her understudy as well. With what, Holly didn't know. How many times could she be sick?

As the others moved about, adjusting chairs and so on, Holly leaned towards the laptop and said, 'You're in the wars, Genevieve. It isn't as serious as last time, I hope?'

Genevieve gave her a frosty stare. 'It's just a cold,' she said. 'It's nothing.'

'All good?' said Miles. 'Cool, let's crack on.'

Holly knew some of the other faces there, people she'd worked with or met before. The script was an adaptation of an early Chekhov play, an unfinished, untitled work that was rarely performed. The main male character was named Platonov, so this was what the play tended to be called in English. Genevieve was playing his young love interest, Holly the widow of a general.

'So,' said Miles, 'we're in a big garden in the spring of 1881. The background is that Anna is the (still smoking hot) widow of a once-great general.'

'Thank you, thank you,' Holly said.

'She's had to mortgage the house and hasn't paid the servants, but she's throwing a party for her friends, because why not. Remember, this is the first time we hear about this friend of theirs, Platonov. We haven't met him yet. We've heard of his reputation. He's supposed to be a man who exemplifies the modern age.'

They resumed the reading from where they were up to.

'"In fact,"' said someone sitting across the circle from Holly, '"Platonov put this rather well. I remember he once said: 'We have advanced in our attitude to women. But even advance turns out to be a kind of retreat.'"'

The actor playing Nikolai Triletzky, the doctor, read, '"Yes, well, that sounds like pure, unadulterated Platonov. What was he? Drunk?"'

It was Holly's turn. '"What do you think, my friend? What is your view of Platonov?"'

'So,' broke in Miles, 'what *do* we think about Platonov at this point?'

'I feel he's the kind of guy who would wear a fedora,' said Holly.

'I have a fedora, I could bring it in,' said Rhys Bateman, who was playing Platonov. Rhys was a tousle-haired actor of some talent and good looks.

'Let's leave that thought for now, but I love these ideas,' said Miles.

In this way the reading continued, with much boisterous interrupting. Genevieve alone was quiet, sticking strictly to her lines. Visible onscreen, she sat sipping a mug of tea and kept tucking a strand of hair behind her ear, only to have it swing loose again. Her once long hair was now a bluntly cropped bob, an anti-style statement that also managed to be stylish. Holly thought it looked annoyingly excellent.

'Sorry, this connection's a bit dodgy,' Genevieve said as they took a break. 'If it freezes I'll call back.'

'Are you living in the country?' Holly asked.

'Oh god, no. We're in Chiswick.'

Holly blinked. Genevieve was just down the road, ten minutes from the theatre. Everyone else had schlepped across London. For Holly, who lived in Bethnal Green, the commute took an hour each way, a walk to Whitechapel tube station and then the District Line.

Genevieve was wooden as she read her lines that day. 'It was hard reading by Skype,' Miles conceded later. 'And she's not feeling a hundred per cent. It's early days.'

*

They couldn't find the rest of Pickles, she and Ben, when they looked that night. There was no doubt the pelt was his; it was distinctive, mottled and silvery like the trunk of a birch tree. Holly was angry at Ben, blaming him for the rabbit's death. In truth, she was angry at them both, for their shared failure as a couple to protect the animal in their charge, their first additional family member.

Later, in bed, she woke Ben. 'It was me,' she said.

'Say what?' He was groggy.

'I think *I* let the rabbit out. I was up late last night, learning my lines in the courtyard. I'm sorry. Oh god. Poor Pickles.'

She should have been more careful. She was anxious about the play, that was the problem. And she was right to be anxious.

She was starting to realise why *Platonov* was rarely performed. Who in their right mind would attempt to stage such a play, with its convoluted plot and impossibly large cast? Miles was still cutting the script down, refining the adaptation. He went back and forth on how much was necessary. Should they cut the scene where Platonov harassed a woman and she fell back into the caviar cart? If they kept it, how could they fake a whole cart full of caviar, and was it necessary for it to be a caviar cart *as such*?

On day two of the read-through, Holly made a point of arriving early. Genevieve dialled in again, smiling bravely and dabbing a tissue at her nose. By late afternoon, when they finished the final act, the group's initial high spirits had given way to a flatter mood. No one admitted to feeling daunted, but the reality of the task was making itself felt.

The following week, they started rehearsals. Holly travelled to Hammersmith every morning, taking her lunch in her bag and loading her phone with podcasts. Before she got up, Ben, who left before she did, doodled on her banana with a Sharpie: an all-capitals message along the lines of *Ben is fit*, or a dick-and-balls cartoon with a few straggly pubes. Genevieve deigned to join them in person, but remained brittle and aloof. In rehearsals she talked in a lofty way about 'making an offer', when what she really meant was coming up with a way to do something in a scene, like delivering a line while pacing about or dropping into a chair with a heavy sigh. During breaks she gave little away. That was the peculiar thing about acting: it was necessary to show vulnerability at times, but you were also very careful to keep some things out of view. Look at this, don't look at that. Revealing and concealing, the two sides of the same coin.

Genevieve always left rehearsals as soon as they finished, never hanging around or coming to the pub. When the rest of the cast were going to a Turkish restaurant one lunchtime, Holly made a point of inviting her but she refused, saying she was vegetarian.

'So am I,' said Holly. 'They have felafel.'

'It's okay. I should get going.'

It was around this time that she avoided Holly by the river. If that's how you want it, fine, Holly thought afterwards. She wondered at the fact that she'd ended up in a play that pitted her against Genevieve for the attentions of some womanising dude. Both their characters, Anna and Sofya, were entangled with Platonov, a schoolteacher-cum-poet-cum-self-styled Don Juan. But Holly focused on trying to find her way into the play. It was part of a festival, the London ChekhovFest. Posters would soon go up advertising dates and venues. It was clear which theatres had the most sway. The big guns got the big trio, *Uncle Vanya*, *The Cherry Orchard*, *The Three Sisters*. Of course.

Miles was upbeat, bless him. They didn't have enough people for all the characters, so he had one actor play all the leftover parts, with much changing of hats, lace caps and moustaches, et cetera. In his time at the Schaubühne, he'd absorbed something of the auteur-director style. This meant, among other things, a tendency to put objects like fridges and sunglasses in nineteenth-century plays. Keen to do something outside London's West End, he had leapt at the chance to bring his vision to Hammersmith.

'I only read the play after I said yes,' he quipped. 'And then I thought, fucking hell, what have I got myself into? Six hours long, are you serious? The audience will riot. But honestly,' he told them, 'I was really struck by this portrait of provincial Russians caught between the past and the future. A glorious past, an uncertain future. Each as inaccessible, as remote, as the other.'

At a certain point, they all had to meet with the wardrobe manager, who put them in dresses and toyed thoughtfully with their hair. 'The mum bob,' Genevieve said, scrunching her hair self-consciously. This was the first time Holly had heard her say anything about having a child, and she must have allowed her surprise to show.

'I know, I know,' said Genevieve. 'I've kept it quiet. Partly it's privacy, like what right do I have to plaster my daughter's face all over the internet before she's old enough to tell me to eff off?'

Holly knew she was supposed to ask the baby's age, ask to see pictures. 'And what's the other reason?'

'What?'

'You said partly.'

'Oh, did I?' Genevieve was saved from answering by the wardrobe manager.

'Don't worry,' he said, stroking her hair. 'We want this production to look modern.'

Genevieve smiled winningly. 'Do whatever you need to do.' Radiating trust and commitment to the cause, she made it sound like she was willing to let him hack off all her limbs. Then it was Holly's turn to be scrutinised, with much sighing and tutting over her measurements and hair. The wardrobe manager informed her that her rib cage was very broad, too broad for standard sizing, then he remarked on her dry ends. 'Try a moisturising mask.'

As rehearsals continued into the second week, the play itself remained a puzzle to Holly. Was it really all about Platonov? At the outset, the other characters – his friends – seemed to think that he was somehow the best of them, as an intellectual, modern man, but this was baffling to Holly. 'He's not that great a guy,' she said during one discussion. During the course of the play, she pointed out, Platonov managed to hit on both Sofya and another woman at the party, rebuff Anna's offers of love, ignore his long-suffering wife, persuade Sofya to run off with him to

Paris, and then decide he couldn't be arsed going after all. Finally, he threatened to shoot himself and didn't go through with that either. 'He's really an antihero,' Holly said. 'He's too ineffectual to do anything.'

Rhys had a different interpretation. He said the play was a study of a sex pest, a drama before its time. 'It's amazing,' he said. 'The way Chekhov *gets* it.'

Miles wanted the play to be a comment on a lost generation. 'Much like ours, really.'

'Erm, what *is* our generation?' asked Rhys.

'Elder millennials,' said Holly. She high-fived with Rhys, while Genevieve looked on, saying nothing.

Genevieve was the other puzzle in all this. Watching her rehearse, Holly was struck by a stiffness in her performance, a lack of confidence perhaps. It was strange – she didn't remember her being like this at drama school. She thought back to *Miss Julie*. She hadn't seen her rehearse for that; she was called in only when Genevieve dropped out. It was an eleventh-hour thing, much to Holly's good fortune. There wasn't the budget for an understudy in the true sense – someone who learned the part during rehearsals, ready to step in if needed. Instead, 'understudy' was a euphemism for 'replacement', with Holly coming in cold and learning the part from scratch in days. She got the call because the casting manager happened to know her work. The director told her she made the play more 'interesting', by which she knew he meant that she wasn't as pretty as Genevieve. Reviewers offered more backhanded praise.

In a happy piece of miscasting, we have Holly Murchison as Miss Julie. She turns Strindberg's most biting (and most moralising) play into a thrilling maelstrom. Come for the car-wreck plot, stay for the sparkle and subversion.

There'd been much talk of the chemistry between Holly and the male lead, Owen Rennes, who played the servant Jean. That was a surprise, considering that in real life she found Owen a damp squib. He was very withdrawn; he hardly looked at her, in fact. Anyway, the play had put her on people's radar. She started getting phone calls, invitations to audition. A string of character parts followed, some on stage, some on screen.

Now here was Genevieve condescending to appear in Miles's production. No, that was unfair, putting it like that. Miles was a talented director. Holly knew she tended to downgrade anything she was involved in; it was a bad habit, as Ben said whenever he caught her at it. Nevertheless, she wondered at Genevieve's motives. She was probably doing the play to maintain her cred as a theatre actor after her film and TV roles, wanting to avoid being seen as a starlet. Whatever the reason, here she was with the rest of them, acting the ordinary mortal in a smock-style shirt and glasses, sitting cross-legged with a highlighter at the ready. It was like another actor Holly knew of, a guy who shot to fame with his role in a period drama. He continued to edit a small literary journal, reminding the world that before he was a star he read English at Oxford and was an intellectual, thinky person with intellectual, thinky friends.

Holly wasn't the only one in the cast struggling with the play. It was Chekhov, yes, but Chekhov in his throw-everything-into-the-laundry-basket phase. 'It's a big old jumble, let's be honest,' said Peter Novak, the actor playing Dr Triletzky.

'That's like life, though, isn't it?' Genevieve said.

'Sure, but we're charging money for people to come and see it. I don't think they'll be impressed by three hours of jumble,' said Holly. (By this time, Miles had whittled the play down to three hours, thank god.)

Holly practised delivering her lines with gusto. This was Anna's best quality, she'd decided, her gusto. There was something extraordinary about her, which came from knowing her own desires and voicing them shamelessly. Like the time after the party, when instead of going to sleep she rode over to Platonov's house on her horse and propositioned him in the bushes, saying, 'Smoke me like a cigarette and throw me away.'

Holly loved inhabiting that side of the character, but had trouble with Anna's blind spot when it came to Platonov. 'She doesn't see the problem with his behaviour,' she said to Ben one night. 'She's always excusing him. It's like she's his biggest enabler.'

'She's human,' he said.

This was on one of the nights when he helped her with her lines. It was good of him to do this. It wasn't all that long since he had given up acting himself. He had quit with the idea of doing something easier. Something more *Ben-friendly*, he said. He thought about being a paramedic in the NHS but settled on a job in a commercial property management firm. It was not creative in the slightest and he found this oddly freeing, an unexpected relief after the years of acting. He was always beautifully generous about helping her with her work, however. That's what Ben was like, generous to his core.

*

In this telling of the story, the version that Holly told herself on a daily basis, she disliked Genevieve; that was all. Yet in certain moments she could acknowledge that there were other possible narratives, perhaps more honest ones. A different telling might make it a story about envy.

Did Holly envy her? God, yes. She envied Genevieve's easy ride. No years of slog for her. Whereas Holly just felt tired. For her, acting was never *not* a hustle.

And wasn't this closer to the truth, closer to the bone? Genevieve represented what had eluded her, represented a certain effortlessness. For Holly, who pinned her hopes on a slower-build career, things still felt precarious, every small success hard won. *Platonov* had come when she was getting traction, but she didn't yet trust her own success. What if the next role didn't come? Or the one after that, or after that?

Two weeks into rehearsals, on a Friday, Holly took the train out to her old acting school in Guildford, where she'd agreed to give a guest seminar, unpaid, as a favour. Standing at the front of the room, she looked out on the students' hopeful, expectant faces and wondered what she could say to them. Don't do it if you can possibly avoid it?

No, can't say that.

She pulled her notes from her bag and began speaking on the woman's voice in Greek theatre, and the line from there to Ibsen and Tennessee Williams. She zeroed in on Chekhov, since he was front of mind. The students looked bored stiff, the little brats. But she knew this was a cover, a pretence, in the way that boredom often was, and that deep down, underneath, they were utterly petrified. They were all so desperate to make it, and they knew the odds were against them.

Wanting to offer them something more, she read them an article about how Chekhov's modesty, his self-mockery and self-doubt, for a long time persuaded others not to believe in his talents. "'It was only slowly and with great difficulty that he gained a modicum of belief in himself – the belief that is essential if others are to believe in us,'" she finished, quoting Thomas Mann.

So she ended up doing the opposite of what she intended, and left them with this note of encouragement.

In doing *Platonov*, Holly had never considered that Genevieve might stand in need of encouragement or support. The following day, when someone asked Genevieve if she'd be auditioning for a part that was coming up elsewhere, she told them she couldn't. 'I can only do this play because it's close to home,' she said. 'My daughter's seven months old. I hate being away from her, I'm in two minds all the time. Even when I'm here I'm not doing justice to the role. You know, I didn't want it to be known that I've had a child because I worried that people would think I'm distracted. And guess what? They'd be right. They'd be *absolutely* right.'

The penny dropped for Holly, and for the first time she felt some sympathy towards Genevieve. Perhaps it showed. Genevieve turned to her and said, 'I should have said this those times you all went out for lunch, but it's better if I pop home at lunchtime for a feed.'

It took Holly a moment to realise that a feed meant feeding her baby.

'I mean, I've expressed, obviously,' said Genevieve with a downwards smile, 'but it helps to keep the plumbing going. Boobs. What a mega-pain.'

'Right,' said Holly, though nothing about breastfeeding was obvious to her. She thought with regret of their previous exchanges, in which she'd been so ready to drop little barbs for Genevieve. Why hadn't she been kinder when she told her about her daughter?

Yet she did not, for whatever reason, recount this exchange to Ben at home later; she must have felt it didn't work as one of her anecdotes, most of which had a theme of Genevieve-is-the-worst. It didn't fit the picture she had created, and perhaps deep down she didn't want to remake the picture. At the same time, she was absorbed by her own dramas, her own concerns.

There was the sad demise of Pickles and her burden of shame and sorrow. Mourning brought her closer to Ben, something she did not expect. They searched for, but didn't find, the rest of the rabbit carcass. They pondered what to do with the pelt, but there was no way of keeping it that wasn't totally unsanitary, and since it was already starting to get a bit whiffy, they settled on a covert burial by night in Weavers Fields. This meant finding a bushy patch, diving in like a pair of teenagers looking for somewhere to grope each other, and tipping the furry pelt from a shoebox onto the earth. Then, kneeling side by side, they covered it over with dirt. And Ben recited Shelley, something about rose leaves when the rose is dead, being *heaped for the beloved's bed.*

He took her hand as he spoke, and the whole thing was curiously intimate and sad, much more real than the half-ironic funeral they expected it to be. They were drawn together in the night in a slightly grotty East London park, while cars trawled up Vallance Road.

Other things were happening in the world, she noticed that week. Spring, for instance. A magnolia tree in a garden she passed each day burst without warning into full, glorious flower, suddenly simply *there*, demanding wonder and attention. It was enough to raise your spirits or break your heart, or both at once – those great, dishy petals enacting a gorgeous wild unfurling.

Rehearsals grew more intense. Everyone felt it. To lighten the mood, Miles had them do a brainstorming session. 'So what we're looking for is a Reason To Believe,' he said, 'a reason to care about this story now, in the present. If the late general represents a great generation, who would that be for us?'

'Churchill.'

'The Wombles.'

'Tony Benn.' This came from Rhys.

There was more of this sort of talk over lunch at the Turkish restaurant, all about the play's supposed relevance to the present. Everyone was there except Genevieve. People said Brexit-y things, speaking about the fear of being reduced to a province, of people beginning to leave the UK in dribs and drabs. A TV in the corner was playing a news update. It showed the Brexiters' march from Sunderland, people trudging beside a road in unremarkable countryside.

'Where are they up to now?' asked Holly.

'I don't know. Aldfield?'

'Which is where when it's at home? My geography is shit.'

Regrouping after lunch, they rehearsed the final scene, in which Sofya shoots Platonov with a revolver. This was Miles's chance to do blood and gore, his favourite thing; it was the only bloody bit in the play. Before they got going, he spoke to Genevieve, prepping her.

'Platonov has pushed and pushed,' he said. 'He's pushed Sofya to her limit. He's flattered and courted her, then resorted to bullying. He's humiliated her. And what does he care?'

'He doesn't,' Genevieve retorted. 'He doesn't give a toss.'

'So she seizes the gun. It's a moment of reckoning.' Miles looked around soberly, script in hand. 'A reckoning means the avenging of an act of wrongdoing; it comes from the word for settling a bill.'

Holly was half listening. Her thoughts were all of Anna and how to play her in the scene. When Platonov died, Anna would be the one to cradle his body, to hug him tight with disbelief.

'Alright,' said Miles, clapping once. 'From Sofya's line. *Enough . . .*'

And it was over to Genevieve, who entered from stage left. In the last few days, her performances had been gradually improving – she was gaining confidence in the role, and Sofya was starting to seem more like a living, breathing woman. But no one was expecting the performance that followed. Genevieve snatched up the revolver, radiating fury. She appeared completely transformed. The effect was disconcerting.

"'Enough!'" she cried. "'It can't be allowed!'" And, with an involuntary sob, she fired at Platonov. She missed, but moved to shoot him again, point-blank in the chest. He fell to the ground. Her arms shook as she lowered the gun. Then, looking ashen, she dropped the weapon and stepped back.

'Wow, Genevieve,' everyone said. And even Holly was impressed.

*

This should have told her something, she realised later. Genevieve's ashen face that day was a clue of sorts. But she, Holly, carried on oblivious, unseeing. She might never have realised what she was missing, the piece that made the rest of the puzzle fit together. (She'd kicked this piece under the sofa, out of the reach of a vacuum nozzle or the most determined fingers.)

She would probably never have figured it out if not for some loose talk in a restaurant soon afterwards. It was a birthday dinner for Graham, a fellow actor and a friend of Ben's. The inside of the restaurant was dim, the sort of place where waiters dispensed with notebooks and took the orders empty-handed, looking smug. A friend of Genevieve's called Zora was there, sitting on the other side of Ben. The conversation at the table was flippant, gossipy, fast-moving. Someone asked Ben about his work, how he was finding it.

'Never better,' he said. 'Work has stopped being my whole life.' And it was true, thought Holly. He had never been better. There was a contentment to his days. But either his friends couldn't see it, or they did and they didn't trust it.

When Holly mentioned the play, Zora nodded to show she knew already. Talk turned to Chekhov. Was he a dreamboat? someone wondered, bringing out a phone. Heads came together over the screen, a glowing oblong at the table.

'His photo would say yes.'

'He looked good in his skinny phase as a starving student.'

'Zora, you can't say that! He had tuberculosis.'

'Oh, old Anton Chekhov. No, I'm not feeling that.'

'The pince-nez isn't sexy.'

'No, it is not.'

By this time they were, if not drunk, then certainly drunk-adjacent. Graham raised his glass and began a rambling mock-speech, offering the wisdom of his years. He spoke about a visit to a distillery in Scotland. ('I was with straight people, that's what they do.') He'd learned that scotch production relied on old sherry barrels for maturation. The barrels were shipped in from Spain, but with so much demand for scotch and not enough demand for sherry, the balance had been lost. 'And I realised, you know, everything is connected. Like in that song in *The Lion King*, the circle of life,' he finished.

'Like you and Genevieve,' said Zora, leaning across to Holly and raising her own glass to her. 'Coming full circle.' She was wearing a blouse with inexplicably wide sleeves, like flowing skirts for her arms.

'How's that?' asked Holly.

'Well, history, et cetera. When you took her part that time after Owen Rennes was a bit, you know.'

'No, I don't. A bit what?'

'You don't know? Oh wow.' Zora smoothed her sleeves. 'He was . . . overly friendly, shall we say. Then a bit nasty in the end. That's why she quit the show.'

'She quit? I thought she was sick. That's what I was told.' Holly's head started to spin.

'I don't think that's quite what happened.'

Holly leaned behind Ben to talk more confidentially with Zora. This wasn't something for the rest of the table. 'What do you mean? What did happen?' Zora shook her head. 'You have to tell me,' Holly hissed.

'No, I don't have to tell you. That's up to Genevieve.' Zora had suddenly grown a conscience, or at least a sense of discretion.

'Come on, Zora. You can't leave it at that. I need to know why they brought me in.'

But Zora would not be pestered. Making a face, she said, 'Oh, go away, would you, Holly.' She turned to the person on her left and started a conversation.

Ben said nothing at the time, but as he and Holly walked home from the tube, he said, 'So you're a scab.'

'I'm not a scab!'

'You are. That's the definition of a scab! She withdrew her labour. You stepped in, didn't you?'

He was prodding her on purpose, but Holly was not amused. 'Jesus, Ben. I didn't cross the picket line of a strike. I didn't know anything about it, if anything happened. I'm not sure I believe it. Zora can't be right. They would have told me if Owen did anything wrong. They would have warned me.'

She could think of plenty of objections to Zora's version of events. If it was true and something untoward had happened, why didn't the theatre get rid of the offender, instead of letting Genevieve quit?

Another thing – if it was true, Holly thought, why didn't Owen try it on with her? Was it something about her? She wasn't Genevieve, clearly. Could you be offended by the fact that you were *not* harassed?

She wasn't sure if Owen was capable of such behaviour or not. From what she knew, he had done alright in the three years since *Miss Julie*. Her memory of him was curiously hazy, apart from the fact that he'd played a good Jean in the play, a fantasy – or nightmare – of an upwardly mobile villain. Don't trust your servants, the play said. And lock up your daughters.

Still, she couldn't dismiss the thought that something had happened. She was swamped by a feeling of bewilderment. Ben clearly thought there was something in it. Pulling off his boots at home, he shook his head and said, 'I'm so fucked off they didn't tell you. It's shitty that they didn't.'

'It's okay.'

'It's not okay! They told you not to call her, remember?'

'Yeah, that's true,' she said, remembering.

'They probably told her not to speak to you either. Maybe she wanted to, who knows? Maybe she felt bad that she didn't.'

Later that night, she woke up parched. Too much wine at dinner. She got up, made tea, and read over the next day's scene, huddling under the lamp with a blanket about her shoulders.

Ben got up and found her. 'The dark night of the soul,' he said. 'Are you still thinking about Genevieve?'

'Mmm.' She gave him a wobbly smile. 'You have to be mad to do this job.'

'It's a bit weird, isn't it? Pretending to be other people for a living.'

She let the script drop onto the coffee table. 'This play makes Chekhov look like the patron saint of false starts,' she said. 'Which is encouraging, I guess. It shows you that even Chekhov didn't start out being Chekhov. He started out being slightly crap like the rest of us.'

She handed him a photocopied page from some loose papers on the table. 'Look at this. At the time he wrote *Platonov*, he was having trouble publishing his short stories. This is from an editor, get this, "You are fading before you blossom. Great pity."'

'Sick burn.' He squeezed her shoulder and shuffled off to have a pee.

She went back to bed soon after. Tried to dispel her doubts, which were many and varied. About her work, her so-called profession. She had come to acting as if following a magnetic field. It was her calling, she felt, but what was a calling really, except a sense of predestination? It was absolutely crazy when you thought about it. By most rational measures, the path she had chosen did not make sense, and yet she was compelled to keep treading it all the same. Her passion was her passion, and she could not imagine herself without it. It was at the core of who she was, not just an overwhelming need, but her *organising* need.

Her thoughts veered to her successes. Now, though, she was forced to feel guilty about those too. Hadn't she built her career on that chance to do *Miss Julie*? In her accounting of her life, she had to make room for this possibility, at least. And now doubts crept in about her own behaviour. Had she been wilfully blind to what she didn't want to know?

This was the big, persistent question about which the others swirled. She kept coming back to it then cycling madly away again, not wanting to think about it: the question of what she, Holly, knew or should have known.

*

Some acts happened offstage, unseen. That was what life was like. The death of Pickles, for example. They never saw the fox, the culprit. She saw no disappearing tail, no paw prints in the gutter. And maybe it didn't matter whether they saw it or not. What did it matter what sort of fox it was, a thin fox or a fat one, good or evil or in between?

Maybe what mattered was what came next, what you did about it, Holly thought. But that was no comfort if you hadn't a clue about that either.

The day after the birthday dinner was the last day of rehearsals. Holly didn't want to be there. All her being – her joints, her very tissue – protested, and she was overly aware of the muscles in her face. Between scenes, she looked at the others blankly, then compensated by over-acting when they got back to it. Her performance was off-key. Here she was playing Anna, this proud, powerful woman, and yet she felt weaselly and low. Here she was being forced to confront her own massive fucking blind spot. She was not so different from Anna, in this department. The blind spot department.

She was hardly able to look at Genevieve. She messaged Zora: *Does she hate me?*

'Holly,' Miles said as they were wrapping up, 'just checking in. What's happening? Are you okay?'

'Yes,' she said. 'No. My rabbit died.' It was three weeks ago, but he didn't know that.

'Oh geez. Sorry to hear it.'

Genevieve, hearing the exchange, waited for Holly to pass. 'Sorry about your rabbit,' she said. And she did look genuinely sorry.

Behind them, Rhys and Miles continued debating the meaning of the play. 'It's about futility,' said Rhys. 'Don't you think, Holly?'

Holly was sick of the back-and-forth about what it was all supposed to mean. They were scratching around for an idea, a grand theory to resolve the messiness of the work. How would I know? she wanted to snap. And was about to when Genevieve spoke up. She'd been collecting her things, winding the cord of her earphones around her phone, ready to rush off like always. She reminded them of something they had read at the beginning of rehearsals, in the photocopied notes that Miles passed around.

'Don't forget that Chekhov wrote the play for the actress he was in love with, Maria Yermolova,' she said. 'When it comes down to it, it's really a tribute. He wanted her to play Anna, so she's got to be important, maybe more so than Platonov.'

Everyone stopped talking and turned to look at her. It was an insightful thing to say. More than that, it struck Holly as generous. Generous to Anna, and therefore to her.

Holly cleared her throat. 'Genevieve,' she said. 'I'll walk you.'

'Okay. If you like.' Genevieve was nonplussed. 'I'll just be a minute. I need the loo.'

'I'll be outside,' said Holly.

Waiting on the street, she thought of what she would say. Cars were spitting past in the bright afternoon sun. She repeated words in her head, learning them like lines, but she wasn't sure if she could say them. Then Genevieve came out and Holly saw her face, which was a mirror of how she was feeling herself, apprehensive and wary and relieved at the same time.

She was doing this, wasn't she? Seize the day. Because (and she only knew this when the moment came) this was the scene she'd been preparing for, here, on the street outside the theatre in the cool spring air.

Unsuccessful breakup

Phoebe had no reason to think the breakup wouldn't stick. Why shouldn't it? Jimmy didn't depend on her for his happiness. He didn't depend on her for anything whatsoever. He was, had always been, a self-sufficient person. He would move on smoothly, like a train leaving a station, slow at first, then gradually gathering pace and speeding out of view.

Having summoned her resolve, she met him on a night in May. It had just stopped raining and the air was clear and fresh. She waited outside the Soho restaurant where he worked most nights. A fashionable French place with big windows. She could see him at the bar, polishing glasses with deft movements, wearing a snug-fitting black shirt with the sleeves rolled up. He was tall and lanky with grown-out hair. Flicking a white cloth over the bar, he looked up, saw her there and nodded.

'Coming,' he mouthed, stepping neatly around the large floral arrangement on the end of the bar, a potentially hazardous concoction of red and orange spears.

Clever, handsome Jimmy! It wasn't that she didn't love him.

He came out in his jeans and his Vans, pulling his jacket on. 'Hey,' he said.

'Hey. How was your shift?'

'Good. Busy. Full house.'

He had to lean down to kiss her. She was small, even scrawny. Early on, Jimmy had remarked that her bony jutting shoulders, prominent collarbone, and closely shorn dark hair created a *Les Mis* effect, giving her the air of a street urchin or orphan. But this was only an effect – in fact, she had two parents, a mother living in Hong Kong, in what had been their family flat, and a father now at large as a travelling salesman.

Kissing Jimmy, Phoebe tasted peppermint Extra. He rarely tasted of alcohol, even when they went out. Despite his job, he wasn't much of a drinker. He liked the artistry of the work, not oblivion, he said. And bartending wouldn't be his final destination, which was another reason he took such pleasure in it.

He entwined his long, elegant fingers – artist's fingers, she always thought – in hers. As they started walking, the clarity of the night after the rain enlivened her senses, or maybe it was the knowledge of what she was going to do. The street lamps shone like grubby jewels strung out on dark cloth, and the occasional black cab sloshed past through the puddles.

They chatted about his shift as she thought of how to say it. She filled the gaps when he fell silent; this was one of the things she did, a role that fell to her in their division of labour. Being talkative by nature, she normally didn't mind. She explained the machinations of the prac rotations in her program. The details were intricate, Machiavellian even, although later she would forget how intense the whole thing was, the need to jostle for a place in a cut-throat competition.

'Don't let them rattle you, Pheebs,' he said. 'It's mind games 101. Get what you need, get out. Simple as that.'

No one got past Jimmy's guard. He was the son of a gambler, and this gave him the advantage of an impassive poker face. A second-generation poker face, he sometimes joked.

Their usual M.O. when she met him after work was to go to her room, in halls at Goodenough. They'd walk past several book-shops, and often stopped to browse. He usually dragged her into Emerson's Book Arcade, a triple-storey townhouse that stayed open the latest and was filled to the rafters with second-hand books of all ages. Jimmy had grown up in London but his family was from Shanghai, and it was his habit to skim the Chinese-language section, running a finger along the spines. The shop bored Phoebe, who liked new books. Tonight she was glad when a brief return of the rain gave her an excuse to hail the bus and skip the session in Emerson's.

'Wasn't that weird?' she said cheerfully when they were safely on board. 'The shower came out of nowhere. The clouds looked like they were clearing.' She heard herself talking, she knew her chit-chat was inane, and from his distracted look she could see he had tuned out. She clamped her mouth shut, thinking, Well, why don't you carry the conversation for a change? If I didn't have to do this I could seem enigmatic too.

She wanted to tell him there and then, get the breakup done and sorted, but no – there were too many people around them, swaying silently in the aisle, and anyway it would be awful in the overly bright lighting from the light-sabre-style tubes that ran along the ceiling.

Did ambience matter for a breakup? It shouldn't, yet it did. Well, she couldn't help it if she had standards.

They got off after a few stops, at Lamb's Conduit Street. They walked until they reached the edge of Coram's Fields, where an iron picket fence marked out the perimeter and a sign pointed the way to the Foundling Museum. When they reached the brown-brick college, she turned and said abruptly, 'I think we should break up.'

'Oh,' he said. 'Okay. That's probably a good idea.'

'Really?'

'Yes.' She watched him breathe in, then nod slowly. 'You have exams,' he said reasonably, graciously, 'and after that who knows? We might end up in different places.' He made this sound quite casual, though she knew there was nothing remotely casual about the way Jimmy pursued his goals. He was older than she was, having taken two years out to save for his uni fees and living expenses. But he would soon be graduating.

'Right, that's what I thought,' she said with a spurt of courage. This was good. He was agreeing. She should have been relieved. She was about to say more when the traffic light changed, commanding them to walk with its intrusive, harassing ticking. Oh shit, she thought, this is really it. The traffic light was urging them to go their separate ways. She would go to her room, and he would walk through the back streets to his aunt and uncle's flat above their corner shop. The shop was a treasure trove, stuffed with everything you could think of, from shoelaces to bath plugs, exercise books, and the daily pallets of soft white bread that elderly customers preferred.

She had expected him to argue, or at least look upset. After three years together, how could that be it? People said that Hong Kong expat brats discarded relationships with hardly a moment's thought, but when it came to it she had nothing on Jimmy. As she went up the steps to put in her pin code, he merely turned the other way to walk home in the dark.

Afterwards Phoebe went over their conversation in her mind. She wished he had said something meaningful, or even something vaguely on the spectrum of meaningful, a comment to parse later and find beauty in. But he'd given her nothing to work with. His reaction – or lack thereof – made her question whether he'd ever cared. Her insecurities flared up like a recurring rash.

'He could have had the decency to pretend,' she complained to her friend Grace. 'He could have sworn at me. Or *something*.'

'He cares a lot, you know.'

'Right, of course. I know.'

*

When news of the breakup reached the rest of their friends, it caused a ripple of surprise. As a pair they were seen as an institution, an immutable fact of life. Their years together seemed a geological span of time. The Triassic, the Jurassic, the Cretaceous period . . . she'd spent more time in Geology gazing out the window than studying the Earth's epochs. The campus of the International School in Hong Kong looked across the water to the stony spine of the Shek O Country Park, which in outline resembled a sleeping dinosaur or dragon. Meanwhile, the teacher went into great detail on the splitting of the continents, when they were carved off and mashed together in new configurations.

Against the ruptures of continents, what did human dramas matter? What possible consequence did her little breakup have? It wasn't so momentous, she told herself severely. She put aside all reminders of Jimmy, including the silver fob bracelet he'd recently given her. She didn't especially like it, and thought of giving it to her sister. Actually, the gift was puzzling. It was not his style or hers (she favoured stacks of bangles). He bought it at Tiffany, the Bond Street store, and this made her think of the glossy couples in the Tiffany ads on buses. The couples were always blond and dynastic-looking. She would rather he had given her a cheap and cheerful candy necklace, which you could wear or eat or both, and cost next to nothing.

It was lonely being single, but nowhere near as lonely as she'd felt in the relationship. In the months before the breakup, the dynamic between them had been increasingly lopsided, and she had tired of being the chatty one. At times she felt shown up by Jimmy's steadiness, as though by comparison she was somehow frivolous. He had become more and more serious, less and less playful. And once the fun was gone – well, what was the point? It was like trying to hang onto a day-old helium balloon, one of the pitiful gift-shop ones she sometimes saw in wards, tied to bedside rails or the wrist of a young patient. Sinking, not rising. Getting in the way.

Feeling strangely vindicated, she busied herself in her studies. This was easy enough to do, she had textbooks to pore over, and it was only at odd moments that her thoughts strayed to Jimmy and the times they'd spent together. They'd met at a mutual friend's house party, where of course he'd commandeered the bar, really the kitchen bench. That year everyone was drinking sugary cocktails – caipirinhas and caipiroskas – but he made her a martini without asking what she wanted. It was easy to fall in love with him in his bartender guise. He was good at it and he knew it, allowing himself a tactile pleasure in the act of making drinks. This was when he was most relaxed, when the weight of other things in his life was temporarily suspended.

It was curious the way he hated sugary cocktails. When it came to sweets he devoured them like a child. They often stopped at his uncle's shop to raid the jars on the counter. It made his aunt and uncle happy to be able to give him something, so he and Phoebe would always leave with their pockets full. They went for

Astro Belts (her sour favourite) and chewy Poppets toffees. Musk sticks and pastilles (the blackcurrant ones, not the green ones, which were vile). And white chocolate Disco Discs the size of periwinkle shells, crusted with sprinkles.

This was something they shared, a synthetic pleasure payload. Sometimes they ate the sweets in the park. Other times they ate them in front of the TV in the lounge at Goodenough. They liked watching crappy sitcoms of suburban family life, though neither of them came from families like that, the nuclear kind that lived together as a unit.

Early on, Jimmy told her that his mother had passed away. His father, a writer, made his living translating books but lost most of his money gambling. Three years before, he'd broken into Jimmy's flat and stolen most of his life savings, the wads of banknotes he'd kept from cash-in-hand jobs. This was why Jimmy had to take time out of his studies to tend bar full-time. It was why he'd moved in with his aunt and uncle. He showed them his appreciation by helping in their shop, taking care as he stacked the shelves to face the labels outwards.

They had come to rely on him, Jimmy told her, and asked his advice on where to send their son to school, what the new tax rules meant, what the different political parties were sounding off about on TV. Jimmy was dismissive – uninterested – when it came to the last point, and Phoebe was not much better. She had grown up in a Hong Kong that had no direct elections and this had left her apathetic about politics in general. In years to come, when fresh-faced high school students started rallying en masse, she would feel moved to see them doing what adults hadn't done. But that year – that run of years – she was wrapped up in her own concerns, focused on getting through medicine and coming out the other side alive.

Jimmy was right about one thing. Term was coming to an end. In a frigid dissection room, working late, she finished with her cadaver. It was not the one from first year, but a new one she was assigned for a respiratory module. When she was done, she said farewell. Not knowing the dead man's name, she thought of him as Ross (from certain angles he resembled the character on *Friends*). She sat her exams the following week, then called her mother to say she was coming home.

'Not now, sweetie,' she was told. 'I'm having the floors repolished.' So Phoebe went out of town instead – to green and hazy Hampshire, where Grace's parents had a house. She spent several days being fussed over. 'You poor thing,' they said, 'here in England by yourself, with your parents in Hong Kong.'

She didn't set them straight on her father's whereabouts. They were only being kind.

Then Jimmy called, out of the blue, and asked to meet. She found herself saying, 'Sure, okay.' This was when she realised he was like a drug to her. Not sugar, not alcohol; Jimmy. From a module on addiction medicine, she grimly recalled the William S. Burroughs quote on drugs: *'Wouldn't you? Yes, you would.'*

Yes, you would, and yes, she did. She met him at a cafe. She felt sweaty, bothered, wary. He wanted to tell her that he was leaving London. He'd accepted a job at a Hong Kong bank, a department with a name that meant nothing to her.

A job in finance in the East – this was what he'd always wanted.

'Another kind of gambling?' she asked.

'Only with other people's money.'

So: Hong Kong for him and a placement for her. Phoebe was going to Boston for a rotation, as part of an exchange program with Massachusetts General. She had plans to do postgrad after that, then apply for a specialisation. She wanted to be an anaesthetist. (Don't be a GP, her lecturers had told her early on. As a female GP, you'll spend your life doing Pap smears.)

She made Jimmy the offer in the cafe before she knew what she was doing. It just came naturally; she wanted to help him, look out for him. She said he could stay at her mother's place when he first landed if he liked. Deborah liked Jimmy. Phoebe knew she wouldn't mind.

'Thanks, Pheebs,' he said. 'If you're sure.'

'I'll give her a call.'

*

They were no longer in touch when she next visited the island, some months later, flying back for a break between one rotation and the next. Fifteen hours from Boston on Cathay Pacific. She landed in a bleary state. Her hair had got longer, more feathery, since London, and she fluffed it with her fingers as she waited at the airport.

'Good to see you, sweetie,' said her mother, meeting her in the car park. 'You look well. Rather better fed.'

'Thanks, I think,' she said.

Deborah talked at her the whole drive, mainly about the dog she was planning to get. Phoebe thought she had aged since her divorce. When Phoebe's father had moved to Thailand with his new wife and their baby, Deborah took over the family business, selling medical supplies. She pushed new product lines, selling eye-lasering equipment and training doctors in how to use it. She often laughed at the fact that people still asked her when she was going home, meaning the UK. 'I *am* home,' Deborah told them with jolly-hockey-sticks good cheer.

The sun was coming up, dismissing the quiet pre-dawn hour. It rose over the hills as they crossed the Tsing Ma Bridge and came down past West Kowloon. Deborah looped back after the tunnel and then made a succession of quick turns that took them uphill to Caine Road. The flat was in Mid-Levels, in a squarish fifties building. An old banyan tree grew near the stone retaining wall by the road, determinedly hanging on, a stalwart of old Hong Kong. (It would do so until years later when, after heavy rains, it finally crashed down on a car, and the driver, a woman, had to be cut out by an emergency crew.)

Inside the poky, single-level flat Phoebe couldn't miss the newly polished parquetry floor, which for as long as she could remember had been scuffed and dull. She had a sudden recollection of playing with a stethoscope on the floor and her father crouching next to her, hands on knees, affectionate, playful. 'Look at you, our little doctor. Is that what you're going to be?' She blinked away the memory.

'You're in your sister's room,' said her mother in a stage whisper, opening the door to the smaller bedroom, not much bigger than a cupboard.

'Why? Who's in my room?'

'Shhh, he works late.'

'Who does?'

'Jimmy.'

'*Jimmy?*'

'I thought you knew.'

'I thought he was only staying till he found somewhere. Has he been here all this time?' Deborah hadn't said anything on the phone.

Phoebe put her case in her sister's old room and came out to confront her mother in the kitchen. It took two cups of tea to get some straight answers. Her ex had been living in the flat since his arrival in Hong Kong. With both her daughters having flown the coop, Deborah liked the feeling of having someone else around.

Phoebe rubbed her face, exhausted, and retreated for a nap. When she woke, Jimmy had gone out. He was out for the whole day. There were signs of his presence: a toothbrush in the bathroom, blueberries in the fridge (that was her mum going all out), and on the bench a fluffy loaf of Baker's Choice from the ParknShop. Deborah had always made them eat multigrain, for fibre, as if her otherwise healthy daughters were at risk of constipation.

'I thought you knew, sweetie,' her mother said again, feigning innocence as only she knew how. As if to complete her performance, she sneaked a slice of the white bread, ignoring her virtuous dark rye. When Phoebe looked surprised, she said, 'Might as well live a little.'

That night, Jimmy came back late. It seemed he still kept unsociable hours, just as he had as a bartender. Lying awake in her sister's room, Phoebe heard him enter and go to bed. The next morning, a Friday, he left early. He did the same on Saturday. The financial markets were shut but he went to work anyway; there would be deals to put together, bosses to impress, tycoons to supply with loans. She heard him flush the toilet in the mornings, run the tap, clean his teeth, but never heard the shower – he must be showering at the office or the gym. He slipped in and out of the flat like a ghost. When he came home at night, there was no rummaging in the kitchen; he must have been eating elsewhere too. The Baker's Choice was untouched.

On Sunday he slept late, well past midday, a marathon sleep for Jimmy. Something about the flat must be agreeing with him, thought Phoebe.

Deborah fretted about his hours. 'I suppose that's how it is in banking. He'll be wanting to make his mark.'

It was she who picked up his dry-cleaning; Phoebe caught her coming home with garment bags on hangers.

'Poor Jimmy, he's never had anyone to do these things for him.' This from a woman who had forced her girls to be self-reliant!

'He can't stay here,' Phoebe told her. 'What if I want to bring someone home with me next time?'

'Like who?' her mother asked.

'*Someone*. No one. I don't know.' She tried another tack. 'You need to understand we're not getting back together.'

'Oh, I know *that*. Of course I know. It's the way of things, isn't it.'

Phoebe felt trapped in the flat with Jimmy's here-but-not-here presence. She asked her sister to intervene, and Selena duly rang their mother.

'I said, if he's not going to be part of our family, what is he doing there, Mum? She said it's not all about you girls. And anyway, it's not for long.'

It wasn't until Sunday afternoon, almost four days into her stay, that Phoebe encountered Jimmy in person. He was in the living room, chatting to two of her mother's friends who had come to pick her up to go out.

'Hi, Jimmy,' she said, frowning. She took off her glasses, feeling sour. She'd been holed up in her room – her sister's room – reviewing edits on a paper about hospital infection rates.

'Phoebe, there you are,' he replied, calmly. He had a man-pony now, a fact that took her several long moments to accept. His hair was glossy and sleek, with a slight cowlick at the temples, and she found herself wondering if he kept a comb in his desk at the office.

They exchanged awkward cheek kisses in front of their audience. Phoebe didn't know her mother's friends, a French woman from her AquaExercise classes at the USRC pool, and her Cantonese husband, an oncologist. The woman was wrapped in mysterious folds of linen arranged like a swami's robes, while the doctor played it safe in a sports coat. Deborah, in a new dress of a peculiar rusty colour, moved to the drinks trolley, but Jimmy swiftly intervened, saying, 'I'll do that.'

'Oh, would you?' She turned to her friends. 'James makes a great cocktail,' she told them. 'It's one of many talents. He works in finance.'

'For my sins,' he said comfortably. He commandeered the trolley, which for Phoebe dredged up memories of her parents' long-ago drinks parties.

Deborah had a minor ankle complaint, but she stayed on her feet to study his movements as he contented himself with bottles and glasses.

'I need ice.'

'He needs ice!' she said. She brought the ice.

'Do you have lemons?'

She brought lemons.

It was excruciating. Phoebe, for some reason nervous in Jimmy's presence, felt the awakening of old pathways in her brain, old patterns of attraction. She took a sweet from the bowl on the coffee table and ate it hurriedly, then another. She was meant to be cutting back. She had made this resolution on seeing that all her fellow doctors consumed was sugar and Coke. This was their crack, their fuel. '*I saw the best minds of my generation . . .*'

Jimmy was clearly enjoying being the centre of attention.

'What kind of finance are you in?' asked the doctor.

'Structured equity. It's mostly US dollar loans secured against stocks.'

Deborah continued to laud his accomplishments. 'Jimmy had offers at four banks. He had his pick.' She corrected herself. '*James*'s father is a writer. He's very clever. He translates books.'

She made it sound quite chic, having a writer for a father, but Jimmy's smile faltered. In truth, his father had not done well out of being a writer. He had spent time in a labour camp during the Cultural Revolution and afterwards had lived a peripatetic life, before settling in London. Then came his gambling, which Jimmy hated with a passion.

The guests, knowing none of this, looked approvingly at Jimmy and Phoebe. You've done well, their faces said.

'We're not —' she began.

'James is like family,' said her mother, giving his shoulders a quick squeeze.

'I go by James now,' he said in an aside to Phoebe.

The conversation turned, as sooner or later it always did, to the topic of Hong Kong's future under the one-country, two-systems rule. Deborah made it known she thought Hong Kong would be safe, it would retain its special freedoms. The way she spoke, Phoebe observed, you'd have thought the island had been a bastion of liberty, not a British colony.

'China won't really clamp down,' her mother scoffed, flapping a hand. Pressed for reasons, she said, 'Why, because of the money! There's too much here to mess with.'

Phoebe glanced at Jimmy. She knew what he thought; he would have said that was naive. But he demurred: 'I'm new to Hong Kong. I'm not the type to go to protests. I'm more comfortable with spreadsheets.'

'I'm with you there,' said the older man with a companionable laugh.

Finishing with the shaker, Jimmy presented their cocktails. He'd made sidecars this time.

'Go on, try it,' urged Deborah.

Her linen-swaddled friend took an obliging sip. Jimmy's face was suffused with warmth. His cheeks and forehead gleamed. Going outside, he joined the guests in smoking a cigarette on the balcony, dropping ash on the foliage below. Phoebe tried to think of a way to talk to him in private. She could hear the doctor deferring to him, the way some men did when talking to people who dealt with obscene amounts of money. '. . . but you would know all about that, in your line of work . . .'

She managed to corner Jimmy when he came in. 'I need to talk to you. Alone.'

Of course her mother interrupted. Seeing them, she sang out, 'One for you, Phoebe? A drink?'

'No, thanks.'

'Oh, go on. Don't be a stick in the mud, sweets!'

So she met Jimmy later, on neutral ground, after Deborah and her friends had gone out to eat. The bar, a few streets away, had little to recommend it, and Jimmy looked around sceptically. They ordered drinks but did not touch them, mineral water with rings of lime.

'You don't want anything else?' she asked.

'Not here,' he said with disdain. Phoebe figured he would normally go to the bars and clubs along Wyndham Street, with his colleagues. She knew of bankers who morphed into barflies, making the most of the island's nightlife. Hedonists took things to the next level in Hong Kong. This thought strengthened her resolve. 'You have to move out,' she said.

'I offered to leave, Phoebe,' he protested. 'Deb . . . your mum said no, not to be silly, I should stay. And it's her place.' He paused. 'You don't live there, remember.'

'I visit. I'm here now.' She didn't care if she sounded selfish; she was determined to get her way. 'You need to find your own place,' she said. 'Call a realtor. Go online.'

For goodness' sake, she thought. She was asking him to leave *her* family home, not his.

Jimmy took a sip of mineral water and set the glass back down. As he did so his eyelid pulsed. It was an involuntary tic, a rare sign of emotion.

This was his tell, she realised. She'd seen it before, just once.

It was on one of those nights at Emerson's Book Arcade in Soho. Jimmy was standing in the Chinese-language section. She was trying to read to him from an old-timey joke book she'd found: *'If all the girls at this party were laid end to end, I wouldn't be at all surprised.'* But he wasn't laughing – or even listening. He was holding a slim, dusty-looking book, and had an odd expression on his face.

'What is it?'

He wouldn't say. He didn't buy the book, but slotted it back on the shelf. That was when, under the bright lights, she saw his eyelid pulse. Was it a vein, showing itself under the skin? It pulsed and then disappeared. Then he walked out of the shop. It was one of his father's books, he told her later as they lay in her darkened room. 'A book of poems.'

'You didn't want to buy it?'

'No.'

Imagine looking for the book, only to leave it once he found it! Even after that, he kept up his late-night bookshop habit, searching for his father's other books so he could refuse to buy those too.

Now it was back, that little throb, giving him away. Was this harder for him than their actual breakup?

'Anyway,' she went on, rationalising her position, 'it can't be great living with Mum.' She wanted him to see that she had his interests at heart. 'Doesn't it cramp your style? Your . . . social life?' She wondered whether he was seeing anyone. 'You're living in Mid-Levels playing happy families. How can you stand it? It's not your speed.'

He laughed at this. 'My social life? My speed? Come off it, Pheebs. You're making me out to be a player, but I would have settled down if that was what you wanted. You *knew* that, don't pretend. It's what made you break things off.'

She coughed as her mineral water went down the wrong way. The damn bubbles. She looked up through watery eyes. Shaking her head, she found she couldn't speak. He gave her a knowing smile. Was that pity in his face? She wanted to say, Now just hang on, and contest his version of events. But he stood up, pulled out his platinum Amex and paid the bill. Then he strode out into the evening, which had suddenly turned gloomy, and a squally wind swept him along with the other pedestrians in the lane.

After that, Jimmy moved out. Phoebe had already returned to Boston, but she guessed her mother helped him. Soon afterwards, Deborah brought home a dog, a Cavalier King Charles spaniel. The animal promptly scratched her floors and was promptly forgiven, with an 'Oh, you're a naughty boy, aren't you, Nelson.'

Nelson. That was the name her mum gave to the dog, after Lord Nelson, the hero of Trafalgar. It was a silly little thing, not remotely independent, let alone heroic: it was pathetic, floppy-eared, with a beseeching expression. It turned out to be quite active, needing a lot of walking.

At least this would do some good, Phoebe supposed. Yet the next time she announced she was bringing someone home, her mother said casually, as if it was no big deal, 'Well, just so you know, James will come by to walk the dog.'

Fox face

Much later, June found ways to talk about her upbringing. In explaining what the Family was, she would bring up Julian Assange, the WikiLeaks guy.

'You know how he spent his childhood trying to get away from a cult, going from place to place with his mother? The centre I grew up in was kind of like that, the way they sucked you in and made it hard to leave. They even used the same name, the Family.'

Oh yeah, people would say, vaguely remembering having read about Assange's beginnings.

June thought it was strange that Assange should spend years trying to get away from a cult then create an organisation that wound up being so cult-like.

Or maybe it wasn't strange. Some days, in a certain mood or light, it made complete sense.

*

To begin with, though, June didn't know what happened to people who left. If anyone left the centre where she lived – a collection of houses and smallholdings on the outskirts of Osaka, populated by families and singles, some foreign, some Japanese – they were either brought back in disgrace or never spoken of openly again. Her friend Alastair, for example, had gone out to buy a lawnmower part one weekday in October and failed to come back. In his mid-twenties, Alastair had always seemed to June enthusiastic about life in the Family. The extraordinary fact of his departure split her being in two. She felt frightened – petrified – and at the same time emboldened.

A few months after this, she turned eighteen. She didn't tell anyone her plans. One cold night, she slipped away after dinner in the communal hall, took a bus, and then another, to get to the ferry terminal on the other side of Osaka, and bought a one-way ticket for eight thousand yen in cash. The ferry was cheaper than a flight and she didn't need to book. That night, she stretched out to sleep in a large dormitory-style room with other women, all strangers. She hardly slept on the passage, tossing and turning on her mat. The ferry tossed and turned as well, making its way south through a choppy swell. In the morning, industrial-strength lights came on to rouse any passengers who were still asleep, prising eyelids open and forcing a reckoning with the day. Around her, everyone was gathering their possessions, getting ready, looking like they knew exactly what the coming hours would bring.

For June, who was uncertain about what lay ahead, there was something sickening in the sound of the engines churning. She pulled on her boots and rucksack and left the women's dorm. Crossing the beer-stained carpet, she passed the chirping pachinko machines where several players still sat captive, bought a coffee at the vending machine and stirred in two sticks of sugar. Then she pushed forcefully through a door to meet the wind on the front deck.

So what if it was cold, if the sea was grey and rough? This was freedom, she decided, feeling a fierce, defiant joy. They had entered a wide bay and the rough swell had levelled out. She saw a small city with palm trees, a promenade, blockish mid-rise buildings, and a few snow-dusted peaks. The mountains threw her a little: she had no memory of them, and she certainly wasn't expecting snow. It was an onsen town, and here and there the steam from the hot springs rose like drifts of smoke, making it look as if countless fires were burning out of sight.

When the ferry docked, she got off and strode past the waiting cars, casting a wary eye over the vehicles just to be sure, but she felt certain that no one was waiting for her. No one knew her here. No one knew where she was. Not her parents, who would never guess that she remembered the city's name or how to get here. It was a good ten years since they'd brought her here, on a rare trip away from the centre. She had vivid memories of that summer visit – the old house with the paper sliding doors, and the alleyways where she played and bickered with her sister – but nothing near the seafront looked familiar.

Hands jammed in pockets, she headed to the highway, where rush-hour traffic streamed towards Oita, the larger city to the southeast, further along the bay. She'd expected Kyushu to be warm, a southern oasis, but it was bleak and rather shabby. The sky was a dirty pigeon grey and even the hills themselves looked cold, their desolate flanks showing above the line of trees.

The town should have been familiar. Should have been but wasn't. It took fifteen minutes to walk downtown, passing the dated trappings of a pleasure destination: souvenir shops, hotels, a triple-storey pachinko parlour, the sort of places the Family regarded as dens of sin and weakness. The streets looked more down-at-heel than those she'd seen in Osaka. She passed a cocktail bar; a sign gave its name as the Tropicana. She was drawn to the tiki decor, which promised warmth and fruit cocktails, the music and film posters plastering the walls, and a blackboard showing drinks chalked up in English, but the bar was closed.

At the train station she gravitated to the Mister Donut counter, where she bought two steaming donuts and devoured them on the spot. Looking back the way she'd come, she realised with a jolt that she knew this street. From a different angle – *this* angle – the town was familiar again, the place of that childhood visit. She knew the way from here.

Brushing cinnamon sugar from her mouth, she eagerly backtracked half a block, turned at an antiques store and cut through an arcade. Emerging in the old part of town, she found what she was seeking. A hulking wooden house, two storeys, tiled roof.

She knocked.

No answer.

Knocked again.

Something didn't seem right. A pane of glass by the door was broken; she saw shards on the floor inside. She wasn't going to stand there for the neighbours to see her, so she wrapped her hand in her jacket, reached in and unlocked the door.

'Hello?'

Still no answer. She stepped inside, past the neat row of shoes along the wall, and went up the stairs to the main part of the house. The house was too big for her grandmother, and she had long ago closed up the rooms downstairs. Upstairs, June started opening doors. The formal sitting room was shuttered and dark and crowded with heavy Manchurian furniture. Imperialist loot, June's mother had observed the last time they were here. June's father had agreed, saying he'd never liked the pieces.

No one had been here in a while, from the look of it. Something else had, though – the couch gave off a foul smell, as though an animal had soiled the cushions. A cat?

Recoiling, June shut the doors to contain the stench and checked the other rooms. No sign of her grandmother. In the main bedroom, she looked in a few drawers, finding a pouch of banknotes, a thin fold. In the kitchen she found a box of rice cakes, the kind you cook in the microwave. The electricity was still on and she warmed one on high, then chewed the rubbery result. The table in the adjoining sunroom was bare except for a newspaper, folded once. Paging through a photo album on a side table in the hall, she saw photos of her late grandfather's war: a tour of the Pacific, island beaches in blazing sun, crisply uniformed young sailors standing in a row.

Why was the house abandoned? June checked the shuttered lower floor. More dark furniture stored away. Near the entry, a bicycle with a broken chain lying beside it on the floor. The bath in a separate room, a big stone tub set into the floor. When she tried the tap there was no water, just a nasty honk of steam. Thwarted, she went back upstairs, stripped off by the kitchen sink and washed herself with a flannel. Afterwards, in the TV room, she made her best find yet: the low *kotatsu* table with its built-in heater. Turning it on, she sat down, crossed her legs under the table and arranged the rug-like covering around her to contain the heat. She sat like this, shivering, and warming up by degrees. It was only then, with a start, that she noticed the shrine on the far wall.

The last time she was here, the shrine had given pride of place to her late grandfather's stern-faced photograph. She remembered studying the black and white image as a child, not quite believing that this man with his combed-back hair had once been alive, like her. His photo was still there, but now it was not alone. It was accompanied by one of his wife, who looked out with a calm gaze from her own picture frame, and this was how June knew that her grandmother was dead.

*

The cocktail bar was empty, just a young woman wiping tables. June's age or a little older, her wide eyes made even bigger with eyeliner. And her height – she was very tall, June saw when she straightened up.

'We don't open until five,' she said in Japanese.

The Tropicana was already brightly lit, with lamps and coloured lanterns. It was the day after June's arrival, and she had returned to the bar at the seafront.

'Is there a manager I can speak to?' she asked. 'I'm looking for work.'

'Sure. The owner's here.' The waitress stepped behind a curtain and in a moment a man emerged. Fortyish and floppy-haired, with tobacco-yellowed fingers, he looked sceptically at June. What was her name, her age, he wanted to know, her bartending experience? Where did she live? June did her best to answer in her basic Japanese.

He peered at her. 'You're not Japanese?' he demanded.

'Yes, I am,' she said stubbornly.

'*Uso.* You can't be. What are you, American? Well, have it your way. There's no job for you here.' Throwing a dishcloth over his shoulder, he walked away, muttering under his breath, 'She must be soft in the head or something.'

June turned to leave, humiliated. She hated him for being what she'd been warned about, the sort of person she could expect to find outside the Family.

The waitress tailed her outside. 'You really don't speak Japanese?'

'Some,' June said and shrugged. At the centre, they had always spoken English. Everyone did. Her Distance Ed lessons were in English. And her family spoke English among themselves at home, in the cottage; June's mother was American, and her Japanese father was comfortable in the language, though he spoke it with an accent. She and Naomi switched between mimicking their mother's way of speaking, with all the expressions she'd hung onto from the counterculture of her youth, and the slang they picked up watching their stash of films on VHS. The only time the two of them went out of the centre's compound was to go shopping with their mother, to buy whatever they couldn't make or grow. Milk, chocolates, shampoo, shaving razors, soap.

Even that was only allowed because June's mother was who she was. Rachel, ever the firm believer, the staunchest member of the Family. She criticised life outside the centre, criticised consumerism, said the world had lost its way in blinkered self-interest. They were better off in the Family. They were *setting an example.* Growing up as a diplomat's daughter, she had always sought out causes, and had met June's father through the peace movement in Kyoto. Together they were active in anti-Vietnam demonstrations, protesting against the war, the use of Japanese islands as staging posts, militarism in general. Then they came into the orbit of some pacifist Christians. Increasingly drawn to a fringe existence, they fell in with members of the Family and helped set up the centre.

All this was history. There was no way to explain it to the waitress. June frowned and hunched her shoulders. A cold wind whipped her hair against her neck.

'You don't want to work here anyway,' the waitress said, looking over her shoulder. 'Give me your number, I'll ask around for you.'

Such kindness from a stranger was almost unknown to June. 'But I don't have a phone,' she said.

The waitress blinked. She took the order pad from her pocket and wrote her number and her name, Chiharu and gave June the page. 'I have to go.'

June went back to the house feeling optimistic. Had she made a friend? Pulling off her boots in the entryway, she left the lights off; it was better that no one knew she was staying here.

Reaching the foot of the stairs, she noticed a sharp new smell, artificial pine. At the same time she heard a sound. Maybe it was the cat, back on the sofa, she thought – but then she heard footfalls, human ones.

Instantly, all her fears rushed back; this was danger, come to find her. Her first, panicked thought was that it was someone from the centre. She thought of running but she had nowhere to go. Casting about in the entryway, she grabbed the only thing she could find, the greasy old bike chain that she was meaning to toss out.

Climbing the stairs, concentrating on her soft tread, she almost didn't see the man in the dark. He was crouched in the hallway, bent over something. As he straightened, she acted almost without thinking. In a stride she was behind him and had the chain around his neck. With a yank she dragged him backwards. She was surprised that she could do this, surprised that he gave way, his knees splaying out in front. He twisted and struggled, trying to grab her hands, grab the chain.

'*Nan darou*, what's this?' he yelled. He was old but still strong; the chain broke when he wrenched it.

He rose to his feet, staggered. Now it was June who'd fallen, forward onto her knees. Standing over her, the man flicked the light switch on. She saw a wrinkled skeletal figure in a dirty undershirt and jeans, with black grease on his throat from the bicycle chain.

How old could he be? He could be dangerous, deranged.

'Junko.' He stared and laughed, an incongruous response. His laugh turned into a wheeze. He raised a hand – to strike, she thought, and flinched. Instead he tapped her cheek. 'So it is. You're Junko.' He spoke in Japanese and used the Japanese form of her name. 'I recognise you, heh-heh.'

She stared back at him, shocked. How could he possibly know who she was?

He banged his hand on his chest. 'Koji,' he said. He swivelled abruptly to the album on the hall table, thumbed through the pages until he found what he was looking for, and jabbed with apparent meaning at a black and white photograph. It showed two kids with bowl cuts standing on a street. The boy was the smaller of the pair, scrawny but cocky. The girl wore a dress with a sweetheart neckline.

'Now I'm old Koji.' He grinned. 'But it's a pity, you're too late.' He stroked the print wistfully. 'Sister has gone.' He glanced up at June and added, 'You look like her, you know.'

So that was who he was. Or claimed to be anyway. Her great-uncle. She surveyed him with suspicion. She had never met him before. At least he wasn't a vagrant, but he might be more of a risk. What if he called her parents?

'What are you doing here?' she asked him.

'What are you doing here, she asks! Young people have no manners. But that's the way of it, isn't it. That's just how it goes.' He looked at her through narrowing eyes.

He had a right to be irate, she thought; she had attacked him, after all. She wondered why he hadn't asked why she was here.

It was now she noticed his box of cleaning products. The old man picked up the bike chain, put it on a news sheet and wiped his hands with a rag. In the sitting room, she saw that the couch cushions were propped up, airing. The windows were open to the night, the wood surfaces had been oiled and a bottle of disinfectant sat on the carved chest. She had caught the old man cleaning.

And she noticed something else. A bowling bag sitting on the floor, a clean shirt draped across it. These were his clothes, his things. So he planned to stay?

'Still, it's Junko,' he said. 'Imagine!' He shook his head, amazed. And she suddenly guessed that he had no right to be here either. Was he as worried as she was about being flushed out?

Alright, dude, she thought. Maybe they'd have to hide out together. But she kept him in her sights as she bent for the rag to clean her hands.

*

The old man made himself at home in the days that followed, getting up early to start his passive-aggressive cleaning. June would find him stripped down to a pair of shorts to vacuum or scrub. He was ancient and tireless, an energetic bag of bones, darting back and forth to make violent thrusts at cobwebs. His manner let June know she was to blame for the dirt and dust. He washed the sofa cushions repeatedly and was angry about the cat. He seemed to blame her for that too, as if she'd let it in.

As uneasy cohabitants, they staked out separate domains. Koji slept in the TV room, which had the *kotatsu* for keeping warm. He claimed the room by hanging his shirt and trousers from a hook. June remained in the second bedroom. The larger bedroom, her grandmother's, they left conspicuously empty. For some reason he stopped calling her by her name and resorted to 'you', and she returned the compliment by not calling him anything. Actually, she didn't know what she was meant to call him. What *were* you supposed to call such a strange and ancient person?

By day, she went out in the cold looking for work. She tried Mister Donut and the shops around the station. She tried the antiques store. The dealer was polite, a fastidious-looking man in middle age. He regarded her as he might an artefact on offer, one which was (sadly, regrettably) unsuitable for sale. The exhilaration of her escape was starting to wear off. What if she couldn't find a job? She had nothing to fall back on, no one to advise her what to do. She had wanted her independence. Now here it is, she thought grimly.

Two days later, growing desperate, she decided to call Chiharu. She had little expectation, feeling sure the waitress had just been polite, but as it turned out, she'd heard of something. She couldn't talk for long – she was at the university, she said, about to go into a lecture – but she took down June's address and said she would drop by soon.

June hung up the payphone at the station and returned to the house feeling lighter, although she told herself not to get her hopes up too much.

During the evenings that first week, June heard the old man eating in his room. He appeared to subsist on *adzuki-meshi*, rice boiled with red beans. It was cheap, she supposed. And easy to chew. He liked to eat sitting under the *kotatsu* and cackle at the television. One night it was *Law and Order*, dubbed in Japanese, the next it was *The Stinger*, a reality program in which women conspired to test the fidelity of their boyfriends by setting up elaborate sting operations. Koji loved this show and kept up a running commentary, trying to warn the hapless men. 'Look out! Don't fall for it, idiot!'

She worried he'd rat her out. She also worried he might die just from being so thin and old, and then she would have to report his death and deal with officialdom. The risk that he might perish of extreme skinniness motivated her to cook dinner for him one night, a simple pasta and green salad, an effort that scored no points with Koji. He complained about the chilli in the arrabiata sauce and was angered by the uncut iceberg lettuce in the salad. He had trouble with the bowl-shaped leaves, which with their coating of oily dressing slipped between his chopsticks. He disliked Western food, he told her petulantly, and she was sorry she'd bothered.

After dinner that evening, Chiharu came around. She brought a bag of vegetables and some pastries, and her kindness was again almost overwhelming. June was struck by her thoughtfulness. For so many years, June had had it drummed into her that society was harsh, people were out for themselves, not to be trusted. And yet here was Chiharu, a near stranger, bringing gifts.

Chiharu, she learned, was studying to be a teacher. With a Peruvian mother and a Japanese father, she was fluent in Japanese, Spanish and English.

'And you,' she prompted June, 'you've lived in America?'

June thought about telling the truth. She could have described the centre and the way she'd been raised, living close to Osaka and yet entirely apart. Instead she tried to think of someplace appealing. She thought of saying California but this made her think of Father David, the founder of the Family, who had started his activities in Huntington Beach.

'Hawaii,' she said, picturing palm trees and white beaches.

'*Sugoi ne*. I'd love to go.' Chiharu looked around the kitchen. 'So this is your family's house?'

'It belonged to my grandmother until she passed away. My great-uncle is staying here too. I don't think he likes me much.'

'And your parents, are they here?'

June shook her head no. 'They haven't been back to this house in years.'

June put the vegetables in the fridge, eggplants, radishes, cucumbers and cabbage. At the dining table, Koji glowered and drank his beer. Chiharu greeted him politely, which appeased him a little. He looked more interested when the pastries came out, and his face lit up with happiness when he was offered one. But after they joined him at the table he started to lecture them. Conscripting Chiharu as his translator, he spoke quickly and jabbed the air.

'He's talking about the war, the time after the war. He's saying, "We had no food. I had to walk across Kyushu, looking for work, for food."'

Chiharu listened and nodded, her face appropriately grave as Koji warmed to his theme. He shot June blameful looks, as though he looked on her as the architect of the war. Cramming the last pastry in his mouth, he kept talking about the war and the West and America.

'He says the Americans who were held by the Japanese as prisoners of war complained about their mistreatment, about being given – how do you say it? – inedible roots to eat. But he says the Japanese were eating roots as well. He says, "To us this is food, they didn't understand, just because in America they eat McDonald's every day."'

They let him talk and talk, because what could they say? Chiharu knew the right way to listen, which was to assume an expression of perfect docility.

As Chiharu was leaving, June asked in a low voice, 'Do you think he's alright? I mean, how old do you think he is?'

'He's fine,' said Chiharu, pulling on her coat. 'Look at him. My aunt, she's a nurse, she works in Fukuoka. She says people that age are indestructible. They managed to survive the war. It's like nothing can kill them now. They keep hanging on. But wait, I almost forgot to tell you about the job. It's at a nightclub called the Hit Parade, they're looking for someone to clear glasses. I've written down the details.'

'Alright, I'll check it out,' June said gamely, although she'd never been in a nightclub in her life.

As she saw Chiharu off, Uncle Koji retired, closing the doors to the TV room. June saw that he'd left his cellphone by the plate of pastry crumbs. Picking it up, she shut herself in the toilet, checked the time and dialled home. As it rang, she pictured the phone ringing in the hall of the small cottage.

'Hello,' her sister said.

June had been ready to hang up if it was either of her parents. 'Hey, it's me.'

She heard a sharp inhalation. Then, 'Where *are* you?'

Naomi was sixteen and a half, two years younger than June, with a babyish quality that made her seem even younger. She still read books about horses, and girls who solved mysteries. And she had other harmless passions, which didn't worry their parents so much as leave them bemused. She idolised the actor River Phoenix, putting his pictures on her wall. She lay looking up at him from the rug between the beds in their shared room, careless of making June tread awkwardly around her. She had *My Own Private Idaho*, one of his films, on VHS, and she watched and rewatched the tape until the stupid thing got stuck.

'June, they are flipping out! How could you do this?'

'Naomi, listen —'

But she wouldn't listen. 'I don't want you to call me. I won't cover for you. I won't!' Before hanging up, she hissed, 'If you call again, I'll tell them. I'll tell them where you are.'

June stood there feeling shaken. Had Naomi guessed where she was? It wouldn't be hard for her to figure out, though it would take their parents longer. Would Naomi give her away, betray her to their parents and the centre? She was angry enough, June thought. She'd merely wanted to let her sister know she was alright, let her know she hadn't forgotten her. But it was stupid to think she could trust Naomi.

She put the cellphone back on the table, hoping the old man would be none the wiser. In the morning, it was gone and he didn't speak to her when she came into the kitchen. Then she saw what he was eating for breakfast. Lettuce! This from the man who objected to her Italian salad. He had piled the leaves on a plate with toast and a fried egg. He stared at her boldly, daring her to object as he took bites of a lettuce leaf and a piece of toast by turns.

That afternoon, she walked several blocks to find the night-club. She didn't know what to expect, but when she went inside it didn't look like a gateway to hell. It had cheerful fifties-style decor – red walls, padded booths, the sort of thing she'd seen in films of the era. Saccharine girl-group pop was playing, the kind of music Naomi liked.

Mustering her courage, she fronted up to the studded bar and asked about the job. The broad-faced bartender looked at her. 'Ah, so you're Junko. Good.'

She was told to come back at six. The club had an older crowd, and most of them seemed to be regulars, going by the way they greeted each other. A few patrons got rowdy as the night wore on, cheering and swaying and mock-waltzing with each other. June wasn't used to dealing with drunk people; the only person she had seen drinking at the centre was old Mr Kumamoto who did the gardening. He sometimes hid behind the hedge to sink part of a bottle of whiskey. Once she saw that the club's patrons were good-natured rather than threatening, she moved among them deftly, saying, 'Look out, coming through!'

It wasn't glamorous or well-paid but she found the time passed quickly. At the end of the shift, Ito, the bartender, asked her to come back the following night. Soon she was working five or six nights a week, knocking off at midnight after they kicked the stragglers out.

*

Her great-uncle stayed long enough to see to things around the house, sorting through the downstairs rooms and carting junk away. Some days he went out on errands that were mysterious to June. She didn't know if he had a home elsewhere, and he was evasive on the topic, always grinning and sidestepping. He had few possessions, just his clothes and a shaving kit. Coming across his wallet lying open one day, she checked his driver's licence. She couldn't read the characters for his address but she knew they did not say Ōita prefecture.

Another time she saw him with what might have been his mail, although it was equally possible it was her grandmother's. She figured he was handling his late sister's affairs; someone had to be doing it, paying the bills at least, because the power and water were still on.

June gathered from his comments that it had been more than a month since her grandmother's death, and she wondered whether the news had reached her father. He hadn't said anything to June at the time, before she left, hadn't suggested they go to the funeral. But she figured he had to know by now, if he didn't before.

As to what Koji knew of June's situation, she couldn't tell how much he guessed. He didn't ask about her parents; he seemed to accept that she was on her own. He did ask about Naomi, saying, 'Don't you have a sister? Where is she?'

She wondered what to tell him. 'In Osaka,' she said cautiously, watching his expression.

'Ah. In Osaka. I see.' He gave her a hard stare, then walked away mumbling cryptically to himself.

It was possible he was *trying* to make her uncomfortable. His presence made things tricky in other ways too. As long as he was there, she could not bathe in the kitchen. With the bath still out of action, she was forced to go to the bathhouse in the laneway, two doors down. Even on her first visit, the neighbourhood women knew exactly who she was. She should have realised they were all gossiping about her. She also learned what was wrong with her bath at home: a neighbour across the alley had dug down to the spring and diverted the water for himself. June didn't really care; the bathhouse was cheap and close and it was the best place to warm up. She could never get her grandmother's draughty house properly warm, and while Koji was there he hogged the *kotatsu*.

After two and a half weeks, the old man moved on. He left while she was out, taking his bowling bag of possessions. She had no idea where he'd gone. She suspected he travelled by train; she hadn't seen a car and the idea of him driving was alarming to think about.

Finally! Alone at last.

June loved living by herself. Chiharu would come over or they went out with her friends, a circle of students and musicians.

They drank at the Tropicana or the tiny bar that Satoshi, Chiharu's boyfriend, opened some nights. Satoshi was older than Chiharu, in his mid-thirties, a reedy-voiced singer who played sets with a ska band.

There were a few foreigners in the circle, including Canadian Terence, an ESL teacher. He took it upon himself to teach June some colloquial Japanese.

'Knowledge is never wasted,' he insisted. 'It's a shame your parents didn't teach you, but now that you're living in Japan, you're out of excuses,' he told her. He started with his favourite, the expression *tachi-shoben*, 'which basically refers to some old dude pissing in public.'

'Got it,' said June. 'Great. That is good to know.'

It was from Terence that Chiharu had heard about the job at the Hit Parade. He did an Elvis act there on Thursday nights, and was a minor celebrity in his own right, having once appeared on national TV as a guest on the show *Koko ga Hen da yo Nihonjin*, or 'Here Are These Weird Japanese People'. This was a panel discussion program in which foreigners discussed their grievances about living in Japan, and Terence had gone on in his leather jacket and argued loudly with everyone. For his standing gig at the Hit Parade, he wore a spangled jumpsuit and jumped about onstage.

June disliked the Tropicana because of her brush with the owner. She preferred Satoshi's bar, which felt more like a private party. Once, heading out to buy mixers, he asked her to mind the bar. She felt inordinately pleased at this small gesture of trust – she was one of them! – then suppressed a shudder of guilt. These people were her friends but she was an imposter in their midst. She still hadn't told anyone about the centre.

It wasn't that she didn't miss her family; she did. She missed her father and his placid manner, his calm face that looked so much like her grandmother's photo. She missed her mother too, and tried to picture her narrow face, her close-set eyes and watchful gaze. She felt sad and sorry for herself. She worried about Naomi, who she knew would be getting a lot of heat.

That was the worst thing, the way she'd left Naomi.

One day in July, she came clean to Chiharu. The conversation had turned to Hawaii, and Chiharu asked why she'd left. June admitted she'd never been there. 'I've never been anywhere,' she said, and went on to tell her friend about the Family.

'But what about your parents?' Chiharu asked, taken aback.

'The centre was their life. Still is.'

'Weren't you ever allowed out?'

'For shopping, sure. Other than that, forget it.'

'And no internet, nothing? Far out,' Chiharu said. 'But you're worried about your sister. What are you going to do?'

'That's the problem. I don't know!'

At least nothing changed with Chiharu. June's life went on as before, as one of the group, sometimes drinking too much and roaming the streets. One morning she woke up beside a pachinko poster, an ugly thing she had ripped from a wall in a run-by the night before. It was hard to get rid of it without the neighbours seeing. The trash and recycling bags were made of clear plastic so she had to tear it up and dispose of it gradually, bit by bit, to conceal the evidence of her theft.

She'd almost forgotten about Koji when he showed up again. She came home one day to find him at the table, eating her peanut butter out of the jar with a spoon. Looking up, he smiled and said, '*Ojamashimasu.*' The visitor's greeting: 'I am getting in your way, I am here to disturb you.'

A few days later, however, it was he who was disturbed. Battling a cold, June took a night off work. She lay in bed listening to the old man's shuffling movements. Having finished his dinner at the kitchen table, he went into the TV room and clapped his hands twice at the altar. June heard him channel-surfing the television before she fell asleep.

She woke to shouting. It was the small hours of the morning and someone was in the alley, calling her name.

'June, June!'

A man's voice.

She froze. Finally, someone had come to find her, someone from the centre.

'June!' he shouted again. 'Are you home?'

It was in fact Canadian Terence. He sounded drunk, must have come from his set at the Hit Parade.

Everyone in the neighbourhood must be awake by now. This can't be happening, she thought, and so she acted as if it wasn't, just lay there in denial. Then she heard a window opening in the house and Koji shouting, 'No, thank you!' in English. His words rang in the night, Terence fell quiet and stumbled on, and June lay cringing in bed. She had never been so mortified in her life.

In the morning, when she passed Uncle Koji in the hall, he turned his old stare on her. Once again she was to blame, this time for her rowdy friends and an interruption to his sleep.

Whatever the purpose of his stay, he ended it promptly, leaving the house mid-morning with his bowling bag and jacket.

*

Summer came with an eggy smell, courtesy of the springs. Tourists descended, strolling in the old neighbourhoods.

June rode her grandmother's bicycle, now sporting a new chain. With Chiharu on university break, they tagged along to Satoshi's gigs. One day they drove to a music festival, driving on winding mountain roads. June had no idea where they were. They passed a convoy of military vehicles carrying self-defence force cadets in camouflage gear to a remote spot for training exercises. At length, a sign declared they were entering Jamaica Village. It didn't seem to June like this should be real, but people were wandering around in rasta hats and dreadlocks, and dancing to a line-up of reggae and ska bands. This was nothing like the performances at the Hit Parade, nothing at all like the music of her childhood, the singing of songs backed by digital piano.

The humidity was oppressive. When the weather broke and it started raining, the guitarists stepped back under the cover of the half-roof over the stage, but the band continued playing, and the dancers kept dancing. Water streamed off faces and brass instruments. June was dancing too, moving with the others, swept up in a shared cathartic joy.

She thought of Naomi more often as the weeks passed by. She knew very well she'd made things hard for her sister by leaving. June, being older, had always been the one who got them into trouble; this was how it had been since they were small. There was the time they were punished for sneaking out and playing chicken with cars out on the road and were shut in a storeroom overnight by the furious leaders. Their mother was incensed, dragging them by the wrists to the storeroom herself. 'You could have been killed! Or caused an accident!'

But it had been worth it, for June at least. There was something thrilling about standing in the middle of the road and watching the cars brake, watching the drivers' stricken faces. The act was dizzyingly close to waving down a ride, something she always stopped just short of actually doing. She wondered later about those people she saw behind the windscreens, about the lives they had, the jobs they went to, their families and their innermost desires, the songs they played while driving to wherever they were going.

Naomi blamed June for the punishment, and that was fair enough. 'I hate you,' Naomi told her. 'Why do you have to break the rules?' And June had felt guilty the whole night they sat in that storeroom, among the boxes of dried goods, broomsticks and dust. After that, they were enemies, then allies, then enemies by turns. Naomi never let herself be persuaded to sneak out again. She stuck to the straight and narrow, and that was fair enough as well.

June thought of home again the afternoon they drove to the town of Yufuin to visit Chiharu's parents. Yufuin was as tasteful as their city was kitsch. Chiharu's parents lived in a house with a manicured garden. They were sweet people, very kind. Knowing June was on her own, they told her she would always be welcome there, to come back anytime. Afterwards, driving back, she fell into a funk and sat staring in silence out the window.

'Is something wrong?' Chiharu asked.

'No. I liked meeting your parents, they're nice.'

In truth, she was angry. With her own parents. She had been treated to a glimpse of what a family could be, an experience that left her with a sense of waste. To think it was possible to have a normal, supportive family, who didn't lock you away and tell you lies about the world!

She said none of this to Chiharu. She didn't trust herself not to cry if she tried to explain how she was feeling.

They went out that night as usual. They had a drink at Satoshi's bar and later went to get a snack at the pancake cart. On the way, an old man by the road looked up at them guiltily. Believing himself to be alone, he had taken a leak and June saw him finishing and zipping up his trousers.

'Sorry, sorry,' he said, bowing and walking unsteadily away.

'What was that about?' asked Chiharu, who hadn't been looking. 'What was he sorry for?'

'*Tachi-shoben*,' she told her friend, using the phrase Terence had taught her for pissing in public. Knowledge is never wasted, she thought. Nothing is ever wasted.

'Oh,' Chiharu laughed. 'Hey, you're sounding Japanese now.'

The right word at the right time. This brought a flush of satisfaction. But June still felt bothered, dragged down by her thoughts after meeting Chiharu's parents. Then she suddenly saw clearly: she had to try again with Naomi.

The following day she made a call. She picked the time carefully. When her sister realised it was her, she was silent for a time.

'Can't you just come back?' Naomi finally asked, sounding resentful. Or she started with resentment; her voice changed halfway through and made the question a plea.

'I can't. You know I can't.'

Not because of the punishment she knew would await her, not because of her mother's anger or the condemnation from the leaders. It was just that she was done. The Family was not for her.

And so her sister hung up again. The conversation stayed with June for a while after that, sitting heavily on her heart whenever she thought of it.

*

At summer's end, there was news.

'I'm pregnant,' Chiharu said.

'What?' June floundered. 'What will you do? What does Satoshi think?'

'He's excited. I am too, now I've thought about it.'

'What about your studies?'

'I don't know. I haven't told my parents yet.' She and Satoshi might move to Yufuin, she said. She wouldn't have her job at the Tropicana for much longer anyway.

'You think they'll fire you?'

'Didn't you hear? The bar's for sale. The owner's moving away.'

That night, June hurried home and knelt to count her savings. It wasn't enough, she thought bitterly. It would never be enough. She felt desperate, too, at the thought of Chiharu leaving. Once she'd had the baby, she would have other concerns, and June would be on her own again. The thought was too much to bear. Tears pricked at her eyes and she wiped them with her sleeve.

To make things worse, Uncle Koji came back the same night. Oblivious to her despair, he went about making himself at home in a buoyant mood. Perhaps it was the continuing warm weather or the fact that her Japanese was better and they could understand each other, but the next morning over coffee he told her there was something he wished to do, the two of them together before the season got too late. He was going to gather clams and he wanted her help.

Surprised, she agreed. The next day was her day off. She thought maybe he'd mellowed; they'd reached an understanding. He hadn't given her away so far, and she figured she could trust him.

The next morning at the beach, they combed the sand at the shoreline for telltale dimpling or bubbles. Like scientists extracting core samples, they used a cylindrical metal pump to suck up tubes of sand, then fossicked through it to find the clams, each the size of a small coin. June had a distant memory of doing this as a child, but didn't remember it being such hard work, all the bending and squatting. Uncle Koji insisted they keep at it. How could he need so many clams? He was pulling up sand like his life depended on it.

After an unreasonably long day, they collected their dripping bags and hailed a taxi. The driver gave them a dirty look when he saw their dripping bags, but Koji berated him. 'Don't worry! Do you think we won't be careful?' And promptly knocked a clod of sand over the seat as he got in.

June sat slumped against the door until they pulled up at an apartment building. 'Whose place is this?' she asked.

He chuckled and wouldn't say. After buzzing, he led her up to a small flat where an old woman met them. Koji gave her a bag of clams, which made her beam and pat his arm. Wondering if she was Koji's girlfriend, June looked around for clues. The woman made them stay so she could fix them noodles with the clams. She gave Koji a tall can of beer, and then another when he'd finished. She hovered to wait on him, smiling coquettishly, while June felt like she was about to perish from fatigue.

To top the day off, when they got home he shoved the bags of clams at her and said, 'Do something with these, girl.'

'Do what?' she protested.

'Don't you know anything? What did your parents teach you? Nothing.' He banged around through his tirade. 'Have you even told them you're here? No.' The beer seemed to have loosened his tongue. 'You have no respect. Just like your father. Where was he when his mother died? Not here, I can tell you that. Poor Mrs Kuriyama had to ring the police. She was the one who noticed when Sister stopped going to bathe.'

He was really angry now. This time she understood his anger, which was mixed up with his grief. Dumping the clams out in the sink, he rounded on her. 'No respect, no duty. And what about *your* sister? Where is she while you're having fun, larking about with your so-called friends?'

But June could do anger too. 'I'll go back for her!'

'And do what? Bring her here? Your parents won't let you.'

She stared at him. So he knew about the Family. He clearly knew a lot more than he'd been letting on.

'Your father's covered for you so far, keeping your little secret. Watch how long that lasts if you bring Naomi here.'

June froze, her mind reeling. Her father knew where she was?

'What did you think, that he wouldn't guess? It wasn't me who told him,' Koji continued. 'You know that this house has gone to him? Sister left it to him. Beats me why! Hah-hah. The way he ran off with your mother, that terrible fox-faced woman.' He peered at her in the dim. 'And you're no different,' he added, then all but spat the accusation: '*Kitsune.*'

'You're just a crazy old man!'

'I know,' he said. 'I know. Don't worry about that.'

He turned abruptly to the sink and started running the tap over the clams. Of course he'd leave again in the morning, she had no doubt of that. Go off again, who knew where – roaming over Kyushu, going from place to place as if the war had never ended. Yet there was something in his manner, a touch of sheep-ishness, she thought, and perhaps he already regretted what he'd said.

He couldn't take it back; he didn't have it in him. 'Anyway,' he muttered as he washed the clams, 'that's how it is, I'll do it myself. Don't worry, old Koji will do it by himself.'

*

Chiharu's belly grew. Her sculpted features thickened. When she walked, she leaned backwards a little to balance the weight. Together she and Satoshi prepared to move to Yufuin. June helped them pack, she saw them off, and all of a sudden she was alone.

214

It was a year since her arrival. She lived in the empty house. Uncle Koji had indeed left the morning after their argument, and she didn't bank on him showing up again. Maybe he felt bad about calling her a fox. While June did not know much about the old folktales, she knew enough to understand what he was getting at. A *kitsune* could be a shapeshifter, a spirit being. It could appear in human form if this suited its purposes; it could come and go as it pleased, play tricks, lead men astray. So this was what Koji believed her mother had done, playing the part of a fox spirit to lure her father. But if anyone was like a fox spirit, June thought, it was Koji, the way he came and went, appearing and disappearing.

She didn't know if she'd be here the next time he came, still living in the house that neither of them owned. At odd moments, she even found herself craving the certainty of her old life. The rules, the sense of purpose. The relief of surrender, of relinquishing the need to find her way in the world. Then she caught herself. Oh no you don't, she thought. Never again, kiddo.

If she hadn't left the Family, she wouldn't have met Chiharu. She wouldn't have found out how to make an independent living for herself. And for Naomi.

The answer to this problem came to her like a bolt of lightning, making her wonder why she hadn't thought of it before. She carried out the transaction not long afterwards. The men came at the appointed time and she let them in. The antiques dealer was there too. He'd been through each room already, giving little verdicts. 'Very good.' (The ornate chest.) 'A lovely piece.' (The bureau.) 'Superb condition for its age.' (The dining setting.) 'Siamese rosewood, it looks like.' (The finely worked folding screen.) There was a whole trove of the stuff downstairs, stored away in the shuttered rooms. At the end, he had given her a tally. She read it, nodded and said, 'Good.'

Now the men carried the things from the laneway to the street. They loaded them into a truck, swaddling everything with blankets. When they were done, the dealer gave her an envelope full of banknotes, completing the sale in the room with the family altar, under the gaze of her grandmother's photo, but June felt no regret as she thanked the dealer. She watched the truck drive away, then she set off on her bicycle. The money was in her satchel, carefully counted.

As she rode through the city, snow started to fall. The flakes were soft and light and somehow never landed; hitting the warm air from the springs, they swirled up again, rising instead of falling.

She rode on to the seafront, to the dormant Tropicana, where she got off her bike. The owner was moving about inside, doing a final clean-up. Peering in, June saw him taking down a picture, and smiled to think of what might go up in its place. A poster of River Phoenix – Naomi would like that.

First order of business, she thought. And without stopping to lock the bike, she stepped into the bar.

Catch and release

It's been a long day for Lee Prescott – busy, interrupted, fractious.

'Oh, come on then,' he tells the client who accosts him in reception.

The guy is pale-skinned, taller than he remembers, in his late teens. When he smiles he looks sly, but also bashful and excited. A *hello mate* was his opening gambit, his way of stopping Lee near the doors.

Darren Kemp. The name comes to Lee. It's stuck with him from last time. Kemp is saying he needs his help, he's in *a bit of a situation*. Lee's heart sinks when he hears this. Kemp doesn't have an appointment; he's walked in off the street. He has the same jittery manner as when Lee last saw him, two, maybe three years ago, although the scar cutting through his left eyebrow and running slantwise across his cheek is new. He's lucky to have the eye, Lee thinks. Kemp's nervousness flays the air, leaping off him like electricity off a damaged power line.

What does it matter, Lee thinks, resigning himself. It's one of those days already.

'Four-thirty, they said.'

'How did you get here?'

'Walked.'

'Right. We'll take my car.'

Lee hasn't even managed to get back to his desk. Since eight-thirty this morning, he has been, in no particular order, leaned on by his boss to take on still more cases, on top of those he's already covering for colleagues; chewed out by a barrister in a courtroom for being ill-prepared; and forced to listen to various tall stories from his clients, all of whom think they should get a stay or have their case dismissed.

'You know the trouble with our clients?' his boss had asked him. Giving Lee's crumpled suit a disapproving stare, he said, 'If you don't look out, Prescott, they'll bring you down to their level.'

Lee drops his files at reception. 'Back in an hour,' he tells the new receptionist, the one with the fingernails. Today they're acid green, a colour that makes Lee wince. She nods and goes on tapping without giving him a glance.

It's a sweltering late-August day outside, over thirty. Lee's client follows him to the car park at the side of the building; he's carrying a heavy rucksack and looks like he hasn't been home for days.

'Life's been good to you, has it, Mr Kemp?' Lee asks.

'Yeah, I spose. Hah-hah.' He offers, 'You look older.'

'I am older,' Lee replies.

'You want to go on a holiday now and then.'

'I'll do that, Mr Kemp.' If only! He isn't taking one this year. Half his colleagues are still on theirs, poaching themselves in the warm waters of Sardinia and Spain.

'It's just Darren. Plain old Daz.' He has a skittish sort of charm and a rangy way of moving. He has a scab or a sore on one side

218

of his jaw, and he keeps touching it with his fingers, giving it exploratory little strokes. Kemp is a user. Lee knows that. He has the user's demeanour, the eyes that are sometimes lively, sometimes calculating, even sly, in the classic bait and switch that is particular to addicts. Normally, the knowledge that a client is using wouldn't throw Lee. It shouldn't bother him with Kemp. It shouldn't – but it does.

'Here,' he says, when he reaches his car, 'it's this one.'

The phone in his pocket pulses. He checks it and sees a text. *So what's it to be? You coming?* Ignoring this, he gets into the airless car. Once Kemp has done the same, he starts the ignition and pulls out onto the road.

'What's the charge?' he asks Kemp.

'There isn't one. They haven't charged me yet.'

'Okay, so what's it about then?'

'Dealing.'

'What substance?'

'Meth.'

They're in the stop-start traffic of the arse end of the day. From Enfield, Lee takes the Lea Valley Road, passing between two reservoirs and crossing the River Lea. It's leafier on the other side, where the streets rise gently towards Chingford. Lee isn't normally in the business of playing cabbie to his clients. More used to driving alone, he has got into the habit, now and then, of imagining that he is running over pedestrians, the way he used to do accidentally when playing an old computer game called *Vette!*, short for Corvette. 'Boom,' he might say, 'boom, boom,' at the moment of imagined impact. With Kemp in the car, though, he keeps his serious face on. 'And why've they asked you to come in?'

'Why do you think? I've committed a crime.'

'Are you sure you want to say that?'

'I'll say it to you. I did it.'

Lee screws up his face, lifts a hand to rub his forehead. 'What I mean is, Darren, what do they have on you?'

'Kid's in hospital, isn't he.'

'A kid? What for?'

'Overdose. Eighteen, same age as me.'

Eighteen. That means it's been three years – Kemp was fifteen the last time he defended him. Lee looks across, gauging his bulk, the size of him in his shirt.

'But this is the thing,' Kemp goes on to say, 'I've got to plead not guilty.'

'You just told me you did it. I have a duty to the court.' Seeing what's become of Kemp, Lee is determined to stay firm. He isn't going to make the same mistake as last time.

'No, listen. You're my lawyer. It's what I say it is, isn't it. You have to say what I tell you.'

The words come quickly, compulsively, as if of their own accord. At a set of lights he turns to look hard at his client. Dilated pupils, twitching jaw, jerky movements – he's on the shoulder of a high, still affected by the drug.

Great. They're not far from the station. Speaking clearly and carefully, Lee says, 'Darren, if that's what you've done I've got an obligation to disclose it. When you told me you did it, didn't you know that's what it meant, that you'd have to plead guilty?'

'I take it back.'

Lee sighs and spins the wheel as he turns a corner. 'You'll have to get rid of me.'

'What?'

'Fire me. Get yourself another lawyer. I'm not doing this for you, Darren, not this time. I won't instruct your barrister to enter a not guilty plea. I can't, after you've gone and admitted it. Do you understand?' He still has a moral compass, albeit a battered one. He can't help Kemp by cleaning up his mess again.

'I *haven't* admitted it, you stupid fucking fuck.'

'Alright, Darren. Calm down. Come on, I'm just telling you how it is.'

Kemp winds down the window with a dramatic sigh. 'Why don't you have a fancy car?' he asks. 'You're not a very successful lawyer, are you?'

'Car's okay. It goes.'

'Okay. An okay lawyer in his okay fucking car. Piece of fucking shit more like. A Ford fucking Fiesta.' He lets out a strangled sound of frustration and rage, bangs his fist on the window jamb, and slumps back in his seat. He shuts his eyes to think, must find the effort taxing.

Lee's pocket pulses again. He should have muted the WhatsApp group. Tonight is his twenty-year school reunion. A few guys he knows are going.

Twenty years! An eternity. It's been so long, and not long enough. It shames him, his revulsion at the idea of going. And now here's Kemp, like his id, like the boys he knew in his youth, like someone he could have been if the wind had blown in the wrong direction.

He recalls how his ex-girlfriend's brother, a guy named Nathaniel, used to go on about the problem of 'filter bubbles'. He said it was important to mix with people from other walks of life, by which he meant comfortable, university-educated people like himself who happened to work in a different field. In civil engineering, say, instead of the civil service. If anything, Lee thinks, I want to be in more of a bubble.

'Who were you dealing for, anyway?' Lee asks.

Kemp shakes his head, stays quiet.

'Was it Simpkin?'

A defensive shrug.

'That's not a good move, you know.'

This provokes a new tirade. 'What would you know about it? Think you know everything, driving your fucking Fiesta? I might think about listening to you if you had a decent car instead of something my old pop would drive to the shops and back.'

'Your pop. Is he alive? Why don't you go and live with him? Might be a better scene.'

'Kicked me out, mate, didn't he. Got sick of me nicking stuff.'

He sounds like a child for a moment. He is probably fishing for Lee's pity, but Lee is famous in the office for not feeling sorry for anyone. He takes a dim view of lawyers who ooze sympathy for their clients, buying them lunches and charity shop suits.

'So what do you do with all your money?' Kemp says. 'If you don't spend it on your car?'

'It goes into the mortgage.'

'London, eh?' He grins. Back onside, just like that. Almost reverently, he adds, 'Simmo's got an Audi.' He strokes the scab on his chin.

'Lovely for him, I'm sure.'

'It's an S-Line. S means sport, if you're wondering.'

Lee gives the Fiesta fuel to get it up Kings Head Hill. 'How did you fall in with that lot anyway? Or don't I want to know?'

'I made some friends in Feltham.'

'You were inside? When?' Lee is surprised. The last time he represented Kemp, he got off without a custodial sentence.

'Don't worry, mate. Different lawyer. That was on someone else's watch, bit later. Which is why I've come to you. I need some of the old magic.'

When Lee had handled Kemp's possession charge, he'd considered it a run-of-the-mill offence, nothing serious. Without thinking too much about it, he'd coached Kemp on what to say, giving him a story to repeat. 'That's how it was, wasn't it, Darren? I can see it happening like that.' He thought it was for the best that he stay out of the criminal justice system – the criminal processing system, as it was at its best. On its good days.

'Sorry,' he says now. 'I'm fresh out of magic. You could get another conviction, Darren. Commercial supply. It's not good but it's not the worst.'

'*Bzzt*, wrong answer. Try again. You'll need to do better than that.'

'Not this time. I'm serious!' Fed up, Lee raises his voice. 'What good did it do you last time? And didn't I say I didn't want to see you back on charges? Yet here you are, three years on. And in a fucking state.'

Kemp is grinding his teeth. Lee checks himself. 'Listen, you're young,' he says, softening. 'They'll want to help you. You've got priors and that's not great, but you could get rehab inside, get yourself into a program. Honestly, there are worse things. It's hard to get proper help outside, as you've probably discovered.'

'Can you just shut it? I need to think!' Scowling, Kemp puts his head down to rifle through his bag, and Lee is treated to a glimpse of a glass pipe, the bulbous end a smoky black where the lighter flame has touched it.

Of course. *Of course* it's worked out like this. Shaking his head, Lee looks away. It's times like this he regrets doing criminal work. He wants to do contracts, probate, family trusts, the cushy stuff with well-off clients who send a good bottle of red every Christmas. He thinks of his own clients as People Who Break Things. Where are the people he wants to believe exist, the people who fix things instead of shitting all over them?

The police station looms ahead on the left, a red-brick oblong with a couple of nubby trees out front, the Met's crest in greyish white. The flag hangs limply from the pole, undisturbed by any breeze. Lee feels the need to piss. He should have gone before they left. No good starting an interview by asking for something, even if it's just the men's.

These are his thoughts as he slows to turn, but before he knows what's happening Kemp pulls a knife from his bag, extracting it in one movement, and holds it near Lee's neck. It's a large kitchen knife, a nasty piece of kit.

'Keep driving,' says Kemp.

'What?' Lee forces himself to stay calm. He's been threatened by clients before, but never with a knife. 'But we're at the station.'

'Just keep driving.'

'Okay. Fine. Okay.'

'You didn't hear anything before. You didn't hear anything because I didn't tell you anything.'

'Course you didn't, Darren. No need for the knife, is there.' He doesn't want to aggravate him further. Following the stream of traffic as it merges onto Station Road, he is aware of his client's erratic breathing and the reek of his sweat-stained shirt. He hopes Kemp's hand isn't sweaty. You wouldn't like that knife to slip.

At the same time, while driving, he sees the streetscape sliding by. A heart-shaped helium balloon stuck in a tree in front of the church. An old woman in a beret (an actual beret!) at a cafe with an awning. The locksmith, the tobacconist, the Coral betting shop. Then real estate agencies and hair salons, the stuff of aspirations. These are ridiculous impressions, of no use whatsoever. He has a knife near his jugular and this is what captures his attention!

Or perhaps he is going to die, he thinks, and these are to be his last impressions, in which case they carry more significance.

Here he is, being treated to a glimpse of the ephemera of life, as though this street in Chingford is something to treasure.

*

Trees settle and cool. A white van trundles along the road. Two men sit in the front, talking in low voices. Behind them, the back of the van is sectioned off with wire mesh. The driver is careful with the brakes, which can be a little jumpy. Soon they sink into silence among the debris of their travels: wadded receipts from service stations, a chocolate wrapper glinting, a pair of heavy-duty gloves, a desiccated towel.

Up an incline, along a straight, then through some shallow bends. The sky darkens overhead, shade merges with the night, and trees reach up either side like gothic rib-vaults in a church. The satnav hovers as if suspended, blinking fluorescent green. They are used to the way it gives directions: here and there, and now left then right, and once again onward through the trees.

The forest is unquiet; it is a peopled, well-trodden place. As it empties of the last of the day's joggers and dog walkers, it hoards its groves of rubbish, bins of dogshit in knotted bags. Trees grow taller and denser. The blackening hornbeam branches spread. Oaks expand in earth and sky. (The growth is tangible, of course, from the point of view of the forest.)

What do the men in the van want? The trees want to know their business. The roots of the trees catch the under-wheel vibrations, discerning a subtle music of weight and speed. The leaves grow and test the air, grow some more, then pause. In the pause they apprehend a breeze, a lessening of heat and light and the day's industry and cares.

*

'Quiet! I need quiet!'

'Alright, Mr Kemp.' Fear makes Lee more formal. He's a lawyer, and formality is his comfort zone, default to factory settings.

Don't panic, he tells himself. He has to think of a way to talk Kemp down, persuade him to put the knife away. Lee knows he can be persuasive. *Lee with the smart mouth*: that's what people used to call him around Leyton Grange, years ago in his former life. It wasn't a compliment, he knew. Smart was something to disdain.

Kemp is giving him directions, his gaze flitting ahead. On past the train station. Okay, this isn't good. Another left. A stretch of grassland opens out, then trees close in around the road. Snowy tufts of thistles catch the last rays of the sun. They're entering Epping Forest, which envelops them in green. Lee's need to pee grows more urgent but this is no time to bring it up. He drives on through the forest on a surprisingly busy road; it's probably a rat run for beating the clogged traffic elsewhere.

The big mystery is why Kemp is so on edge about facing a dealing charge. Granted, it isn't great, not how you want your day to go, but pulling a knife? It makes no sense. The meth is fucking with his mind.

Lee risks a comment. 'It'll be alright, Darren. I promise you it will.'

Kemp lets out a cry of anguish. 'It won't be alright, though, will it? They'll know we did the job on Maggot.'

'What?'

Lee knows the name Maggot. How many Maggots can there be? The penny drops. Everything drops – his heart in his chest, his stomach.

'They'll know we offed him!'

'Darren, you didn't. Tell me that wasn't you.' Lee read the story in the paper two or three weeks ago. It was not one of the good papers; it was a tabloid at a cafe next to the court precinct. A man's body had been found in Epping Forest. Identified as Mag 'Maggot' Dordevic, from Walthamstow, known to the police.

Kemp doesn't blink. He looks straight at Lee. 'That's why I can't plead guilty. They can't know I was selling or they'll connect me to Maggot. It puts me in the picture.'

'How will they make that connection?'

'Because it was Maggot's gear I sold. Simmo gave it to me.'

'Jesus Christ,' Lee mutters.

A silence falls between them, until finally Kemp says, 'I mean, that's what they'll *think*. I wasn't confessing. Not for that.'

'No, I know. Of course not.'

'Are you going to say I said that too?'

'I'm not going to tell them anything, Darren.'

'I know you won't. I'll make sure of it.'

This isn't what Lee wants to hear. None of it is what he wants to hear. Not while he's driving through the very forest where Maggot was laid to rest. As he tries to take in what he's heard, they pass more wretched trees. Lee is not a nature person. He doesn't know half of the trees' names, and anyway the forest is whipping past too quickly.

'What have they got on you, Darren, really? For the dealing thing, I mean. Some texts? Let's stop and have a look. Maybe we'll be able to explain them away.'

'It's WhatsApp messages,' he says.

'You'd be better off with a BlackBerry. The police have trouble breaking those.'

'Do they?'

This is news. 'See, Darren? I can help you.' At the same time, he thinks, Christ, it's your business to know these things, not mine. 'Where is Simpkin now, anyway?'

'It's his week minding the kids.'

'Father of the year.'

'You've got a mouth, don't you, Prescott? You'd do better to keep it shut, I would've thought. If I was you. Wait, turn here.'

It's the first time he's used Lee's surname. And it's jarring.

'Turn, I said!'

'Okay, I'm turning.'

Kemp presses the knife close. Lee doesn't believe he'll actually use the weapon, he just wants to look convincing. Then the blade makes contact, a cool flat presence at Lee's neck.

'Fucking Christ!' he says. 'You've cut me!' He puts a hand to his neck. 'I'm bleeding.'

'Fuck.'

'Is it bad?'

'I don't think so. I don't know! The blood, it's on your collar.'

His shirt. That is a shame, he thinks in a disembodied way. Lee is always short of shirts for work. He hates going shopping, stepping into T.M. Lewin where some overzealous teen tries to get him into stripes or a cutaway collar.

'Okay,' Kemp says. 'Stop the car.'

'What?'

'I need to get something for your neck. Hands on the wheel where I can see them.'

Lee does as he's told. Where they stop there is lots of bracken, great clamouring mounds of it. This is a plant Lee can name, not that he likes it much. It seems to him somehow cheap, the bottom-feeder of the woods. Still holding the knife aloft, Kemp uses his free hand to rummage in his bag. But instead of a bandage he fishes out a roll of gaffer tape.

'Oh charming, Darren. Use that on Maggot, did you?'

'Just take the tape,' Kemp says coolly. 'Peel some off.'

It makes an awful unsticking sound as it comes off the roll, and Lee is chastened to see blood on his hands and on the tape. His blood. He looks at it, dazed. At the same time, Kemp, who has clamped the knife in his teeth to go hands-free, swiftly binds his wrists, going around double with the roll. Lee, caught off-guard, struggles, but Kemp is strong.

'Come on, Darren! You don't need to do this.'

'They weren't supposed to find him,' Kemp is saying, as if continuing an argument. 'He was meant to decompose.'

'It's Epping Forest, not the wilds of the Amazon! You've got dog walkers. Mountain bikers. For Christ's sake, you've got doggers.'

Lee sees Kemp's surprise and it makes him want to laugh. Mustn't do that, he thinks. Mustn't laugh. Lee is under no illusions now. What happened to Maggot was no joke. As well as making the front page of the tabloids, the death was on the TV news. Lee saw the scene at Hollow Ponds one night while idly flicking channels. Police lights flickered on the leaves, turning them Ninja Turtle green. It was funny (he thought then) how young officers looked these days; the constables he saw at court had the faces of babies. They were only children, really. It was extraordinary.

'Listen to me,' he tries again, turning to eyeball Kemp. He will debase himself if he has to. He will grovel. 'I don't have to say anything about what you said back there.' Beg, borrow, steal, or lie. He is not too proud.

'You're lying. Or else you were lying to me before. Which is it, Prescott? Your duty, you said it was. That's a way of putting it, isn't it? A way of saying you're going to dob.' The childishness of the word 'dob' cuts against his tough-guy act. 'Out of the car,' he says. 'No, wait.' He eyes Lee's legs.

'If you tape my ankles, Darren, you'll have to carry me,' he points out. 'There's only one of you, remember. You're on your own this time.'

So Kemp tapes his mouth instead, as Lee thrashes about. He feels the tightness on his mouth, the puckering of the tape.

Kemp gets out of the car and comes round to the driver's side, opens the door. 'Get out,' he orders and then points with his head. 'That way. I'm right behind you.'

His cockiness is back in force; it must have been taping Lee's wrists that did it. It has given him a sense of satisfaction at having managed something. Lee knows the feeling: the weird, unexpected thrill of competence when it arrives.

'Keep going.'

'Mm-hmm.'

The cut on his neck is hurting now. It must be worse than he realised. He can feel a throbbing, lateral pain, and his shirt collar is wet. They walk into the forest. Pigeons make unhelpful noises, a low, fruity gargling that Lee figures signals love. The ground is crunchy underfoot with a carpet of dry seed pods, which make it feel like he is walking on outsized Coco Pops.

Then he hears movement ahead and thinks, Oh please, god. His spirits sink when he sees a squirrel. It is a grey squirrel to boot, the less desirable kind of squirrel. It scampers along a log, a tiny acrobat in flight. It's hard to hate a squirrel, but he really wishes it were a dog, being trailed by an owner who would see him and intervene.

There are wheel ruts on the ground, signs that mountain bikes have been here; perhaps a rider will bounce into view. He dislikes mountain bike riders, trail-runners, and extreme sportspeople in general, but he longs to see one now. There are now so many people doing adventure sports, it is practically an epidemic. Apparently Everest is crowded and covered with litter. People are dying in the queues. He thinks of them saying to each other, *after you; no, after you.*

Kemp prods him from behind, insisting they keep going, keep wading through the bracken. He's audibly short of breath, the user's affliction, but has the energy of someone who feels himself to be on the up. He's been speaking as he walks, more to himself than to his captive. 'Don't trouble yourself, Prescott. This is just a game between friends. A mystery tour of the forest. Maybe we'll play some Marco Polo.'

Lee feels a buzzing in his pocket and imagines the messages from his friends at the reunion. *Come on, come for a drink, you miserable prick.* Then, with a few more drinks under their belts, *Think you're too good for us, do you, Prescott?*

Oddly, Kemp comes out with a similar sentiment. 'Not much to say for yourself. Think you're better than me, do you? I bet you like a little glitter at your lawyer dinner parties. Just nip into the bathroom for a line in private.'

Actually, I do think I'm better than you, Darren. But Lee doesn't have to answer; the tape relieves him of this duty. His only task, it seems, is to endure the forced excursion. He goes on hating nature just to have something to focus on. Look! Here's some holly thrusting up beside the trees. Here's a stand of spindly birches. Here's a dip downhill. He hears a bird's falling cry, repeated without answer. Are there no other creatures in this wood apart from that one squirrel? Is that the ring road he can hear? The woods are too quiet and too noisy at the same time. Emptied of wild noises, they reverberate with the distant traffic and, briefly, the *doof doof* of a car stereo somewhere.

Soon they come to a glade of verdant green, an Arcadian vision. Arcadia, the home of Pan, the god of all the wild, thinks Lee. He knows this from trailing his ex-girlfriend through successive art museums. From Pan's name comes the word *panic*. Funny that, he thinks. He glances over his shoulder. Kemp is toting his rucksack like an overgrown schoolboy, is for a moment the fifteen-year-old Lee knew. Back then he had spirit, a bit of pluck. He'd stood out from the parade of sullen defendants.

'This isn't personal, understand,' says Kemp. 'It's just to teach you a lesson.'

'Definitely, I know,' Lee would say if he could speak. Then again, this makes no sense. Of course it's personal. Who is to receive the lesson, if not him, Lee Prescott, in his capacity as a person, a living, breathing being who bleeds when his skin is pierced?

There is no more buzzing in Lee's pocket. His phone, at last, is silent. No one will miss him for days. No one knows where he is. Not his colleagues on holiday. Not his alcoholic boss. Not the receptionist with the gel nails. She'll have gone home by now, or out, wherever she goes of a Friday night. Her office clothes look like nightclub clothes so it's difficult to tell.

He pictures the reunion-goers in the beer garden at the pub, enjoying themselves without him. Up until this evening, he had no desire to be there, but now the scene in the beer garden takes on an unexpected lustre: he thinks of lanterns in the trees, faces turning towards his.

'This'll do,' Kemp announces suddenly. He has Lee sit against a tree, takes out a coil of nylon rope and ties him securely to the trunk. He shakes his head as he knots the rope. In a voice full of regret, he asks, 'Why did you have to say those things? About the barrister, the police?'

Lee makes apologetic noises, fruity, gargling pigeon noises. The ground beneath him is spongy, its damp seeping through his trousers. He feels the knobbly trunk at his back, smells the rich dark earth, and realises that he might die here.

Panic comes with this thought. It has finally found him, caught him up, and it makes itself known to him in an intimate embrace. His panic is a close, constricting thing, closing off his windpipe. He feels warmth in his trousers and knows he has urinated.

Kemp is pacing back and forth now, growing more and more agitated. Lee doesn't know if he will kill him. He doesn't think Kemp knows. He is making a call on his mobile, and Lee can hear the voicemail recording. Simpkin must be busy with his kids. Lee hopes they puke in his car, all over the leather interiors. He knows Simpkin will be livid when he finds out what Kemp has done, the underling taking the initiative in the boss's absence.

Kemp doesn't know this yet, of course. He is too new to the job. He's tapping out a message, then looking stupidly at the screen. He wants someone to tell him what to do. Don't we all, Lee wants to say. And he almost feels for the guy, a fellow craven mortal. But this spark of recognition, instead of making him warm to Kemp, makes him more afraid of him. He sees him for what he is. A dangerous quantity, a wrecking ball of a human being.

Kemp stops stalking back and forth and looks at Lee. Finally he says, 'So what do I do if you won't help me? What am I meant to do?' He is despairing.

Lee makes talking noises.

'What's that? Oh, for fuck's sake. Here.' He rips the tape off Lee's mouth.

It hurts. It feels like he's been punched. Lee's mouth goes slack from the shock of it. He can scream and shout now, but who's going to hear him?

'I'll help you,' he says.

'Why would you do that?'

'Because I know you, Darren. I helped you last time, didn't I?' Lee speaks softly and quickly. He lets him see his fear, the bald edge of his terror. Kemp needs to see that his threats have worked. 'You don't want to make things worse,' he goes on. 'This can be just between you and me. It'll all be fine, I promise, but you've got to let me go.' He adds, 'I've learned my lesson. Promise.'

Kemp stares at him and groans. 'You've ruined my day, Prescott.' Then, 'Okay,' he says. 'Okay.' He crouches before him. 'I'll leave you here, alright?' Taking a penknife from his rucksack, he nicks the tape between Lee's wrists. 'You work away at that, you'll be out of here in no time.'

He taps Lee on the cheek. 'Lighten up, I was only joking in what I said about Maggot. I was joking, that was all. You shouldn't take it so serious.' Then, in one swift movement, he straightens and moves off. 'I'm late for my interview, now, aren't I?' he calls back. 'I'm going to have to get an Uber.'

After a few strides, he stops and turns around. 'I can find out where you live. Where the Fiesta goes at night.'

'You won't need to.'

'Course I won't.' He laughs and offers one last grin. Dangerous Darren, signing out. And he lopes off through the trees.

*

In the back of the white van, there's movement. In the dark, a shape writhes under rough cloth. A gamey smell pervades the vehicle, which hasn't been cleaned in a long time.

'Alright back there?' a voice enquires, one of the men in the front. His crumbly leather jacket chafes against the seat as he swivels to

look back. 'You'll be better off out here,' he says. 'Fewer people to make a fuss.' His voice is soft, cajoling as the van travels through the evening.

The second man chips in, 'It's a lovely wood, you'll see. You won't know yourself in the forest.'

The incline rises gently, nothing to tax the engine. They turn onto one road, then another. The forest marks their progress while knowing nothing of their purpose. It knows only the diesel smell of the van, birdsong, a helicopter's beating wings far off, and the general, distant whine of traffic in an off-key communion. Even these are mere sensations, hardly worth the forest's notice compared with everything it has seen: plague, blight and die-off, years and seasons, et cetera.

Of what consequence is a van winding uphill? The forest has stood here through the ages. It is now a scrap of its former self: it once reached halfway to the coast. But it holds the memory of those times and has a sense of diminished grandeur. It can recall, with some precision, the facts of its life to date. But not human facts. As a species, humans all tend to look the same; they blend into each other.

From the point of view of the forest, the men in the van do not mean much. Still, the forest wants to know – it tries to ascertain – their motives. Why do they bother doing this thing that they are doing? Why bother with anything, when it amounts to so little? The forest is world-weary, but despite itself it wonders. It sends its feeling out towards them. It feels the imprint of the tyres and through them the sounds of the van engine, which is in reasonable running order, someone is keeping it in good nick.

*

In the glade, Lee slumps against the tree, feeling woozy and light-headed but also triumphant. When he hears a crashing sound some way off, he thinks, Fuck. He's back.

Lee pulls at the tape on his wrists. No luck. He is still bound to the tree, so to get to his feet he has to shimmy his back up the trunk. As he does, he hears two men shouting. Neither sounds like Kemp.

'What's that?' one of them calls out. 'What's that you're after?'

'Get on with you. You're alright. It's better than Clapham Common.' Then, 'See? He's mended nicely. Gait's looking much better.'

The rustling draws closer and Lee sees a fox. A long-bodied creature with an unembarrassed stare, it considers him with interest from the edge of the clearing. Behind the fox, the first man shouts again, 'What's he after? Look, there's someone there. Hey! Hello?'

Torch beams bouncing, the men blunder towards Lee. Lee makes them out in the almost-dark. One is unplaceably old and wears a battered leather jacket, while the other one, in a flannel shirt, is closer to middle age.

What on earth are they doing, chasing after a fox? He is exorbitantly happy to see their kind, genial faces, which are rosacea-red and weathered in the light thrown by the torches.

Having found Lee, the fox grows bold, darting close to get a sniff. Lee locks eyes with the animal. It knows he is maimed; this is why it's here.

'Scoot! Get out of it,' the man in the flannel scolds. Lunging, he shoos it with his hands, his boot. 'You're free, don't you understand?'

The fox hesitates, looking off into the middle distance. A knowledge arrives from somewhere and glimmers in its eyes. Yes, it understands. That old, old knowledge: it is free. And it darts away, disappearing into the forest.

'Goodness. Are you alright?'

'Call an ambulance. He's bleeding.'

Wanting to reassure them, Lee tries to form the words. The old man fumbles with his torch as he hastens to dial 999.

This is when a third voice says, 'I didn't want to do this.' The two older men spin around, and Lee peers in the direction of the voice. Darren Kemp is back, phone in hand. A chemical smell wafts off him – acetone, paint stripper – meaning he's had a hit. Oblivious to the two other men, he stares intently at Lee.

I should hate him, Lee decides. And he honestly wants to hate him. He knows why Kemp is back: to finish the job he started.

They bring you down to their level. The words of Lee's boss ring in his head. But it is Kemp who is ascendant, a man brilliantly transformed. In the flash of the high, the sudden dopamine rush, he moves quickly and gracefully, with none of the jerkiness of before. As he approaches, it strikes Lee that he should have been a dancer. He's fleet of foot, old Daz. He could have done swing or rockabilly, in shirtsleeves and flat-fronted trousers and winklepicker shoes, tearing up the dance hall, throwing a partner into a spin. He has the instinctive streak that all good dancers have, and a spring in his gait that says, *This is all a game, and we've won before we've started, and isn't this a lark?*

Then he stops, as of course he must. His pale blue eyes widen as he sees the intruders. The surprise, for both of them, Lee and Darren, is that they have been spared the worst. They grasp this fact at the same time, and Kemp looks terrified and relieved.

'I didn't want to do it,' he says again.

It's true and it isn't true. Lee is eye to eye with Kemp. They're on the same level now, and he hears himself saying, 'It's alright, Daz, I know. Don't worry, okay? I know.'

Day Zero

Sebastian was still in bed when Teena came back from her run. Hearing her come in and put the coffee machine on, he sat up, checked his watch and rubbed his face.

'You should've come,' she said when she looked in. 'It's a beautiful day. No dust.'

He got up. It had been quiet in the flat and he had overslept. His phone had hardly rung all week; everyone thought he'd gone to District 6-13. His packed bag sat on the floor, ready to go. On top sat his press pass and a box of respirator masks. Picking up the box, he turned it over unhappily. He always took the masks on assignments to the outer settlements, but he'd had to cancel this trip at the last minute.

'You didn't sleep well?' called Teena. In the other room, she was opening a window and throwing her running suit over the sill to air.

Sebastian didn't answer, pretending he hadn't heard. In fact, he had lain awake between the hours of three and five. He had occupied himself by plotting his funeral, his favourite pastime during recent sleepless nights. By now he had considered all aspects of the event, giving it the same lavish attention some people gave to weddings. He had thought a lot about the music and, crucially, the venue. He didn't want it to be a church. (He had nothing against Christians.) He didn't want it to be the meditation pavilion next to the school. (He had nothing against Buddhists or mindfulness meditators.) It could be a function room at the convention centre, although that would lack ambience and possibly feel flat.

He heard a loud thwacking sound, then another, which meant Teena had seen a cockroach. 'You little fucker,' she said, and her satisfied tone suggested she'd made a kill. She came back into the bedroom to see him holding the box of masks.

'What'll we do with these?' he asked, looking up.

'Wear them to have sex?' Sweaty from her run, she tipped her head and grinned. Having taken off her suit, she wore briefs and a sports bra. Sinewy muscles gleamed on her abdomen and thighs.

'No. Maybe. No.' He smiled distractedly then frowned. He did not want to be cheered up.

Moving to get dressed, he paused long enough to let Teena take a look at the nape of his neck. This was where the shrapnel had gone in. It had happened three weeks before, during his last trip to the outer districts, where he was visiting bases to report on resourcing concerns. The wound wasn't a big deal – in fact he'd been secretly pleased about it, welcoming it as a sort of battle decoration – and he was due to have the shrapnel cut out in a few days' time. A scan had shown the offending sliver, lodged a half-inch in, an innocuous stroke of black amid the grey of surrounding tissue. But this was not all the scan had shown; there was another, larger mass, the thought of which had been keeping him awake at night.

'Some training exercise,' said Teena, shaking her head as she gently pressed the spot where the shrapnel had entered, and he smiled.

'Well, not everyone can be as competent as you.' He was proud of his girlfriend. Raised by her grandmother in a Hounslow council flat, she had risen through the ranks after joining special forces. Having applied for a transfer several years ago, she now worked at a desk job, handling logistics.

'Lucky, though,' she added. 'It meant you got that scan.'

It was past eleven. 'I've got to get going,' he said.

Teena threw him a look that said it was about time, then went to take a shower. He left the flat before she emerged again.

Outside, he saw Teena was right: the day was clear and unpolluted, the sky a soft sage that rose to a deep olive tone. He crossed the street and hailed a bus. Once he was on board, his phone rang. It was his dad, calling from Leeds, but as soon as he picked up the call dropped out. He wasn't the only one with a bad signal; he heard a girl behind him say, 'I've only got two bars. Make that zero bars. You would think we were on Pluto.'

It was something of a relief not to have to talk. Settling back in his seat, he returned to his thoughts of the early hours, considering again how he would like to be sent off. He knew there was an irony, even hypocrisy, in planning his funeral in his head. Hadn't he often mocked the elaborate preparation that went into his friends' weddings? He had always seen such efforts as stupid and exhausting. Of course he played his part when required. He had shuttled to the nearest moon for a stag weekend, cramming in with the other guys in a rank-smelling cabin. He had been to nuptials in the desert where the guests were made to wear retro bubble helmets, and to a town hall service where the groomsmen were kitted out by the last living Neapolitan tailor (the suits would never be worn again, thanks to a quirky choice of fabric). He had heard the works of Bach played on ruined cellos, their strings brittle from the dry air of the steppes, and the performance of one musician who was also the bride's ex-boyfriend, because his career had really taken off and no hard feelings, right?

It was a sort of advertising, a conscientious display of individuality that was in truth (he'd been heard to say) 'the logical extension of late capitalism'. But here he was indulging the same dubious impulse, enjoying the curation of his ideal funeral. He had been jotting his ideas in a moleskin notebook, eclectic song lists that consisted of a mix of high and low, classical and pop. In the hours when he had the flat to himself, he listened to the tracks on his longlist, assessing the degree to which they evoked a sense of his being. A hard thing to pull off in the space of forty minutes, but he relished the task, treating it like an aesthetic puzzle.

He thought, too, of how things might go if he didn't leave instructions, the awfulness of someone playing some really crappy music, the highly possible disaster of a badly chosen reading. He knew it wasn't a good idea to try to talk about this with Teena, even though he would have liked to rule out a few things up front, like R&B ballads and anything biblical. He figured the best thing was to write out his ideas, make a final list and tuck it safely in a drawer, his last will and testament regarding the event.

*

His phone rang again, breaking into his thoughts. He answered it thinking it was his dad again. Instead, he heard the voice of his friend Dino. Immersed in his own concerns, Dino had forgotten that Sebastian was meant to be away for work.

'Hey, Seb, what's happening? Want to stop by the studio?'

Dino was an artist. He painted the sand dunes, cliffs and caves beyond the settlement's limits, churning out proficient landscapes that were increasingly popular.

'Can't today, Dino. Work is insanely busy.'

'Yeah, I hear you, man. I'm painting like crazy. I've got this retrospective opening on Day Zero.'

A retrospective? Sebastian blinked. He had been looking out the window, ready to tune out, but now he found himself jealous of this mark of acclaim. These past few weeks, he'd been trying not to think about the state of his own career as a freelance journalist. He had always been confident of his eventual success, perhaps a stunning exposé that would spark controversy and debate. He had pictured the future as being ripe with promise, or rather with a thousand different promises. It was a far-off, inviting land, suggestive of a gorgeous superfluity. Now, though, his horizons were closing in, hurtling towards him way before he was ready.

'Aren't you too young to be having a retrospective?' He pictured his scruffy friend, who went everywhere in scuffed Converse high-tops, cords, and a zip-up hoodie. The scar across the bridge of his beakish nose, a legacy of a car accident, gave him the look of an outsized wounded bird. Dino was not yet forty, although he was old enough, as Sebastian now knew, to be the father of a teenager, a boy who had only lately got in touch. It was bizarre to think that Dino had had a son all this time, a kid – his own flesh and blood – walking around New Province.

'Well, it's really a survey show. That's what they call it if you're not dead. And I've been around the traps for a while now, you know.'

'Yeah, but doing what? Picking up art school students?'

Dino was unabashed. 'I don't know what you mean. I've been beavering away on a few new pieces, as it happens.'

243

'Wait. You're making new work for the show? Day Zero is next week.'

'I've got to have something to put up. They've sent out the invites, made me sound like an A-grade dick. *An artist who has succeeded, much more than any other, in finding a fitting visual language for the New Province landscape.*' He said the party was being hosted by the Co-Sec embassy. 'Tell me you'll come to the opening. And I want you to come round and see what you think of this newer stuff I've been doing. I've been staring at it so long I don't know if it's good or what. They're from these magnified slides of extremophiles.'

Sebastian couldn't think about paintings right now, couldn't go to the studio and stroke Dino's ego. He couldn't stomach the idea of the opening, either. The champagne flutes on trays, the speeches and grandstanding, the vapers huddling on a terrace like the last of a dying tribe. And he hated Day Zero, the way people carried on. They would talk of the beauty of the place, the spirit of exploration. No one would mention the outer districts or the long, slow-burning conflict. Day Zero commemorated the settlement's founding. The planting of the flag, the pegging out of the first biodome, the splashing of pictures over the internet to show other hopeful nations that they had been too slow.

'Sounds amazing, Dino.' He squeezed his way off the bus. 'Hey, I'm just heading into a meeting. Call you later, yeah?'

This was stretching the truth. His meeting was really an appointment. Seb entered a low-rise glass building, checked the directory in the lobby, and went up to the second-floor waiting room, which struck him as depressing, a wasteland of humanity. Its seats were occupied by the infirm and the diseased, a blotchy-skinned people with lashless, staring eyes. Sebastian took a seat next to a skeletal-looking man with a protuberance on his cheek.

After studying him for a moment, the man asked, 'What got you, a solar flare?' He leaned close, as if to let Sebastian in on a secret. 'Have you tried the fox's breath diet? I've got the cold-pressed juice on order.'

Sebastian hadn't tried any diets, fox's breath or otherwise. He had heard of fox's breath, of course, a rare flower used to make a medicine of sorts. A delicate amber-coloured blossom that still grew in a small number of surviving habitats on Earth, it was said to give off a rank odour, like the smell of rotting flesh. Doctors maintained the plant was a dangerous toxin, but an army of devotees sang its praises on web forums.

The man leaned even closer. 'I have a source, a guy who knows a guy, you get me?'

If this was meant as an invitation, Sebastian didn't take it. He wanted to get away from the old man and his messed-up face, repelled by his suggestion that they were in this thing together. Congenitally sceptical, Sebastian hated – no, he abhorred – being forced into the role of a wide-eyed miracle seeker. Everything inside him bucked against starting a quest (onerous, all-consuming, time-sucking, never-ending) for some new and transformative alchemy.

He was saved from the conversation when his name was called, and he went in to meet Dr Seymour, a slightly built American in a button-down shirt and a bad tie. An expensive bicycle leaned against his office wall under a row of certificates.

He proved to be chatty, even slightly manic, but his opening line was encouraging. 'The young are the most deserving,' he said. 'Well, they have the most to gain or lose.' Scrolling through the scan cross-sections on a screen in front of him, he kept up a commentary that required little of his patient. 'Do you have any symptoms? No? So you were just going along, shoulders back, and then this tripped you up. A splodge on a scan. It's a weird thing, isn't it, technology. Just surreal. You wouldn't otherwise have had any idea.'

Dr Seymour kept scrolling and scrolling. 'You're being very cool about it, cooler than I would be. It's very courageous of you.'

Courageous. Sebastian stiffened, not liking where this was going.

'Look, I won't say it's inoperable. It's eminently operable; it's just a question of what that will achieve. You see, this is now recurrent cancer. Here and here, you see.' He pointed. To the left of the small black mark that represented the piece of shrapnel, Sebastian saw the offending splodge. 'In the spinal cord. Which means you're resistant to the drugs you took last time, and unless we can find something to stop the spread of microscopic disease, we are kidding ourselves. If you were seventy-one instead of thirty-one, we wouldn't even be talking about doing anything about it. We'd be saying the horse has bolted.'

'Right,' said Sebastian, reeling in his seat.

'I have to take this to our panel,' Dr Seymour said. 'If I had my way, I'd operate. I mean, otherwise it's just a self-fulfilling prophecy, isn't it. I had one patient, we decided we couldn't go in, I always think that we failed him . . .' Here the surgeon began to ramble, and his gaze moved restlessly about the room, unable to settle, as he described how the patient died 'a horrible, painful death' as a quadriplegic.

Sebastian listened, appalled. He didn't want to hear a story about a man dying. He wanted to hate the surgeon for dumping it on him, but at the same time he was conscious of a struggle taking place within the man across the desk, some compulsive inner battle the surgeon seemed to be losing. He's breaking up, Sebastian thought. The guy is having an episode.

By the end of the consultation, Dr Seymour could not even look him in the eye. He averted his face as he shook hands, so that Sebastian was reminded of old exorcism films, in which the person who is possessed recoils from a priest.

*

The first time Sebastian had cancer, he had taken a course of pills. They were meant to clear it up and had appeared to do the trick; it was almost like taking antibiotics for a nasty flu.

He had been diagnosed soon after his twenty-seventh birthday after suffering from headaches and severe vertigo. It was a primary brain tumour, malignant, in the cerebellum, which was the lower back part of his brain. He had cancelled a work trip that time as well, had let everybody think he was away at the conflict zone when in reality he was sitting on his couch, smoking joints to relieve the nausea from the pills and enduring an acne rash that spread over his face and chest. The experience as a whole was like regressing to teenagedom – being grounded, getting stoned all day long.

After that, he'd had a scan showing that everything was fine. He had come to regard that day as his personal day zero, the first day in what would be his new calendar. That was two years ago, or four Gregorian years. He thought he had seen the back of the disease, and every so often, when he caught himself getting bored on a bus or at a checkpoint, as he waited for some official to okay his credentials, he would draw himself up and think, That's right. I won. I fucking *won*. He had once said this to Teena, to be met with the dry response: 'Well, you know, Sebastian, no one wins forever.' Which wasn't an attempt to rain on his parade – it was just her way to tell the truth.

This time around, he knew straight off it was different. Not because he felt sick. Weirdly, he felt fine. Nothing had changed and yet everything had changed. The recurrence meant he had hit stage four, which made things serious. Getting the news a week ago, in a windowless doctor's office, he had sat there soberly, almost impassively. He had listened and nodded without asking a lot of questions. He didn't need to ask to know what the news meant: a slow or fast decline, with perhaps a stab at surgery, and the brute use of drugs with decreasing effectiveness. Actually, the news had broken his heart, a quiet event that he had kept to himself, not letting on even to Teena. Aside from having to cancel his trip to District 6-13, he went about his days and found he could function fine. Maybe this was the difference between being twenty-one and thirty-one, knowing that he could live pretty well even with a broken heart.

As much as he thought about his funeral, he didn't actually want to die. He had briefly thought about suicide but only as an abstract prospect. He had thought about the writer Hunter S. Thompson, who had shot himself in the head rather than endure a slow decline, and who'd then been sent off with a cannon salute paid for by Johnny Depp. In Sebastian's estimation, this was over the top. Plus, he would not want to do the deed unless it was really time. Even then, he was pretty sure he didn't have it in him; he didn't think he could end his life when it came down to it. It comforted him that Teena would know what to do. This was another subject he had not raised with her yet. But he knew she would help him if the situation called for it. She would carry things off with her unfailing competence. He could trust her to kill him – painlessly, efficiently, undetectably.

For the moment, he took some satisfaction in the way he was keeping things together. He had the ability to live with uncertainty, something he came to think set him apart from other people. After that first diagnosis, he had tried seeing a counsellor.

It had seemed like the thing to do, plus it made him feel important, sitting on a couch like someone in a film. Ultimately, though,
he couldn't get into it. He could never quite believe that talking
did anything. Nor could he warm to the psychologist, a well-
heeled looking woman with a thing for beige. She always wanted
to circle back to his relationship. 'And how is your girlfriend
faring?' she would ask with a concerned look, as if she couldn't
believe that Teena was not a teary mess.

'Teena? Teena's great,' he'd answer truthfully.

'Is she talking to anyone?'

'You mean as in counselling? About me?'

'About you or about her . . . experiences.'

'No. She's a trooper. In both senses, ha-ha.'

One thing that worried him this time was that people would
find out. He worried that no one would give him work, that his
phone would stop ringing. So far only Teena knew what was
going on. They had always based their relationship on telling
the truth, and more specifically on an absence of sentimentality.
This was something on which they prided themselves, although
the problem then became one of how to show affection, how to
make romantic gestures that were non-schmaltzy and authentic.
The risk was lapsing into a codependent indifference, living in
close proximity like two neutral adjacent atoms, having no need
to bond by swapping electrons. Luckily, this problem fell away
during the night. This was when they spooned in bed (Sebastian
liked to be big spoon), or when he wriggled blindly across the
wide cool sheet to find Teena where she lay at the other side,
poised as if to roll off the edge of a continent.

When they had found out about his new scan, she had cried a
little. He had told her she should leave him, saying, 'I'm so sorry.
I didn't want this for you.'

She shook her head and wiped her tears. She said, 'I already did my thinking.'

'What do you mean? When?'

'Last time around.'

'Oh.' He was surprised to hear this and also a bit put out.

'As you can see, I am still here.'

'Yes,' he said, nodding, but he felt far from reassured. He tried to keep a childish note from creeping into his voice. 'Well, maybe it's time for you to think about it again.'

*

It took an hour to get to the desert, taking a series of unsealed roads. They suited up before the checkpoint, pulling on pliable moulded masks, snapping on ventilators, and got back into the buggy. He had never learned to drive, and there was something comforting about being chauffeured by Teena, who drove with a technical competence that showed her years of training. As they left the gravity field, she changed down through the gears. The sound system died when they lost connectivity but Sebastian was happy to do without music. There was the sound of the throaty engine, the tyres eating up the road, and the rushing of cold air at the reinforced windscreen.

He had rung Teena on getting out from seeing the surgeon that afternoon. 'Want to get out of town for a bit?' he'd asked. 'I'm sick of this joint.'

She had come to pick him up. As they got going, she asked, 'Want to talk about it?'

'Later,' he replied. 'Did you bring my suit, the lighter one?'

'Yes.' She glanced at his feet. 'You wore those sneakers to see the doctor? I thought you were getting new ones.'

He looked down. On both feet, his little toes were pushing

through the worn-out mesh, showing the grey fabric of his socks. 'I'm making these last.'

'Last until what?' Teena made a face as she drove. 'Just buy new sneakers, will you?'

The day was getting on; soon it would be dusk, and the temperature was dropping. On reaching a shallow crater rimmed by rocky cliffs, they entered through a narrow pass between eroding tiers of stone. There was an isolated hut, a basic can-shaped structure with a stand-alone latrine. Campers weren't supposed to use it – it was for work crews – but Dino had coaxed the keypad code out of someone he knew. He made it his base for his sketching excursions, making forays to the cliffs and fossicking in the caves. The hut was an open secret among their group of friends; Sebastian and Teena used it to get away. They both felt lighter in the desert, and Teena especially craved the relief of low gravity when her leg gave her trouble.

On arriving, they threw their gear into the hut, shut the door as the air processor cranked up, and pulled off their headgear to down a couple of cold beers. They looked out the window at the cliffs, which were popular with rock climbers. 'That reminds me,' Teena said. 'I've got to ring Zoe. She's been wanting to go climbing.'

Zoe was a friend from her time in special forces. She had sought to remake herself as an adventure tour operator, but it seemed to Sebastian that she had a lot of time to burn. 'Well, another time,' said Teena. 'The cliffs aren't going anywhere.'

'No, they are not.' Sebastian went to take a leak. He was glad to have his mask – the latrine had not been cleaned. He would have thought that the work crews would be used to urinating in a low-gravity environment, but the stained wall showed where they had overshot.

Escaping the cubicle, he found the magnesium sticks and kero and got a campfire going, just for the hell of it, coaxing the flame until it took and burned cheerfully. He squatted before it and looked across the shallow valley to the cliffs that were just then catching the last of the sun. People rhapsodised about the quality of light that was distinctive to New Province – the streakiness of the sky, the delicate colours, a golden haze that was in fact the sign of noxious gases. It was almost a religion, and sometimes he thought there was something more at play in these protestations, something almost competitive, a need to definitively prove an attachment to the place. Still, there was something to it. He wasn't unaffected. He watched with a quiet awe as the sun sank, then disappeared, its dying rays turning the sky an electric blue.

At that point the quiet was rudely broken when a large RV pulled up. It came to a shuddering stop a short distance from the hut. A generator churned into life, dubstep pumped from a loudspeaker, and spotlights burned through the dark to illuminate a swathe of ground. A half-dozen guys wearing technical fabric suits jogged down the vehicle's steps, fanned out in a V formation and, calling to each other, started doing frisbee drills. You've got to be kidding, Sebastian thought. He had forgotten that sports teams sometimes trained in the valley, making use of the natural amphitheatre for low-gravity sessions. As one of the frisbee guys waved at him, he smiled back politely even though he wore a mask and actually felt like crying.

'We've got company,' he told Teena, going back inside the hut. Having passed through the airlock, he pulled his headgear off.

'I saw,' she said wryly. She was warming soup on the burner. They sat on the lower bunk to wait for it to be ready. When he adjusted his position, rolling up a sweater to put behind his back, she said, 'Is it bothering you, the shrapnel?'

'No, it's fine.'

'You're a better man than me.'

'That has never been true, except biologically speaking.'

'Ha.' She zipped her suit open from the ankle to the thigh and took off her prosthesis. He knew the rubber bands that secured it cut into her skin, and she was always relieved to remove it. 'I'm still glad we came,' she said. 'I like it here. Although do you remember that time we came and that other couple was here, and the guy was going on about their dehydrated meals, how he made them all himself using a solar-powered oven?'

'Ugh. Don't remind me. I wanted to punch him in the face.'

'And the way he talked over her, like could you be more pompous?' Picking up a sheaf of documents she had brought with her from work, she idly ran her gaze down some sort of supply list. Stopping at a line item for sanitary products, she looked up with a smirk and said, 'You know, I read that early on, when NASA was going to put some woman astronaut in space, the engineers had to know the weight of everything, right, so they asked her how many tampons she'd need for a week. They asked her would a hundred be enough?' Lowering the page, she laughed. 'A hundred! That's so crazy. Dudes have no idea.'

'Well, why should they?' Sebastian asked. 'I don't know how many of those silicon cups you use.'

'I just use the one and wash it.'

'Right, but do you know how many times I shit a day?'

'Well —'

'Do you? How many?'

The soup was sputtering to a boil and Teena hopped up to take it off the burner. He knew not to offer to get it for her, but sat back and took his mug when she handed it to him. They lay back on the bunk to eat, resting on utility blankets that they had folded up like pillows, and warming their hands on the mugs until the soup had cooled a little. At this point, Teena said, 'Tell me what the surgeon said. Tell me what you're thinking. You've been so distant, Sebastian.'

'I'm always distant,' he told her.

'No, you're a smart, engaging guy who cares about people.'

'You've been consistently mistaken about my true nature.' Finishing his soup and putting the mug aside, he massaged her leg where the rubber bands had left their red indentations. Outside, the music had cut out, and they could hear the frisbee players firing up the RV to leave, their voices echoing as the sound bounced off the cliffs. Through the small square window he saw stars spattered across the black, and one of them seemed to pulse, although it was probably just a flaw in the thick glass.

'Oh, and another thing, get this. Did you know Dino is having a retrospective?'

'Yeah? That's fantastic. Be happy for him, won't you?'

'I am happy for him.' A minute passed before he added, 'Why wouldn't I be happy?'

But there was no answer from Teena, who had fallen asleep. He pulled a blanket up to her chin, re-masked to go outside, and there, without anyone to object, used a wasteful amount of kindling in making the campfire blaze.

*

Several nights later, in bed, Sebastian had the idea of going to the conflict zone anyway. The thought came to him just before four-thirty am. It wasn't as if Dr Seymour had settled on a plan. In the meantime, why shouldn't he go? Why shouldn't he jump on the next shuttle?

He finally dropped off to sleep wondering why he hadn't thought of it before. But when he woke to the light of day, he remembered the rules of his insurance. No one was going to certify him as physically fit to go to District 6-13 now. How would that letter read? *To whom it may concern, Sebastian is about to get sliced up for his out-of-control cancer, but prior to that he is good to go. Yours faithfully, A. Doctor.*

He rose that day to go and see a different doctor, the neighbourhood all-rounder who would pull the shrapnel out of his neck. On his way to the clinic, he took a call from his father. Sebastian had called him the night before to break the news about his tumour. As he had expected, the call did not go well; his father had reacted with bewilderment. Now, having taken the night to try to digest the information, he was calling back with specific questions. He prefaced question number one with a convoluted story about a woman stationed in Antarctica who had diagnosed her own cancer and then cut it out herself, following instructions from specialists via Skype. He asked, 'Is that what you're going to have to do?'

'We have doctors here, Dad. We have a hospital.'

'Was it the solar flare, do you think? It was a lot of radiation.'

'Was it the solar flare? How would I know, exactly? There's no label on the tumour. It's not like ordering a wine where you know the provenance.'

The trouble with talking to his dad, Sebastian reflected, was dealing with his questions. Questions Sebastian couldn't answer, that made even his doctors throw up their hands and shrug. When it came to rare conditions, oncology was less a science than an art, and definite answers were thin on the ground.

He ended the call as he fronted up to the clinic. He had been told to take some codeine before coming in, and that morning, after his coffee, he had dutifully popped some tablets and smoked a joint for good measure. The drugs were beginning to take effect as he lay facedown in the small room, and then the doctor, a balding man in a Hawaiian shirt, gave him a jab of local anaesthetic. Sebastian felt no pain as the guy made an excision and went in with a pair of tweezers. Turning his head away, he examined the posters on the wall, advertisements for Botox. Then he moved his gaze to the TV screen, which was playing reruns of *Grand Designs: The Space Edition*. The episode showed a Silicon Valley billionaire creating a fortified bunker. 'The *pièce de résistance?*' the presenter said teasingly. 'The master bedroom is one big hyperbaric chamber.'

Before the big reveal, however, the doctor declared that he had finished. With a flourish, he held up a specimen jar. The artefact visible inside it was disappointingly tiny, Sebastian couldn't help but feel – a dull sliver like the lead out of a drafting pencil.

He was still codeine-drunk when he got back on the bus. Checking his emails on his phone, he clicked on one that bummed him out. His editor said he was killing the piece on corruption in tenders for infrastructure contracts. Sebastian had been working on this for months and had called in a lot of favours to wheedle out the details. The outlet was prestigious; this was the first time they'd said yes to one of his pitches. As a freelancer, he hated having a story spiked; in the hierarchy of all his least favourite things to happen, he would rank this as worse than losing his bond on a rental place or realising his hairline had receded another half-inch in its gradual and inexorable retreat towards his crown. The irony with this particular piece was that it had got longer with successive requests from the editor for more and more information, but now the guy wrote to say: *It turned out to have more of a feature feel than really made sense for us, and now that the facts are known we can't make it work as news.*

Sebastian reread the email before tapping a reply, *Riiiiiiiiii-ight*, and hitting send.

To hell with the editor. He had lost sight of the big picture. The really annoying thing was that there was nowhere else to place the story; other outlets weren't keen to run a detail-heavy piece.

As the bus rattled on, Sebastian began to spiral. It might have been the drugs (it was probably the drugs), but this abstract realisation did nothing to calm his thoughts. He was yanked back to his great fear, the drum of his discontent. He had summoned the courage to let Teena know how he felt, saying the night before in bed, 'I feel like I haven't done enough. And what if I never do enough?' Her response had done nothing to allay his fear. In fact, she had laughed at him. 'You always feel that way,' she had said, rolling onto her side. 'So the world is as it should be. Everything is in its place in the universe.'

The real unfairness, he thought, was that he might turn out to be a failure just by running out of time. If he died anytime soon, he wouldn't just have failed in his work, but in an even more basic way: he would have failed as an organism. There was nothing more essential to succeeding in life than managing to stay alive. His next, unbidden thought, however, was that this might not be strictly true. His memory of high-school biology was admittedly pretty hazy, but he knew that some creatures had evolved to die as they procreated – certain spiders, perhaps? And didn't bees kill themselves when they stung? Which would mean they could realise their destiny even as they died, so long as they went out having sex or spiking someone's arse.

He hit the stop button with some force. The bus was nearing his destination. He had to go directly to his second appointment for the day, this one with some kind of radiographer. It was on

Dr Seymour's say-so, to get more pictures of the blob. Sebastian had scheduled his appointments back-to-back to get things over with, and as he arrived at the clinic he felt pleased about how efficient he was being. The radiographer wore jeans and had too much product in his hair. He led him to a lair-like room suffused with the bluish light of several computer screens. Sebastian felt a bit weird about letting the guy run a lubricated instrument up and down his neck, but his interest was piqued when the computer next to them started emitting sounds. He heard hissing and whooshing then something like white noise. 'That's what it sounds like in there?' he asked, amazed.

'Yes, or that's how the software interprets it.'

'It sounds like space.' It was a strangely expansive soundscape; he thought of machines raking the galaxies for high and low frequencies, for the faintest disturbance, for the resonances of dust. He thought of the task of these machines as akin to a kind of yearning and therefore as somehow poignant. They were the programmed expression of the human ache to hear something, anything, in a sprawling, inhuman cosmos.

As he sat there listening, a boyhood memory came to him. It was his first time in space. He was struck by the sights and sounds, a sense of limitlessness. Lift-off, a funnelling darkness, space junk spinning close. A classmate, clammy and frightened, urinating in his clothes. They were on a school excursion; Sebastian was embarrassed that his parents had not paid for him to do the extra activities. He pretended he didn't want to hike across a crater or go to a toboggan park. Instead, he fooled around in the dust, flapped his arms to make an angel indentation, looked up and scanned the skies with his portable transmitter. What he heard, to his surprise, was not the chattering of aliens, not an aria or concerto played by an orchestra, but a courier somewhere going about his work and humming to himself, something that might have been David Bowie.

Tears sprang to his eyes as this memory came to him. Even now, as an adult, he was ashamed of his emotions, and his shame made him brusque. 'I have something in my eye,' he said to the radiographer. 'You should know I took drugs this morning. Also, you see that sticking plaster? That is where I was shot.'

'All good.' The guy backed away. 'I'll give you the room.'

*

The next time Dino rang, he spoke about himself again. Still self-absorbed, he didn't seem to have noticed that Sebastian hadn't rung him back last time. He rambled about his paintings, and about a new girl he was seeing – 'Brunette and kind of hot, but in this compelling ugly way, with a fuck-off nose and forehead.' He spoke of his opening, which was almost upon him. 'And my son is coming,' he confided. 'I feel like it might be weird.'

Sebastian's own preoccupations fell away when he heard this. 'Oh Dino, that's huge. I'll be there, don't worry.'

After getting off the phone, he thought about Dino as a father, and then about his own prospects of procreating. He would never have children now; it just wasn't in his future. He felt sorry for himself, and even sorrier for Teena. Then, from the flat below his own, he heard his neighbour berating her toddler, shouting, 'Stop it! Stop it!' with rising desperation, and he couldn't help feeling marginally better.

The buzzer went. He opened the door in his pyjamas, which consisted of trackpants and an old uni T-shirt. It was Zoe, Teena's friend, dropping off a climbing harness that she had borrowed at some point. She said, 'It's been sitting there forever. About time I returned it.'

'Teena's out, I'm afraid. At work.'

'No, no, I know.' She smiled. 'I just wanted to drop it off. I've been clearing things out, lightening the load.'

Sebastian hastily closed the moleskin on the table. Then he looked again at Zoe, who seemed different somehow. He hadn't seen her in a while, so that could have been it, but her face was so fresh and bright, her skin dewy and translucent. It was as if her inner self was fizzing up inside her, brimming closer to the surface than usual. It was a strange thing to think of someone who had once been a soldier, someone he knew to be capable of toughness, yet he was struck by the way she appeared so open and unguarded. And that bright fizzy aura – it made her strangely charismatic. What was Dino's word? Compelling. Unexpectedly he felt something in him responding, like his own inner self was brimming up as well.

Feeling overwhelmed, he surveyed the kitchenette, searching for a distraction. It was always the same: his responses embarrassed him. 'Do you want coffee?' he asked. 'A cookie? They're out of date, I think, although when are they not.'

'No thanks,' she laughed. She moved to the window and looked out.

He followed her gaze, wondering what she was thinking. After a long moment in which they just stood there, he kept his eyes on the scene and asked, 'Was this what you thought it would be like, when we got to be real adults?'

She laughed again, but in a hollow way. Her eyes glittered darkly. 'No,' she said. 'Why, what did you expect? How did you think things would be?'

'I don't know. Maybe more like a Wong Kar-Wai film, with really attractive robots.'

'You're a romantic.'

Was she flirting with him? The thought was enlivening and a charge ran through his body. He didn't want to cheat on Teena but he was afraid of missing out. He feared a future in which no woman would look at him twice, let alone want to have sex with him. (The fact that Teena had sex with him all the time seemed irrelevant for the moment.)

'I don't actually know what I thought it would be like.' She was still thinking about his question, still gazing down on the street below. 'It's a case of the best laid plans, I guess. What we're trying to do here, I'm really not sure it's going to work. To think we've come so far, only to bring our problems with us. We are losing to insurgents. We are losing to the landscape.'

'Wow, somebody is taking a turn to negative town.'

She didn't appear to hear this. 'You know what this is like? It's like how in Soviet Russia they tried to domesticate the silver fox. I read about it once. It was this secret science project, very ambitious, men trying to play God. Taking something wild and trying to tame it, trying to short-cut evolution, the whole order of things.'

'Did they? Did it work?' He widened his eyes, leaned back.

'No, that's what I'm saying. It was never going to work.'

'Because I would definitely be into having a fox as a pet. I would call it Algernon. Algernon the Fifth.'

She gave a quick huffing exhale that wasn't quite a laugh. 'I don't think there's much chance of that happening. It's safe to say we are living in a post-fox environment.'

A post-fox environment. True enough. The thought was a bit depressing. He thought of the fox's breath remedy, made from the rare miracle bloom. Or supposed miracle bloom. He wondered whether it really worked, or if that too was a fantasy, the last shot of the desperate.

He forgot all these thoughts, however, when Zoe turned and met his eyes. She scrutinised him briefly, tilted her head and said, 'It's nice to see you, Sebastian. I've always liked you, you know.'

'Good,' he managed. 'I'm glad to hear it. I like to be liked.' Her words left a pleasant glow; he might have been basking in a sunbeam. Then the thought came to him: she knows, Teena must have told her. He smiled sardonically to cover his dismay. He said, 'Next you'll be asking me if it was the solar flare.'

'What?' She looked blank. He realised his mistake.

'Oh, nothing. Don't worry. It's just . . . words coming out of my mouth, not in any order.'

'Right, sure, of course.' Her eyes darted around the room and he was reminded of his surgeon, the troubled Dr Seymour with his tales of patients past. Then it occurred to him that Zoe had come knowing Teena would be out. Was this meant to be a sex thing? What was he supposed to think?

She patted the harness on the table. 'Well, I had better go.'

'Okay, yes. Of course.'

Perhaps feeling self-conscious, she departed in a hurry. He stood by the door pondering their encounter. The visit left him excited, if a little puzzled, and when Teena came home that evening they had energetic sex. He thought about Zoe, trying to visualise her body, what she would look like without clothes. He did the same the next morning, too, when he and Teena had sex again. This time he found it harder to summon Zoe's image. It didn't matter, he didn't need to. He cupped his girlfriend's breasts and felt an intensifying pleasure. She was not on birth control so he came in her mouth. Afterwards, with her eyes still level with his abdomen, she pulled some lint from his navel and said, 'I don't know why these sheets are shedding so much fluff.'

'It was great for me too,' he said.

'Sorry. I didn't mean —'

'No, I know. Just kidding.'

She moved to get dressed for work, and he got up, invigorated. This was when he floated his new idea: he could go to District 6-13 without worrying about insurance. He mentioned it casually, aware that his night-time logic might not win Teena over. 'Anyway,' he said, 'what do they really cover when it comes down to it?'

'No.' She rounded on him. 'Just no. That is not an option.'

'I'm not doing anything here. It could be just for a few days.'

'Honestly, Sebastian, are you listening to yourself?'

How quickly the mood had flipped. The air was tense between them. Only now did he notice that she had unpacked his travel bag, putting his things away at some point while he was out. A cockroach scuttled across the floor and she lunged at it with a book. She missed, it escaped, and she turned back to him angrily.

'And just so you know, I saw the tabs on your laptop. I know what you're doing, why you're listening to that music. But seriously, Sebastian. "Dido's Lament"? Are you kidding me?'

He froze guiltily. Being caught out planning his funeral made him feel disloyal; it was like planning to give up. She didn't wait for a response. 'And now you want to go to 6-13. Admit it, you're addicted. You're a conflict zone junkie.' She leaned out of the window to pull in the towels she'd hung out. A breeze was making them dance, which meant a crack in the shield and a risk of dust. She tossed the towels down as she went on. 'I've been out three years. You're the one who keeps going back.'

'Someone has to cover it! Even if everyone's stopped reading.'

'Totally, of course. But at this point, is that you?'

Her words stung. He shook his head, growing defensive. When they met, he had been the vehemently anti-war correspondent.

263

That was still who he was, what he was all about. He couldn't believe she would want him to give that up. 'So what, I hang out here, thinking about this shit?'

'Yes, maybe! I know you hate it, but listen, Sebastian, this is not the end. There are always new drugs coming out. Every quarter, every month. This is war and you have to fight.'

'Is it, though? Is it? I know everyone says that. "Such-and-such lost a long battle with cancer." But you've seen warfare, Teena, and you know it's a dumb comparison. The whole thing about war is not just trying to stay alive, it's that you actually have to make other people die. And *then* you stay alive, and afterwards you go home and try to live with yourself, which maybe you can and maybe you can't.'

It wasn't the first time he'd had this thought; he had been developing the idea for the last little while. He had imagined expounding it in front of an audience, perhaps while on a panel or possibly as a guest on a TV program. 'Yes, Bob,' he might say, warming to his theme, 'I would say that is the difference. I would say that is a very salient difference.'

But he wasn't on a panel. He was talking to Teena, and as he said the words out loud and he saw her face close over, he knew he had gone too far.

'You know what,' she said, 'I am going to the gym.'

'I'm sorry,' he said. 'Teena —'

But she was already out the door, she wouldn't wait to hear it. Feeling awful, he tried her phone. It went straight to voicemail. He was trying again when she burst back in.

She stood in the doorway looking shocked and confused. Her phone was buzzing in her hand, and she looked from it to Sebastian as though she didn't know what she should do with it. 'It's Zoe. She's dead.'

'*What?* No. She can't be.'

'Jamal just called to tell me.'

His hands rose to his mouth of their own accord. 'No,' he said again.

'She killed herself.' Teena's face sagged in disbelief, but as soon as she'd said the words Sebastian understood. As horrible as it was, he was all too able to believe it. He thought of how Zoe had seemed when he'd seen her the day before. He thought of the signs he'd missed or wilfully misread. Her restless gaze and mood. Her weird, fizzy charisma.

And then Teena, staring, told him, 'She did it at the cliffs.'

*

Over the next couple of days, they learned more about what had happened. A work crew had spotted her body at the bottom of a hundred-metre drop, not far from the hut. Emergency services came out in a light aircraft, took several attempts to land on a rocky ledge, and at last retrieved her body. Her family would later be told that it would be best to identify her from her dental records, a coded way of saying it would be better not to look at her remains. She was found an unusual distance from the base of the cliff: other rock-climber friends said she must have taken a running jump.

Sebastian tried to picture her doing this; he was struck by her resolve. She hadn't stood at the edge looking over before she leapt. Perhaps she knew that if she looked down she would lose her nerve. Perhaps she knew this from having made earlier attempts.

They went to the memorial three days later, gathering in a public park near a struggling copse of trees. It was late afternoon; a breeze whipped the leaflets that people held in their hands. These bore a photo of Zoe in camouflage gear, the years of her birth and death, and the words 'In memoriam'. It was a no-fuss event, which was partly intentional. Jamal, Zoe's brother, preferred the park to an inside venue, and there wasn't a sound system. 'We didn't want music, anyway,' he said wearily. 'Or readings or poems. We would rather let folks say a few words about Zoe.'

Sebastian stood at Teena's side but she refused to hold his hand. She was brittle and withdrawn, her mouth a thin, firm line. Someone had propped up a framed photo on a folding card table. It showed Zoe smiling in front of some craggy cliffs. Seeing it, Sebastian said, appalled, 'They've got to be joking. A photo of the cliffs?'

'No one's joking,' said Teena crossly. 'She really loved climbing.'

A few people spoke about Zoe in turn. Jamal described his sister's struggle with PTSD, something she'd gone to great lengths to hide, and then a soldier from Zoe's old unit told of how she had always encouraged him. 'Once, when I was having a hard time, she made me watch a video of Arnold Schwarzenegger.' In an attempt at humour, he tried to do Arnie's voice: '"All the time people ask me how many lifts I do, but I only start counting when it begins to hurt."'

It was sobering for Sebastian standing there to listen. He had spent the preceding days thinking obsessively about what Zoe had done. He thought it the most radically free act he'd ever known someone to commit. As he listened, though, it dawned on him that her act was not free at all, that in fact she'd been driven to escape her suffering; her demons had all but chased her over that cliff. He hadn't known about her illness. It must have been terrible.

The other thing that struck him was the glaring contrast between this memorial and his own, imaginary one. All his folly, his vanity, descended on him at once. It wasn't just that he'd been wrong about Zoe's state of mind. He had been totally seduced by the false romance of death. But here and now he was confronting the unadorned fact of it. Envisioning your send-off was an idiotic diversion, he realised. Anyway, who did he think he was trying to impress? Life was the thing, that was all you had, and once it was gone there wasn't anything else.

The trouble was, the question of how to live was a lot less fun to dwell on. Life was repetition, struggle, ordinariness. Its problems were open-ended, defying resolution. You couldn't curate it as you could a big one-off event.

The soldier was still speaking, describing one deployment when they had rolled into a settlement. The place was oddly quiet but then all hell broke loose. They found themselves in an ambush, a unit of eighteen surrounded by upwards of three hundred insurgents and having to withstand five hours of non-stop fire. 'I probably aged ten years that day,' he said. 'I thought, this is it. Game on. Welcome to the war.' He chuckled nervously, without humour. 'You know what? All I wanted to do was go out in a good way. That was my thing. I didn't want to just die on my knees?' He seemed to appeal to those listening, looking from one face to another. Then he turned his eyes to the propped-up photograph of Zoe. 'Well, Zoe,' he said, 'I didn't. And you didn't either.'

Now it was Teena's turn. She moved forward to face the group and began by saying what had made her friend move to New Province. 'She knew that staying where she was meant limited prospects. She tried to make something of herself. She was looking for reinvention.'

Sebastian blinked. He heard himself in this description, and for a brief, shameful moment he wondered if Teena was using her speech about her friend as a way to get through to him. He too had wanted to reinvent himself. This was why he had wanted to go to space, why he had moved, soon after university, to the growing settlement. But what was then a desire was now a necessity: he had to find some new way to reinvent himself, to remake himself so fully as to confound all expectations. This time it was urgent. It was a matter of life and death. He had to find a way to stay ahead of the disease, to inhabit a zone beyond the probable.

It was getting hard to hear what Teena was saying. There was a commotion in the street, some kind of noisy parade. Sebastian strained to hear over the racket. Then Teena stopped and started coughing, having inhaled some dust carried on the breeze. Recovering, she described meeting Zoe on their first deployment. She had been the captain of Zoe's unit. 'I was responsible for her,' she said, her voice cracking.

The parade was getting louder as it approached. 'That might have to do us,' called Jamal.

He comforted Teena, patting her shoulder, and turned to tell the group, 'Please have some coffee and cake.' People lingered and tried to chat. But it was almost impossible.

Sebastian found Teena. 'What is that *noise*?' he asked.

'The Day Zero parade.'

'No. Today's Day Zero?'

'Yes,' she said. 'So?'

He had completely forgotten. Dino's opening. He looked at his watch with a sinking feeling. It was almost six. The function had started an hour ago.

'I've got to go,' he told Teena. 'It's Dino's thing. I'm sorry. Can you drive us?'

Teena looked pissed off. She had every right to be. He should have thought ahead and arranged some other way to get to the opening.

'Really, Sebastian? On today of all days, really?'

But she dashed her coffee on the ground, made her goodbyes and started walking. He had to hurry to keep up with her. Once in the buggy, they took a route they thought would avoid the parade, but had to keep diverting because of road closures. The traffic was a nightmare and Teena was getting agitated. She drove aggressively, angrily, taking the turns at speed. He tried to navigate but this had never been his strong suit. 'Was that Musk Avenue?' he asked. 'Why didn't you take that turn?'

Everything was going wrong. The dust was getting worse: another fissure must have opened on the west side of the shield. They were being subjected to a taste of the outside storm, which darkened the twilight sky as though it was night. Teena switched on the fog lights and leaned forward as she drove, peering through the windscreen. Sebastian looked out too. It was a dystopic scene. He saw pedestrians struggling through the conditions, attempting to find their way, and their hunched figures made him think of the cancer patients he had passed in corridors. The thought came to him that he was looking at his future. He would become one of the craven, the poisoned and irradiated, the hairless, shrunken people grimly hanging on, scouring online forums for miracle drugs and superfoods. This was what lay ahead, he thought. Welcome to the war.

As they swung around a corner he realised where they were. At the top of the street, he discerned the outline of the embassy for the Allied Planetary Co-Security Union, a monolithic stone building topped by a steeple-like flagpole. Teena pulled up and parked.

'Here,' she said. 'Happy?' They got out. She had to shout over the wind and the snarling traffic. 'Well, what does it matter anyway, hanging around for a memorial? Zoe's dead. So what? That doesn't mean anything to you.'

He rounded on her, and spoke with a fierceness that surprised him. 'It means something to me! It means a lot, in fact. Zoe's gone, and I'm really sorry, but I can't change that. Tonight matters to Dino. And life is for . . .' He paused.

'For what?'

'For whoever is still here!'

Teena stopped on the road. He thought she would leave him there, she would turn around and drive off. Maybe she thought so too. Then at last it was as if she had seen something new in him. 'Okay,' she said finally. 'If that's how you feel, okay.' She caught him up, drew her coat about her and shoved her hands into her pockets. 'Come on then.' She still sounded severe, but was beginning to relent. 'Those shoes. It's embarrassing.'

'Dino won't care.'

'No.'

'I'll order a new pair, promise.'

Then the traffic was surging forward, the road having cleared ahead, and tipping their faces against the wind they made for the party.

High country

In the morning, when we set out, Mr Noffey was still asleep. Not because he was lazy; Bea said he'd been up all night trying to deliver a calf that had got all twisted.

'It died,' she concluded. 'He had to shoot the mother.'

And going onto the verandah, we saw the long rubber gloves he had washed and laid out to dry. We examined them clinically, the left and then the right, noting the traces of blood and bovine fluids. Death fascinated us. So did the cruelty of nature, which from then on became linked in my mind with Mr Noffey, who had shot a heifer dead in a field while we slept.

Mr Noffey was Bea's uncle. He lived in the big house on the farm. He was bearded and scowled a lot because his wife had left him. The night before, he had been stern at the dinner table, reprimanding me for feeding the cocker spaniel.

'What do you think you're doing? It's bad manners and unhygienic.'

I resented the dressing-down. I knew about dogs and bacteria. I had been careful not to touch the spaniel's mouth under the table, but being too cowed to say anything in my defence, I had to sit there accused of being ill-bred and uncouth.

Heading to the shed, we found Bea's cousin Benny crashing a Matchbox car into a tyre. Three years younger than Bea and with darker orange hair, he was said to be either special or slow. He wasn't merely mute but mildly brain-damaged as well, and had a teaching assistant to help him in the classroom. When he heard Bea talking about a swim, he signed to say he wanted to come.

'Sorry,' she told him. 'You won't fit on the bike.'

He glared at us as we rode off, but we quickly forgot him. Bea doubled me on her Peewee 80, setting her face against the wind. She had the magnificence of a Viking figurehead, except that her hair did not stream out behind her, having been scraped back severely with gel and water. As well as the motorbike, she used to have a pony, but her parents had sold it. Bea had trained Quincy to bite people on the arms, and then he was palmed off on some fools in Bibbenluke, a family who wanted a dressage pony for their son.

We liked to try to climb the ridge, a distant stair-like rise of hills, although we hadn't yet found a way to the top. We didn't ask permission. Bea's parents were away, as they often were. They were keen travellers and even when they were home they lived like expatriates in their own country, full of poetic sentiments about the beauty of the Australian landscape. They had a smaller house on the property, behind a line of trees. When they were away, Bea stayed with her uncle and cousin. She took her parents' absences as normal; she was very self-sufficient.

At the foot of the ascent, we abandoned the motorbike. The climb up, over craggy ground, was surprisingly difficult. The rise gave way to crevasses and lichen-coloured boulders. The trees stood like sentinels, their trunks shining white against the blue subalpine sky. The only signs of life we found were a cluster of white bones, which Bea matter-of-factly declared were 'animal, not human'. A lamb had sickened or gone lame and been taken by a fox, but the predator itself was nowhere to be seen.

We carried on in the rising heat, but halfway up we were again defeated by the ridge, this time by a chasm that dropped away sharply at our feet. We had a clear view to the west, where the fields in the autumn sun had the blank colour of jute sacking. This was the vast, dry dominion of the Noffey clan. In the midst of it, past the rut of the riverbed, sat the big house. It had been built as a monument to a long wool boom. Up close, it revealed signs of neglect – the peeling paint, the cracks that hinted at subsidence – but distance gave it the neatness of an architect's miniature. Further on yet out of sight, obscured by foothills, was the approach to the alps and Mount Kosciuszko. Or *Kossie Osko*, as we called it. Kosciuszko, a famous Pole, had led his people in rising up against the might of Russia and Prussia, but in true democratic fashion we bastardised his name, giving it four syllables instead of the Polish three.

It was hot and we wanted a swim. We made a scrambling descent and rode to the river, which showed the cracked earth of a long dry spell. We headed for the one spot with enough water to dunk under. Getting back to the house on dusk, we found Benny had been busy. His clothes were wet and muddy and he looked at us defiantly.

He had wanted to swim too. That was the trouble. It was a powerful desire of Benny's, this wish to swim, and it would pave the way to trouble on more than one occasion. Who could blame him, in all fairness? Not me, of all people.

Certainly not me.

But I am getting ahead of things. There was a sequence of events, a progression. Or an escalation. It was one thing and then another, and another and another. Yet even then, at the start of things, I felt apprehensive, like something bad was going to happen.

This time Benny, in our absence, had used the hose to flood a ditch. It was pretty creative really; he'd made a swimming pool of his own. In doing so, we learned later, he'd emptied the water tank by the house.

'Benny!' Bea cried. 'What have you done? Your dad will be angry!'

Bea's uncle was coming back. We heard his tread on the verandah. Having come from around the side, he hadn't seen Benny's pool, but it wouldn't take him long.

'Come on,' Bea said to me, 'let's go wait for your mum.'

Not hanging around to hear the ominous clanking of the pipes, which would be Mr Noffey attempting to wash his hands, we slipped outside to wait for my mother's car. Mercifully, it was then that she arrived to pick me up, bumping over the cattle grate and looking relieved that she'd found the house. I was relieved as well. I was spared Mr Noffey's wrath on this occasion, but even in the abstract the prospect was terrible.

*

To my mind, Mr Noffey was like the troll under the bridge in the fairytale. He was a foe, an opponent. He owned all the land, all the places I wanted so much to explore, and he didn't want to let me pass. When he lost his temper it was like a roar from under the bridge: *Who's that walking on* my *bridge?*

I wasn't the only one to take a dark view of him. He was considered a bad farmer. He allowed footrot to persist in some of his stock when he should have put them in quarantine or slaughtered them straight off, and it was said he'd let it spread to a neighbour's farm. In selling off some of his land, he'd divided up the parcels without a thought to the future owners, leaving sections stranded without proper rights of way. He didn't go to Landcare meetings, didn't nominate for the committee, as secretary or treasurer, and this was at a time when Landcare was the de facto support group for drought-stricken farmers. Much later I heard he knew the site of a mass grave where Aboriginal people had been killed by his forebears, but never reported it or had it investigated.

He was the eldest son of the eldest son. He hadn't wanted – hadn't asked for – any of it. The odd thing was that he had the talents farmers were meant to have. He was a crack shot, for example. At that time there was a lot of talk about gun accidents on farms, which was code for suicide. Mr Noffey was too good with guns for anyone to believe him capable of an accident, and maybe that was what saved him from giving it a go. But more likely he didn't care what people thought and he kept going because he had to, because he had Benny.

Unlike the Noffeys, my family were newcomers, having moved to the area the previous year. The town had a timber mill, a plinth for the two world wars, and a swimming pool for use during the dry summers. Shop windows carried signs declaring 'Greens Cost Jobs', hippies were disliked, and a few weeks after our arrival my father shaved off his beard, collecting the clippings on the pages of the *Sydney Morning Herald*. At the red-brick primary school, my Year Five teacher was Mr Sedden, who peered at us like we were beasts and wouldn't give me my pen licence. He didn't give a reason and I felt it was unjust, being made to go on scratching resentfully in pencil long after the others were allowed to write in ink.

Why did we move there? Not many people did. The men in the town complained that the women moved away. But my parents, outdoor types, lived in fear of suburbia, and they moved every so often to some neglected backwater that butted up against the wild places of the state. On this latest move, we had decamped from the coast because development threatened, meaning specifically the building of a supermarket. My dad took a job at the high school, teaching science and agriculture. He promptly set about making improvements to our house, and for a time we had no front door, only a tarpaulin, and my mother cooked dinner wearing a ski jacket.

As for Mr Noffey, his wife's departure was still fresh. She had left for good reason, people muttered, but they despised her for leaving Benny. They said it went to show the cruelty of the rich. The Noffeys were a notable family in the district, and if they weren't as wealthy as they had been in wool boom days, they were still considerably better off than most. The idea that rich people were cruel was a widely held belief, fed by the fact that affluent farmers sent their children to boarding schools. 'My mum says if you send your kids away you don't deserve to have them,' a girl in our class told Bea, knowing full well, as we all did, that at the end of the following year Bea would be sent away herself.

She got worse from a kid named Adam McDonagh, the son of one of the truck drivers who brought logs to the mill. He puffed up like a rooster and called her 'the rich bitch with a big garden'.

'It's called a *farm*,' Bea told him archly, because she wasn't a weakling. As the year went on, however, I noticed the way she'd try to say 'I seen' for 'I saw', and 'twenny' for 'twenty', though sometimes she slipped and accidentally pronounced the 't'.

This was in the nineties, though you wouldn't have known it. The eighties died hard in that corner of the world. The schoolyard was riven by class. Everybody knew who would be going away to high school and who would attend the local comprehensive down the road. This was the divide that ran through everything; it was the source of more cruelty than our teachers suspected. Animosity ran deep because jobs were under threat. The logging of old-growth forests was out of favour in the cities and there had been calls to put a stop to the convoys of lorries that growled up the winding roads bearing enormous logs. Between the town and the coast, at a point equidistant from Sydney and Melbourne and last in the pincer movement of felling and settlement, stood one of the last great old-growth forests of the eastern seaboard.

Meanwhile, my parents barbecued and dined with other schoolteachers, all of whom seemed to be building mudbrick or straw-bale houses. They were not on the dinner circuit of Bea's parents and their friends. Living at the edge of town, we were neither one thing nor the other, neither landed farmers nor working-class. When I voiced my dislike of Adam McDonagh to my mother, she told me, 'Rowan, you're a snob.' She threw out this accusation in an impulsive way. I was taken aback, and thought the reproach unjust.

I didn't know it at the time but my father's father, Snow, had been a shearer elsewhere. I knew he'd died racing a train, an event I envisioned like a sequence in a Charlie Chaplin film, complete with giddy piano music. In the shot, the light-haired Snow gripped the wheel of a black car. He tore along the tracks, while from behind (also in frame) a huffing engine bore down on him. Years later I had to revise this version when I saw a news bulletin about a motorist's death at a rail crossing. Hearing it said that the crossing had no boom gate, bell or light, I realised that 'racing the train' did not mean what I thought it meant.

In class we were schooled to fear what could do us harm, other Chaplinesque dangers that were standard issue in country towns. These were strange men, dams and silos, roughly in that order. We were told about children who fell into silos, how they flailed about and drowned, their mouths filling with grain. The dangers were real enough but they didn't apply to us: there were no crops in the area, so no one had a silo. As for dams, we had better options – a river that ran with melted snow each spring, and the municipal swimming pool with its lycra and flesh parade. That left only strange men, but there were no strangers in the town, and if any were to come they would be easy to spot.

When school broke up for the summer, the shearers came to town. They moved from one property to the next, dossing in sheds and staying a week or two as needed. This was also when Bea made the startling announcement that she would be away the following year, our final year of primary school, globetrotting with her parents and home-schooling on the road.

She gave me this news when I went over for a visit. Her parents were cooling their heels at home to prepare for the trip. There was her slight, elegant mother, and her father, a charmer in a battered Akubra. Spinning it on his finger, he regaled us with his stories over toast in the breakfast room in the big house, on his way out to help the men in the shearing shed. He boasted about how he used to fly light planes, zooming so low that the treetops all but stroked his fuselage. And he spoke convincingly of his plan to replant the riverbanks with native saplings. Especially ribbon gums, he said, as they were struggling elsewhere. The trees were mysteriously dying, turning bone-white across the district.

From a crowded shelf by my elbow, I picked up a pewter cup that commemorated Mr Noffey's win in the 1968 Thredbo Ski Club Egg and Spoon Race. I could imagine his youthful self on skis, dashing over the finish line, extending his spoon before him like a fencer's foil, but looking closer I saw that the engraved lettering read 'S. Noffey' – for the elder Mr Noffey. This was a surprise and a mystery. It was hard to picture Bea's forbidding uncle engaging in the high silliness of an egg and spoon race in the snow. Yet the trophy showed that he had – and he'd excelled at it.

The elder Mr Noffey, the egg-and-spoon-race winner, ate in the dining room by himself. He was very fastidious, swallowing each mouthful without any sign of pleasure. No one commented on the fact that he ate alone. It wasn't treated as unusual and no one wanted his company.

*

Before school started the next year, some strangers did show up in town. Not men, but women – three Filipina women. Together or separately, through methods unclear, each was matched with a man from our town to marry. Their children came to our school and the eldest, named Moses, took the desk next to mine. He was good-looking, had glossy hair, and smelt of lemon soap. With Bea gone, I needed a new friend and Moses was quick to ingratiate himself, copying the way I arranged things on my desk.

When I went to his house one Saturday, the TV and radio were playing the football, and sun-leathered adults were relaxing in pastel-coloured chairs. They were a tribe of people unknown to me until then, and moving easily among them was Moses's mother, a plump, friendly woman. She laughed when someone told her, 'Take a load off, love.' Moses's stepfather, a speckled man with hazel eyes, introduced me to everyone, then Moses and I went our own way, walking to the pool.

This was a place of spectacle and a fitting stage for Moses. He was otter-like in the water, diving and swimming with an easy grace. He drew glances from the boys as well as the girls and liked the attention. When we stretched out our towels to lie on the grass, he seemed to glow in the greenish shade of the liquidambar trees.

While the other kids stuck to their tribes, Moses and I existed outside the social order, or that was what I thought then. We didn't have to pick sides. Did Moses know better? In line at the newsagent's one time, we heard two men discussing Moses's mum and her compatriots. One was Adam McDonagh's dad, a surprisingly skinny man. He referred to the women as mail-order brides. The other man said he wasn't sure they were, to which Mr McDonagh said, 'You're right, what they are is whores, the three whores of Manila.' His friend observed amiably that Manila had more than just three whores, and both of them laughed until they saw us standing there, and then the girl at the till said, 'Can I help you, please?'

Like this, the year went on. I rarely thought of Bea. I couldn't picture her travels, could not imagine the places she was visiting. In spring, our teacher, Ms Lurie, said she wanted to teach us about life. She had us raise some chicks that had been hatched in an incubator. We housed them in cardboard pens at the back of the classroom, with a light on a timer to keep them warm at night. But one day my chick started acting strangely, jerking compulsively as if to look over its wing. The other chicks noticed; they gave it little pecks. That night, I lay awake in my draughty add-on room, praying that my chick would throw off its affliction.

The next morning I went to school early. My chick had died during the night. Its downy body was stiff and cold and its eyes were squeezed shut in an expression of concentration. I looked around the classroom. Empty. There was nobody to see when

I switched the tag from my dead chick's leg with the tag on Adam McDonagh's chick, a vigorous little bundle. Having made the swap, I sat with my new charge at my desk. It was a lesson about life, though not the one Ms Lurie intended. My fascination with death had paled; how could it compete with life, the thrill of a beating heart?

The bell rang and students entered. They mobbed the cardboard pens. 'One's dead!' someone exclaimed. 'It's Adam's. Look, it's dead!'

'What?' said Adam, barging over. When he saw the fuzzy corpse, he refused to accept it. 'But . . . but . . .' he said, faltering. He let out a violent, ugly sob. He couldn't help it or disguise it, and it was followed by more sobs. His grief was liquid and convulsive, a force of mucus, tears and spittle. Ms Lurie could not console him, not for all the coloured stickers in her storeroom or the world. He shouted that he hated chickens and hated Ms Lurie even more and then he stormed out of the classroom and downhill to the road, where he tore the budding roses off the bushes by the fence.

Moses knew my secret. He'd seen the weakness in my chick. But he never let on to Adam, not even when they started to have more to do with each other, playing football on Saturday mornings. He kept my secret as I later kept his, and when we had our assembly at the end of the term, I stood centre-stage with the grown chicken and accepted the applause as if I had earned it.

*

The end of the year came with a run of sweltering days. Bea came back from her travels like Christopher Columbus; she gave me her report as if to the king of Spain. Her journeys had made her into a sophisticate and she thought nothing of wearing a crop top with her bike shorts. She showed me the sanitary pads she had taken from the plane. 'They're these amazing long cushions you put in your pants.'

'Great,' I said. 'What for?'

'Oh, anything,' she said.

We tried them out that afternoon on the motorbike. Beforehand, as she and Benny tinkered with the bike, I went inside in search of snacks and to grab Bea's boots and socks. 'Not the good socks,' she added. But when I stood at her drawer, I faced an impossible dilemma: here were untold pairs of socks, an abundance of spots and stripes. I picked the least appealing, a plain white pair. As I went back past the dining room I saw Bea's uncle eating lunch. Something about him checked my stride. I hadn't seen him in a year, and he came into focus as a person in his own right; as someone making an effort, drawing himself up, summoning the will to go on with his work. I suddenly wondered what it was like to have his life, his burden of obligations, the care of the farm as well as Benny.

Then, going on, unobserved, I scrounged in the kitchen, selecting and pocketing some Italian chocolate truffles.

Out in the shed, Bea and Benny were still focused on the Peewee 80, squatting in the dirt with their heads together. I was used to seeing Bea leave her cousin out of things, and now their closeness surprised me. Benny had taken off the shift lever, found a buckled part and hammered it flat again, and as I approached he was putting the pieces back. Bea turned and saw the socks I'd brought.

'Those are my school socks,' she said, and took them and turned them over in her hands like stones. *School* did not mean our school, but the one she would start at in a few weeks' time. She added, 'It doesn't matter,' though her tone told me it did.

Off we went. It was just like before, but better cushioned with the sanitary pads. We hurtled over the tussocked ground and the stepped ridge drew close. That was the day we came closest to reaching the top. Or I should say I, because Bea's boots gave her blisters halfway up. I left her airing her feet on a flat rock in the shade, and after climbing for a while I thought I had made it. Then I saw two things that stopped me in my tracks. One was a sharp ravine that dropped away not far ahead; the other was an animal that loped into view. It was a fox, with an orange coat, a supple, elongated body, and a curious, frank gaze that it turned in my direction.

I moved instinctively. Keeping my eyes on the fox, I felt in my pocket for a chocolate truffle, softened now in the heat, and set it on the ground between us as a tribute. It was a disloyal act because the Noffeys hated foxes, but I was already acting from an allegiance to something else. I didn't want to be like the Noffeys, something I wasn't; I hoped to be something else that I hadn't yet defined.

The fox watched me with interest, ears pricked, alert. Taking several steps back, I ceded the ledge and returned the way I'd come. Bea had grown impatient. I didn't tell her about the fox. Going the rest of the way down, we found the motorbike where we'd left it.

'It was the washer that was the problem,' Bea said, lifting it off the ground. 'Behind the switch lever. It had bent out of shape. That's why it wasn't changing gear.'

'Benny's good with bikes,' I said.

'He's better than a mechanic.'

It occurred to me to ask why Benny was the way he was.

'It was an accident of birth,' Bea said, and I pictured her cousin as a slippery newborn baby, being dropped on his head by a careless doctor, or perhaps by his father. I recalled the rubber gloves I had seen after the night of the twisted calf, bearing the traces of blood and fluids, obvious signs of the sliminess of birth. I said it sounded like a thing that could happen to anyone.

*

There were truths as eternal as lichen-covered boulders. My parents moved us on almost absentmindedly and I started high school in a different part of the state. The remaining old-growth forests of the south coast were saved; public feeling grew strong enough to take care of that. Bea went away to her new school, still saying twenty instead of twenny. Moses was more successful at the reinvention game. He remade himself as the town's favourite son: in high school, he was school captain; in adulthood, a member of the Returned Services League club, a ringleader of dirt-biking and pig-shooting expeditions, a go-to organiser of buck's nights and weekends, and a paintball team commander in full camouflage gear. He worked as a foreman at the mill, which was threatened with closure many times, then rescued by the arrival of cheap plantation pine.

I saw Mr Noffey, Benny's dad, years later. In fact, I saw him twice, both times in Sydney. The first time was on a bus in the inner west, and he was helping a guy who was freaking out on ice, verbally abusing the female bus driver. Talking the youth down, Mr Noffey kept saying, 'Now son, now son,' as if soothing a frightened cow. His manner was so gentle, so caring, that I was struck by the difference between this man and his younger self. *Now son, now son.* The tenderness of it somehow made me feel like crying. Before he could see me, I got off the bus at the rear door. This was something that Moses had shown me, years ago: that it is easy to disappear in the midst of a commotion.

The second time I saw Mr Noffey he saw me first. I was back in Australia partly to do a story: the newspaper I worked for had sent me to all manner of countries, but now my boss wanted me to write about Australia. He wanted a story of the country as a harbinger of climate change, the canary in the coalmine. Something gripping, I was told. Fires, storms, floods, trauma and grief. My background reading got me thinking about the drought years of my childhood, precursors to bigger droughts to come. I read that those years marked the point when, in the language of the scientific papers, 'the human fingerprint emerges above natural variability and can be clearly detected through climate models that compare worlds with and without greenhouse gases'.

With these words in my head, I thought back over events. I thought of those dying ribbon gums, turning white against the sky, and of the river on the Noffey property, wending its dry, cracked course below the stony ridge. And now here was Mr Noffey himself, the man in the flesh, at the bottom end of King Street in Newtown, near the auto repair shop.

His face lit up when he stopped me. He took out his earbuds – he said he'd been listening to something on Radio National – and told me he lived nearby, in a flat with his son. He took care of Benny, who had a disability pension, but he got a break on Tuesdays when the Samaritans woman came.

He asked after my parents, remembering their names. I didn't ask about his wife. I don't know if she was helping to care for Benny or was in his life at all. I knew by then what his property had come to: the sale of parcels of land in a piecemeal way at first, then finally the last clutch of fields with the houses. He'd been freed from one duty to assume another.

'And you've done well,' he said to me. He knew I had gone to Oxford on a scholarship and then moved to London. He was pleased for me, generously so. Facing him, I felt like a fraud, as if I was once again standing there holding a chicken, a living, thriving thing to which I had no right.

That stupid chicken. I had not stopped feeling guilty about it. I had swapped a dead chicken for a live one, one loyalty for another, and I couldn't shake the thought that in doing so I had somehow opened the way to the ugly thing that happened next.

'And how's Benny doing?' I asked hesitantly.

'He has his moments. Don't we all.' Mr Noffey shifted and smiled. 'You wouldn't have seen him since the ... accident.' That slightest of pauses before he said *accident* made my heart plummet, as I realised he knew. He knew what the boys had done, and he knew that I knew too.

'You can see him if you like. If you don't need to go, that is.' His brow furrowed slightly and a shadow crossed his features. He tried to give me a way out. 'Or next time, if you're in a hurry.'

I was afraid to go with him. I was afraid to see Benny. I felt responsible, complicit. But the troll under the bridge was finally offering me a way across. 'No, I'll come,' I said. 'I'd like to.'

He smiled again and said, 'Alright then,' and untangled his earbuds, then we fell into step together. He was not unhappy, I realised. That was the difference. It opened something in me to see him so transformed, because I understood what despair could do to a person, what a disfiguring force unhappiness can be.

*

That in-between summer, we had all glimpsed something of the lives to which we would lay claim. All except Benny, whose future was decided for him, taken away and twisted and turned into something else.

It happened on a Sunday at the swimming pool. Benny was standing behind the block, waiting to dive. He watched the kid in front make a slick efficient entry and didn't notice Moses and Adam sidling up and exchanging glances. As he stepped onto the block, they mouthed, 'One two three,' and pushed. They were a half-moment too early to push him clear into the pool, and his foot caught on the edge. He tripped, windmilling forward. It was another Chaplin sequence, this time in lurid colour. Benny's block was near the side, and the angle at which he fell meant his head struck the edge of the pool. So did his arm; I winced to think of the graze. Then he was facedown in the water and his head was bleeding, releasing an ink-red plume into the turquoise pool.

That was the moment when things changed again for Benny, when his mild brain damage became something more severe. He lay in a coma in Canberra Hospital for three months. The swelling on his brain would certainly have killed him if not for the quick actions of a visiting specialist, a South African surgeon who was an expert in head trauma. He excised a four-inch section from the front of the patient's skull then sewed the flap of skin back over his forehead. His brain expanded to fill the gap where the bone had been. When the swelling went down, Benny woke up and the doctors patched his skull with a special metal plate.

I had seen what happened at the pool. I saw Moses jerk backwards. Adam McDonagh visibly shrivelled, losing his bantam chest. Their movements brought other movements, which came in quick succession. Two bigger boys running up and lifting Benny from the water. Mr Sedden rushing over, dropping the apple he'd been eating. And then the man who ran the pool sprinting over too, to start the CPR he had once shown us on a dummy.

Shortly afterwards Mr Sedden, as the first adult on the scene, asked me to write down what I had witnessed. He was distracted as he gave me a pen and paper, too distracted in that moment to distrust what I would write. My statement was to be given to a policeman, who had already been called and was driving down from Cooma. But before I could write anything, I saw Mr Noffey through the wire fence. He had just pulled into the car park and was doing that thing he did, taking a breath and drawing himself up. He didn't know anything yet, he was oblivious. Then I turned to see Moses, who had so far gone unnoticed. He was standing in the shade of the liquidambar trees, close to the gathering knot of people and yet apart from them.

It was an accident, I thought. It could happen to anyone. Then I looked at the page and wrote what I had to say.

Acknowledgements

Thanks to:

Claire Conrad and everyone at Janklow & Nesbit, Ben Ball, Siobhán Cantrill and the Simon & Schuster team, Nicholas Jose, Brian Castro and the writing community at the University of Adelaide, the Norman Mailer Centre in Provincetown, the Residencia Internacional de Arte Can Serrat, Varuna the Writers' House in Katoomba, Tegan Bennett Daylight, Luke Carr, Geraldine Hakewill, Kyra Henley, Tessa Khan, Jonathan Pearlman, Nadia Rosenman, Laura Scrivano and Andrew Nolan.

Earlier versions of the story 'How is your great life?' appeared in *Meanjin* and Black Inc's *Best Australian Stories 2015*.

The landscapes and skyscapes of the Mars-like planet in 'Day Zero' were informed by Sean McMahon's writings, especially the essay, 'The aesthetic objection to terraforming Mars,' which appeared in James SJ Schwartz and Tony Milligan (eds), *The Ethics of Space Exploration* (Springer, Switzerland, 2016), pp. 209–218. All errors and liberties are my own.

Sources for the quotations in the stories are as follows:

p. 16: Kenneth Grahame, *The Wind in the Willows* (Modern Library, New York, 2005), pp. 4 and 35.

p. 33: Dr Seuss, *The Cat in the Hat* (Random House, New York, 1985), p. 18.

p. 87: William Shakespeare, *Henry V*, Act 3, Scene 1.

p. 94: Isaiah Berlin, *The Hedgehog and the Fox* (Weidenfeld & Nicolson, London, 1967), p. 1.

p. 101: Quotations adapted from Thomas Nagel, 'What is it like to be a bat?' *The Philosophical Review*, Vol. 83, No. 4 (Oct., 1974), pp. 435–450 at pp. 438–9, 441. Used with the permission of Thomas Nagel.

pp. 150, 157: Various lines from the untitled Anton Chekhov play known as *Platonov*, written in 1878 and first published in 1923, as translated by David Hare in *Young Chekhov: Platonov; Ivanov; The Seagull* (Faber & Faber Ltd, Bloomsbury, 2015).

p. 158: Thomas Mann, in the essay, 'Versuch ueber Tschechow', originally published in *Sinn und Form* in 1954, as quoted in *The Undiscovered Chekhov: Thirty-Eight New Stories*, trans. Peter Constantine (Seven Stories Press, New York, 1998), p. xvii.

p. 160: Percy Bysshe Shelley, 'Music, when soft voices die', in Mary Shelley (ed), *Posthumous Poems* (John and Henry L. Hunt, London, 1824), p. 214.

p. 178: William S. Burroughs, *The Naked Lunch* (John Calder, London, 1982), p. 3.

p. 183: Allen Ginsberg, 'Howl', in *Howl and Other Poems* (City Lights Books, San Francisco, 1956), p. 9.

ACKNOWLEDGEMENTS

p. 186: Joke attributed to Dorothy Parker in Paul Hammond and Patrick Hughes, *Upon the Pun: Dual Meaning in Words and Pictures* (W. H. Allen, London, 1978), p. 4.

p. 285: This extract is reproduced from Joëlle Gergis, *Sunburnt Country: The History and Future of Climate Change in Australia* (Melbourne University Press, Carlton, 2018), p. 102.

Born in Wollongong, Jo Lennan studied in Sydney and Oxford. She has worked as a lawyer and writer, contributing to *The Economist*, *1843*, *Time Magazine* and *The Monthly*. Her work has featured in the *Best Australian Stories* and *Best Australian Essays* anthologies.